CLARKE[ ]D

C000097083

FICTION

NON-FICTION

Neil Clarke: Publisher/Editor-in-Chief
Sean Wallace: Editor
Kate Baker: Non-Fiction Editor/Podcast Director
Gardner Dozois: Reprint Editor

Clarkesworld Magazine (ISSN: 1937-7843) • Issue 102 • March 2015

FICTION

NON-FICTION

Slowly Builds An Empire
NAIM KABIR

There was no need for talk in Tokyo, so the streets were silent.

The loudest features were the colors of the electric motorcars and the styles of the eclectic fashions—polychromatic shells that switched from lip-pucker lemon to cut-grass green and double-cut polymer skirts alongside old-fold silk suits.

Shinsuke Takinami stood above and apart from it all, teetering on the edge of a ledge and wanting to yell down below, but swaying silent and still. They wouldn't hear him anyway. Where his world was quiet, theirs was boisterous and noisy. Vibrant. Lively.

Lovely.

For a moment he considered letting the breeze pluck him from the rooftop like the floret of a dandelion, but a tone from his phone made him think better of it. Money had just come from what he called the Department of Pay. Shinsuke could have always let the yen funnel directly into his personal account, but he preferred walking on the marble floor of the brick-and-mortar building, where perhaps he had a chance of interaction.

He took the mechanical elevator down twelve stories, walked past faded yellow wallpaper, through a set of double wood-and-glass doors, and onto the glistening street below.

The taxis there had either forgotten how to interpret a hand signal or were willfully ignoring him. After fifteen limp minutes of flailing on the sidewalk, he stepped in front of a vehicle and watched it automatically roll to a stop. Shinsuke cleared his throat and whisper-yelled, "Oye! I need to go somewhere!"

The driver's eyes widened at the use of a mouth and tongue and forced air, but he remembered the rudiments of language and opened the door, thinking all the while that he had picked up an oddity.

Shinsuke offered an address and they were off.

The sun was high in the sky by the time they arrived, and Shinsuke squinted in the glare from the road. But the shade of the concrete pillars fell coolly over his eyes as he moved to enter the building, just one of three hundred people in lines feeding into a faraway desk.

All was quiet.

He wondered what they must've been saying to each other, these people. In intimate shades of sound and thought passed from mind to mind, with no need for facial twitches or a squeezed throat to speak. He wondered what they must be saying, these people so unlike him.

He tried offering a smile, but was met with a glacial wall of empty face, all flat lines and smooth skin. Inscrutable.

For the rest of the wait he kept his head down, wondering if they were trying to talk to him. Maybe they were giving him mental nudges that he just couldn't feel, and maybe he was surrounded by hellos.

He stared at his shoes, hoping he wasn't being rude. Those hellos could turn into a collective hatred, the type felt by all tight-knit tribes as they came upon an outsider. They might have been thinking he was one of those loud, bad ones—those angry ones that roam at night and vandalize the city.

Or maybe they were feeling pity; as they basked in the warmth of each other's thoughts, perhaps they felt sorry for this poor hikikomori, this puppy left alone and afraid in the cold.

He looked at the floor until he reached a desk, where there was an awkward silence as the attendant stared through him. Shinsuke whispered a word and the attendant seemed to catch on, presenting him a small electronic tablet.

He pressed a button that transferred the money to his account—something he could have easily done at home—and was shooed out of the line and back onto the street. This always ended the same way, but he kept coming back.

It gave him something to do.

The screen at home shouted a constant stream of entertainment from the Misinformation Age, with bombastic characters and honorable warfighters yelling and jumping and trying their hardest to make Shinsuke feel like he wasn't alone.

It worked, sometimes.

But Shinsuke's greatest secret was the little black box nestled beneath the screen, connected illicitly with a tangle of wire and two paperclips. His father, Haru, had installed it some twenty years ago with a screwdriver

2

tucked behind his ear and his tongue peeking out from the corner of his mouth, long before Shinsuke decided to run away from home.

Deep into the afternoons Shinsuke would roll wire from a controller, plug it in, and roam through virtual worlds and talk to virtual people who spoke to him, joined him, fought with him, against him, and all those wonderful things he imagined must have gone on before the war on social parasites.

His mother, Aiko, had told him the story while he played with his father. As they roamed through a dungeon she recounted the camp they escaped with shovels and wirecutters. While they waded through the inevitable sewer level she talked about how dank and cold and smelly it could actually be underground, among hundreds who lacked the "complete empathy" of their countrymen and were forced into hiding.

When a god-emperor granted them three wishes as reward for defeating the demon king, Aiko told them how their only reward for survival was the sudden cessation of mass killings and an uptick of forced sterilizations instead.

Shinsuke always lived in a sort of awe and loving respect for his parents, and then Shinjuku happened. A group of hikikomori gunmen had crashed into a surgery suite and destroyed the equipment with lead bullets before being neutralized by hyperefficient police machines. They had called themselves the Nation, and Shinsuke was convinced they all lived out in the countryside together. He wanted to set off at once.

His parents said no. His mother hugged his head to her chest and just repeated the word, "No, no, no, no . . . " She called him a miracle, their one miracle in a life of curses, and told him please not to go, he was a miracle, he couldn't.

Haru stood gruffly at the door with his arms crossed and his eyes closed, a bouncer meant to keep him inside. His mother tugged at his arm and said, "Shin, you have to stay, you're a mir—" And that's when he started yelling.

He yelled that he couldn't just be cooed at like that, that he wasn't special, and that they could shut up trying to make him feel like he could be anything in this world when he was branded hikikomori, social recluse, parasite, insect who could never truly love someone.

Shinsuke made to throw a lamp at the video game console and his father bolted to it with his arms flailing wildly, and then he dropped it to the floor and hurried out the door. Haru chased him a good three miles to the metro, but Shinsuke finally lost him in the crowd.

After roaming for months in search of the Nation, he realized that his mother must've only been twenty years old when the sterilization procedures had been rolled out. They would have used an injection, radiation, or some surgery—but six years later there was a drooling baby boy who'd learn to talk and smile in their tiny apartment.

Miracle. That's what she called him the day he left.

To the government's credit, local law enforcement didn't take any action when they found out about new hikikomori children. The experts weighed in and stated there was too tiny a population of nonpathics to affect the rest of the country, as long as they were spread far apart.

So they let baby Shinsuke bounce, grow up, and tell his parents that he could never truly love.

Sighing, he spun up the usual disk and sat at the usual rocking chair. Long into the night, he played through dungeons and wide-open landscapes, fighting, dancing, and singing along with his party of colorful friends.

Shinsuke. Mama. Papa.

Molotov cocktails can hardly mark a supercrete wall, but they made for an impressive lightshow. Shinsuke watched from his rooftop as a column of shouting hikikomori rode down the block on ancient revving motorcycles coughing black smoke, launching fiery bottles at the walls as they passed.

They exploded deep unnatural red over the empty street: the color of the Nation Within a Nation, the Peoples Without Voice. Their shouts held a certain rhythm:

Call, "We, the folk of Nihon-koku!"

Response, "The Sun in the midst of the Cold White Field!"

Call, "We, the folk of Nihon-koku!"

Response, "Blood-drop red and the People's shield!"

Unwittingly, Shinsuke found himself mouthing along, wondering how these riders found each other, wondering how he could find them and belong. Was there really a city of them out there?

The rumble of the thirty-person column echoed through the avenue and faded to silence, scarlet flames dying down in their path. The LED red and blue of a pursuing police machine and the whistle of a siren came later, much too late to catch them.

The hallucinations started in summer.

Twin suns in a slow waltz and a rust-brown sky. Volcanoes throwing ice twenty meters into the air, golden-brown lakes, soaked spongy islands, a smart clean smell that whipped the air.

Then it was gone, as quickly as it had come.

He was told in impersonal government letters that social isolation had its costs, and that some year he would begin to develop a sort of dementia. This, the letters said, was the line between a hikikomori who was a commensal symbiote of society and a hikikomori who was a parasite. To keep from becoming a parasite, he'd have to visit his city's counselor.

Thankfully, for this appointment Shinsuke could travel by train. It was a red and white rocket that floated on an invisible cushion, pushing off underneath the dense intersection at Shibuya. He bumped into padded shoulders and he scuffed a hundred polished shoes while everyone around him moved in rehearsed lockstep. After a few moments a circle of space bubbled around him as he walked, the crowd retreating and rerouting like a school of fish. He smiled meekly in gratitude and made his way to the platform as the masses parted ways.

He got off at Yamato, deferentially bowing to the crowd that swirled around and blebbed him out into the open-air prefecture with rolling green hills and a sweet yellow sun.

The counselor's office here in Kanagawa was meant to serve the nonpathics of Tokyo and all of its wards and outlying towns, too. It was quite sufficient for this task.

For the first time in a long time, he was addressed by name, spoken aloud.

"Shinsuke Takinami."

The counselor was a brusque, short man in a bad brown suit and golden glasses, with a square moustache over tight lips. "You are here today because you have begun to see things."

The man had been trained well in speech, though his facial expressions were a little exaggerated, as if he were a player in a traditional kabuki history. For all Shinsuke knew, traditional theater actually *was* where he'd gotten his vocal training—this was a common practice for nonpath-liaison positions within the government.

The man continued with a too-wide smile, "I am Dr. Otani, would you like to come into my office?"

Shinsuke nodded meekly and entered, lowering himself onto a plastic chair as the counselor took his seat at the desk.

"How long have you been alone at home? You are quite young to have these problems now," said the doctor, jotting down a few notes on a yellow pad.

Shinsuke answered in a hoarse whisper, "Maybe eight years, now."

The doctor frowned comically deep. "Ah, that's a painfully long time. Perhaps that explains all these young people becoming sick so soon." He

5

put down the pencil and his face went to a stone neutral. "This year we have a new initiative. My colleagues and I have convinced the State to allow group meetings for many such as yourself."

Shinsuke's eyes brightened. A group?

"The problems are caused by extreme isolation. Conventional wisdom says that screen-entertainment helps you avoid this, but we've seen this isn't true. We've convinced the government to allay this acute isolation by having meetings where you may speak to each other. Of course, there are limitations, but overall this sounds like a good idea, neh?"

Shinsuke nodded vigorously, almost obsessively.

Dr. Otani's face lit up with a smile that could've been seen from the last row of an amphitheater. "Good, good. For now we will just take some tests and perform a short interview. But I will see you here again, in one week. Be prepared to socialize."

A vaulted sky of swirling red and yellow, like jelly spooned through cream. Dark spots of passing moons, thin sounds of music like wet thumbs on a wine glass. What sounded like a voice but was more like a thought being born, saying: Here is a part of Us, who are part of You.

The train ride to Kanagawa was quiet like the streets were quiet, and the lobby of the counsel building was, too. But when Shinsuke shouldered through the doors to his first group meeting, the noise washed over him like a hot breath in wintertime.

Shuffling chairs, men and women, boys and girls, all speaking to each other in voices loud and hushed. He basked in it.

Some paused as he came through the door, and he forgot how to introduce himself. He said, "Hello, hello," and they fell silent before a girl asked:

"Nice to meet you. I am Saeko Inamasu. What's your name?"

"Ah, ah, Shinsuke Takinami!" he whispered back, smiling the warmest he had in years. The others introduced themselves. Rena Hasegawa, Ayano Nojima, Eiichiro Matsushita.

Dr. Otani moved to the front of the room and rapped on a blackboard.

"Before you get too friendly, some rules. You may not," he fumbled with a piece of paper from his jacket pocket, "exchange addresses. Trade phone numbers. You may not leave together, or . . . " He squinted at the page, "Engage in physical affection."

Shinsuke looked nervously at Saeko as she listened attentively. Dr. Otani continued reading, "If you are suspected of doing any of these, you will be forcibly removed from your home and sterilized. If your offense is especially grievous, you will be killed." The room was silent, and then the counselor smiled that rubber-mask smile of his. "With that, continue introducing yourselves! In a few moments you will tell each other your stories!"

The first story was an old man's. He had survived the first wave of the war against social parasites but had been kidnapped and operated on during the second. He had a wife, once, and now she was back. That was why he was here.

Shinsuke furrowed his brow. This was unfamiliar: the man was seeing ghosts?

The second story was a gray-haired woman's. She had always spoken to her cats, but it was only recently that they had begun to talk back.

Shinsuke was glad for a moment that nobody in this room could read his mind, fully aware of the irony.

Dr. Otani cleared his throat, "The dementia of a nonpathic always comes in this form. The human mind craves company, and when it does not receive it, it creates it. It is cruel of the State to discourage nonpathic communities, I know. But hopefully this meeting can make you feel better!"

It was a bitter tragedy that even in this room full of hikikomori Shinsuke still did not belong. When his turn finally came, he went to the front of the room and spoke in a waver.

"Sometimes, when I am alone at home . . . " He inhaled deep as if he could breathe in more time to think, as if he could inspire a good lie.

"Sometimes when I am alone at home I see my parents still there." And the rushing gurgle of a dark current, a city lit by heat alone, and the warm sour taste of hydrogen sulfide. "I have not seen them for many years, but now I can finally talk to them." A voice as old as starlight, saying, Look. "My last words to them were that I could never truly love someone, but now I can tell them that's not true." You are Us. "I can finally touch them and hug them." We are You. "I can tell them I love them." You belong.

His audience nodded silently. He bobbed his head and returned to his seat so the next person could speak.

When the meeting was concluded, they were let out one-by-one, at fifteen-minute intervals. Shinsuke left the same way he'd come and boarded a metro car.

Partway to Shibuya, he felt a tug on his pinky. He whirled around to see Saeko staring dead ahead, her face blank like everyone else's. But she had his pinky pinched between her thumb and forefinger. He looked dead ahead, too, trying not to blush. If anyone suspected two hikikomori meeting together, the news could travel at the speed of thought to someone who could stop it with an electric rifle and a plastic club. Who could have them thrown in a hospital and forcibly treated, down where Shinsuke wanted no scalpel to ever touch.

When they reached Nagatsuta station she briefly tugged on his finger before floating away with the crowd. He did his best to follow, but was soon lost and spat out alone into the wide-open Midori ward, empty hill-country of Kanagawa prefecture.

Then he saw her standing perfectly still, ten meters away. When she caught his gaze she was off again, and he followed. This time it was much easier: the crush of the crowd disappeared and it was just the two of them, beating a path from the cracked concrete sidewalks of Midori proper and into a hilly wilderness.

When they crested the first peak she stopped and turned around to face him.

"You see them too," she said, in a voice strong and clear. She'd had more practice than he had in recent years. "The other worlds."

He whispered hoarsely, "How did you know?"

"Your story was so much a lie. You didn't shed a single tear. That's how I knew," she said, glancing periodically at the way they'd come. "There are more of us, at the camps. Not many, but more than just two."

"Camps?" This was very much illegal, and could very much get Shinsuke killed. But it was the dream he'd searched for as a young man, dropped into his lap. A commune. A place to be together.

She grabbed his hand and jerked her head southwest.

"Camps."

Hexagons of hard and warm, smells like a homecooked meal and a mother's hair, and the comforting vibrato press of family. A hive. Even here, he was told, A revolution can take hold. We are You, You are Us, You belong.

The camps were built from wooden planks and plastic bags, with the doorways draped in deep red flags and guarded by hard grown men and women. Motorcycles and jeeps girded the perimeter in a makeshift fence of headlights and black tires.

"Welcome to the capital of Nihon-koku." Saeko took him to one of the larger wooden cabins while he let out a hoarse, amazed sigh. This was the home of the Nation Within A Nation—the Peoples Without a Voice. He had actually found it.

A big man with scars came out of the cabin and saw Shinsuke next to Saeko. The man had a stern face and what seemed like a permanent squint aimed right at him. Shinsuke had watched enough streams to know that this was when the newcomer would get grilled about his loyalties, his origins—everything. He needed to build trust or else he'd be turned away.

The scarred man stomped through the dirt, Saeko averted her eyes, and Shinsuke braced himself. Then he was hugged tighter than he could remember, so firmly that he let his legs hang limp as he was lifted off the ground. So tightly that he saw stars, that the knots in his back unraveled and he was as soft as steamed rice in this big man's arms.

"You will never be alone again." Shinsuke was placed gently back on the ground. "Welcome to our family."

Asteroids peppering a small red moon, craters like pinpricks in its skin. Then a massive barge, dragging rocks in a net of gravity, crushing them closer like fingers folded into a fist. A flick of a gravitic wrist, a sudden squeeze of gees, and the stone let loose from its sling to wreck that lunar face.

"What are they?"

Shinsuke was sitting on the dirt floor of a hut along with Saeko, Grace Ueda, and Keigo Naktani. All of them had the visions, and those bubbling thoughts that felt almost theirs but were far, far too old.

Keigo explained as if he already knew, in a deep gravel voice: "They are voices from other worlds." Shinsuke had already suspected this, but hearing it said aloud gave it a strange and terrifying life. He shuddered, and Grace smiled at him with wrinkles around her eyes.

"We were each afraid, too," she said. "How strange to find that we aren't alone in this life!" She touched her fingers to her temple: "But think also how wonderful."

Keigo smiled and his thick bushy moustache curled up like a caterpillar reaching to nibble at his nose. "Think of what this means. Not only that we have friends in faraway places, but that it is possible to even hear them at all." He put a fist over his heart, "The me inside can talk to someone millions of miles and millions of years away, someone as distant as the faintest star—and they can talk to me. We've seen their worlds, so unlike ours, and yet . . . "

Grace continued, "And yet here we are. Inside we are all the same."

Saeko had been silently nodding while sipping at a bowl of soup, but she lifted her head to lazily say, "Grace and Keigo think that means we have souls."

Shinsuke turned to her. "You don't agree?"

Her eyes were hard. "It would also mean there was a God, and what kind of God would make us live like this?"

"Perhaps the same kind who would connect us with beings so far away," Keigo offered. "One who is now giving us an opportunity."

Shinsuke's brow crumpled in puzzlement. "What opportunity?"

"Haven't you understood? They've been talking to us about a revolution."

Upwells of deep ocean churning the thermocline, catalytic magnesium bubbling liquid in a vial, a diamond planet pecked just right and shattered into a trillion shining pieces throwing rainbows into space for light-minutes in every direction.

Shinsuke had been learning how to be useful. In the mornings he helped cut a terrace from a hill and soak its soil with water for the rice paddies. After a nap 'till noon, Keigo would take him to the hives to collect honey from the bees. Some horrifying days he'd have to wear a thick jacket with a netted hat and wield a wooden racket. Hornets the size and width of his thumb would sometimes come to steal bee-children, and he and Keigo and some others would need to swat them out of the sky. Their stings were brutal, and their biting jaws were just as bad.

Today, Keigo asked him to do something he knew he couldn't do. The pig was tied to a post and squealing like a child might cry, desperately tugging at the rope and lying limp in the dirt in awful alternations. Shinsuke was handed a small rifle and told to make it quick and painless.

He shook his head no. "I can't do this, Keigo." His voice had gone from hoarse to the smooth timbre of a young man's. "Give me another terrace to dig, or more rice to plant. But I can't do this."

Keigo smiled and gently placed his hand on Shinsuke's shoulder. Then he breathed in deep and asked, "Do you know why the countrymen use machines to fight for them? To act as their police, to hunt down their dissenters?"

Shinsuke shook his head.

"It's because they are afraid of accountability. To their own feelings." He drew a circle in the air with two fingers: "They are all connected like this, and if one of them commits a violence they all feel the guilt. So they give that job to their machines."

He gestured to the tied pig with an open palm. "You've eaten pork every week. You've spoken with, danced with, and played with everyone here who is happy to be well fed. And now it is time for you to pay for that pleasure." Keigo pushed the rifle deeper into Shinsuke's grip. "Will you be like the countrymen, too afraid of their feelings to do what is necessary? Or will you be like the men and women of the Nation?"

Shaking, Shinsuke raised the weapon to his shoulder and took careful aim. The iron sights jitteringly aligned above the snorting creature's eyes. He tightened his finger slowly, let go a long breath, and with one deft move he squeezed the trigger.

Fire exploded from a bonfire and the week's big feast was underway. Keigo cleared his throat in front of the crowd and publicly thanked Shinsuke for bringing them all a delicious dinner. And then the drums began.

Everyone talked, ate, drank. When the time was right they danced on the flats that had been stamped down by the weeks of dancing that had come before. Saeko came by to lure Shinsuke away from the tables, but he remained and ate slow and shuddering everything but the pork.

Monsters the size of subaquatic mountains lumbering through trenches in the sea, blankness in cold pursuit and a promise to unmake, spores released that latch on and change the very shape of the mind.

Shinsuke awoke to find Keigo in moth-eaten fatigues and slung with a very large gun. Saeko was there, too, with grenades strapped to her belt and a long rifle strapped to her bulging pack. They gave him clothes and told him to get into the jeep outside.

A girl was already there. Shinsuke knew she was named Namiyo, and that her father was an engineer. He traded awkward hellos and asked where they were going. She opened her mouth as if she were about to speak, but fell silent and told him to just wait.

They spent a few minutes looking at the pre-dawn tease of orange across the cold gray sky before Keigo jumped into the driver's seat and the jeep rumbled to life. Saeko joined them and they set off, tumbling through the hills.

"Shinsuke, tell me—what happens when we miss a hornet and he makes his way into the hive?" He aimed his question over his shoulder, since the jeep's mirror was missing.

"He kills anything in his way," Shinsuke said.

"But?"

"But then the hive will come together, surround the hornet with their bodies, and cook him until he dies." Keigo slapped the steering wheel and laughed as they rolled between hills and onto an overgrown road.

"Yes! Yes, that is perfect. And, what occurs if a fire is left too close to a hive when this happens?" Namiyo, the engineer's daughter, blushed at this. Two weeks ago she left a torch next to a hive when hornets came looking for food.

Shinsuke put his hand on her shoulder and answered, "The whole hive dies. Even a little more warmth is enough to kill every single one of them."

The vehicle bounced over cracks in the road and pieces of broken stone from the curb. Mottled light fell between leaves that blotted out the sun, flashing in a golden strobe when Shinsuke cared to look up.

"The key to causing a defensive reaction like this is singular. Saeko, what is that key?" Creaking metal towers whipped by amidst the overgrowth, sagging under powerlines and leaning at dangerous angles.

Saeko answered, "Abject fear."

"Precisely. Fear from a single hornet can kill the whole hive, under the right conditions. And we," he said, setting his jaw, "We can be the hornet to the countrymen's hive." They arrived in a time-shattered lot of an old facility when Keigo snapped up the brake and jumped outside.

"But the hornet dies," said Shinsuke.

Keigo waved away the thought and beckoned him inside the building. Hulking police machines stood limp at the gates, seventeen feet and sixteen tons of metal left deactivated to rust. Namiyo produced a small screen and began to swivel oddly with it as they proceeded through the facility.

They finally reached a room designed like half of a stadium, with raised platforms filled with desks and chairs and a giant screen dominating the wall. Namiyo pressed a button, there was a loud rumble, and the room came to life. Panels turned on, the screen grew bright, and the loud tortured thrum of an old fan beat noise through the walls.

Shinsuke wondered for a moment what the guns were for. Perhaps a safety precaution in the event this place was less abandoned than it seemed.

Keigo gripped him by the elbows and looked at him with pride and knowing. "Shinsuke." He took a deep breath. "Though you are our newest member, I know you're the right man for the job." He gripped harder. "I know you will act without hesitation—like a true man of the Nation—because I've seen you do it before." Shinsuke had killed many pigs in his time with the Nation. And other animals, too.

Namiyo dusted off a console and presented Shinsuke with a seat. Keigo guided him to it and sat him down.

"This is where countrymen once piloted their machines themselves. Today, that job is yours." Keigo patted Shinsuke on the back. Shinsuke threw Saeko a bewildered stare, but her face was blank. "You need to remind them what it is to hurt, Shinsuke. And then they'll rush to defend themselves so hard and clumsy that we can take them all out with ease." He did not elaborate.

A control-stick slid out of the console with an aching whir. Shinsuke grasped it and asked, "What do I have to do?"

Keigo sighed. "You are going to have to kill a lot of people."

· · ·

An ocean boiled, a continent charred, a planet sliced open like an orange, a system sucked into a black hole, all necessary, all horrible, death that paved the way for new life, a spreading fire with revitalizing ash.

Saeko and Keigo stayed until Shinsuke reached his first target. The controls were easy, like a game's. They were all surprised that Shinsuke could pilot the rusted heaps so gracefully. Many of the guns attached to the walking mech-machines had long since been jammed, but the rockets and sheer mechanical force provided by the limbs were enough to smash a building to pieces. This target was simple enough: Shinsuke could see no bodies in the rubble and went on guilt-free.

Keigo left his list of targets and said he and Saeko needed to attend to other business. "Don't lose focus," he said. "Keep going. If one machine is destroyed, engage another." He glanced at Namiyo and unslung his rifle. "Trust only your senses, and do what is needed."

Their footsteps disappeared and the loud shunk of a metal door slamming shut followed their exit.

Namiyo finally spoke. "They're tricking you."

Shinsuke looked away from his screen and the growing scene of a chaotic crowd pulling at the rubble to find hands and feet crushed beneath. "They're tricking me? Tricking me how?"

"They never intended to wipe out these people. Right now they're going to warn them, in exchange for replacing their police force with unconnected people like us. A hikikomori tribe that countrymen would encourage to grow, as protection."

"How do you know this?" Shinsuke's hands left the machine's controls. He saw the red-and-blue lights flash in the distance on-screen as the engineer answered.

"I heard. Keigo finished yelling at me for being so stupid with the hive, and when I left, I heard him whisper to Saeko and Grace. This was always the plan."

Shinsuke closed his eyes and asked a question he already knew the answer to. "And what exactly will happen to us now?"

"Keigo, Saeko, and a contingent of others from the Nation will come here with their big guns and destroy this entire facility." She sank into her seat with what could only be described as acceptance. "They've locked us inside."

Shinsuke didn't feel any roaring hot anger. It was cold, like a sword left in a quenching pool. It was sharp.

He snapped up the controls just as an autonomous police machine approached his own, ready to fight, but instead it simply bent down to help the people with the rubble.

"Your robot's friend-or-foe identification is still valid." She crinkled her nose. "Strangely enough. They won't attack you."

"Perfect." Shinsuke activated another machine close to the facility and followed the tire tracks in the road. He dropped his mech into full-transport modality and sped like a sportscar after Keigo and Saeko's jeep.

"Namiyo, what capabilities for speech are on board these machines?" Shinsuke flipped a few switches and returned his attention to the main screen.

"Both audio and visual. Only audio when in transport mode. Speak into the microphone and press the green talk button to broadcast your message."

Shinsuke nodded, "Good. Now pull up a console and take a mech to Kanagawa prefecture, at this address." He wrote down a street number and slid it to her desk. His machine was rolling at two-hundred kilometers per hour, bouncing high into the air when it hit ruts and ridges in the concrete. The jeep's dust trail was only a few hundred meters away, and Shinsuke spun up the engine as fast as it could go.

A defunct space station hanging derelict around a shattered star, a glowing glass world left devoid of life, a great machine sparking and blown to smithereens upon first touch. First Plans, first Results.

Shinsuke activated another machine and commanded it to follow the jeep as well. His first mech was coming up close from behind, now. At a meter away, he swerved around the speeding vehicle and went perpendicular to the road in front of it. The spherical wheels slowed and the moving barrier ran the jeep off the steep shoulder of the road.

Keigo and Saeko picked themselves out of the dirt while Shinsuke punched the talk button and calmly said, "Namiyo told me what you were planning."

Their voices streamed in as if through tin.

"Shinsuke? What are you doing? What did Namiyo tell you?" Keigo stepped in front of Saeko and said, "I thought I could trust you to stay focused on your targets?"

"She said your ultimate plan was to join with them, Keigo. To come back here and blow us to pieces. It's a good plan." Keigo raised his hands above his head, slowly.

"We would never do that to you, Shinsuke. You're family." Shinsuke turned to look at Namiyo, who was still busy performing the task he'd asked her. When he looked back at the screen, he saw Saeko had slipped the big gun from under Keigo's raised arms and was aiming directly at his mech. The barrel was as dark and deep as a black hole: until she fired and the camera feed burst into static.

Cold, cold anger.

The second machine was already within a hundred meters and he saw the smoldering wreckage of the first smoking in a junked heap. He jumped the mech into full-combat functionality and it rolled out into a heavy six-limbed titan in mid-air, swiping wildly at Keigo and Saeko and forcing them to dodge and drop their weapons. The mech landed with a thump and an explosion of dirt, with the two cowering at its feet.

Phospholipid bubbles effervescing out of primordial ooze, the scaled predator hunting the fat prey, one set of teeth gnashing better than the last. Strong rules over Weak.

Shinsuke smashed them into puddles of red mud almost without thinking, burying them deep with thirty-ton stomps of piston-legs and sealing their graves with jets of flame. Then he dropped back into transport mode and sped down the overgrown roadway, trying to remember the path back to the camps.

Namiyo had finally made it to Dr. Otani's office in Kanagawa prefecture, and was waiting for Shinsuke's command.

"Give me the microphone, and put me at full volume." Namiyo complied.

"Dr. Otani!" he called, and the mech's speakers thumped with every syllable.

The counselor emerged from his office and looked curiously at the big machine.

"Shinsuke? We have been missing you at our meetings. What are you doing in that vehicle?" He puffed up in a show of indignant confusion, with his hands on his hips.

"Never mind that, Doctor. There has been a crisis to your people, and I've managed to resolve it." Otani made one of his classic thinking faces, with his fingers rubbing at his chin and a single eyebrow raised higher than should physiologically be possible. "Your machines no longer seem to be an effective tool for your protection and defense. I have a proposition for you. For all of you."

The old mech stood at full height in the middle of the Nation town. It had been draped with red flags and its metal shell was painted white with war stripes.

In six months Shinsuke had taken the Nation from a cluster of huts in Midori to a pre-fabricated town named Haruaiko, with running water, electricity, and an academy for training the new generation of nonpathic protectors.

His people had risen to control every war-machine produced by Tokyo's factories, and they were growing larger. They sent for nonpaths from other cities, and the Nation's glory finally matched its name. In a few years, towns like this were expected to pair with every major city in Japan. Strategic positions.

A gas giant, a yellow rock, a blue-green marble swinging wildly around a star. Mountains like shards, nacreous clouds, spheres teased open in space and time; bent light and bridged minds—an infinity of minds that wove webs a galaxy in span. All connected. All united.

It would take generations for this planet to be readied for Shinsuke's faraway family: for enough conductive minds to be nurtured and enough defective ones to be culled. And it would take decades for the first arrivals to ever make landfall.

Patience.

Stars born over long centuries, systems resolving from spinning discs, planets coalescing from cosmic beads of molten rock.

Slowly does Greatness come from Meanness.

Comets splashing down in melting balls of carbonated snow, bilayered bubbles emerging from the morass, lightning striking cyanide and aminated soup.

Slowly grows the Large from the Small, the Significant from the Worthless.

Fire turning night to day on the eve of a rocket launch, accelerating strobes of dazzling light from inside a superluminal bubble, the great awe of touching the face of an other for the first time.

Slowly.

ABOUT THE AUTHOR

Naim Kabir is a novice who was lucky enough to get noticed: by *Beneath Ceaseless Skies, the Journal of Unlikely Stories,* and *The Dark Magazine.* When he's not busy with University life he's working on his debut novel, and hey–maybe you'll see more from him soon.

Cassandra

KEN LIU

πόλλ' οἶδ' ἀλώπηξ, ἀλλ' ἐχῖνος ἕν μέγα
The fox knows many things, but the hedgehog knows one big thing.
—Archilochus

"Just doing my job." He mugs for the cameras, that magnificent smile, that ridiculous cape and costume, that stupid quirk of the brow. Behind him is the unharmed research center building. Overhead the brilliant fireworks of the bomb he had heaved into the sky light up the scene, the sparks drifting down over his shoulders like confetti.

He could have tossed the bomb into the river, of course, but this makes for better TV. This is why I've taken to calling him *Showboat*, which happens to also work well with the soaring "S" on his chest.

"What do you have to say to her?" some reporter shouts.

"Villainy doesn't pay," he says, like some baseball player with a repertoire of a dozen clichés that will play well for any purpose. *Don't be evil. Surrender and face a fair trial. The American people will not tolerate terrorism. Open your heart to the goodness around you.*

I flick off the TV. He had probably figured out my plans with the city's help. With thousands of surveillance cameras everywhere these days, it's almost inevitable that my image was captured by some of them. Computers and his super-vision would have done the rest. He does believe in at least one form of anticipatory knowledge then, the kind that concerns me.

I'll keep on trying, though I'll need a better disguise.

The apartment is well appointed, comfortable. The man who owns this place won't be back until tomorrow morning; I'll be safe here. I fall asleep almost immediately after a long day of crawling through ventilation ducts and utility crawlspaces carrying explosives.

I dream about the building I failed to blow up, about the humming servers and cluttered labs I saw, about the knowledge that is stored within, about automated drones sweeping across the sky, over a busy market, over a remote hamlet, raining death upon the people below implacably. I feel the terror of the man through whose eyes I see these things, and the knowledge that it is wrong, all wrong, and yet also necessary, because war has its own logic, the perennial excuse of cowards trying to evade responsibility.

But *I* am the villain. Right?

You want to hear some dark, twisted origin story, some formative experience that explains how I've come to be me. That's what Showboat wants, too. "I feel sorry for her," he tells the cameras. "No one is born evil." I want to throw the remote at the TV every time he says that.

The real story is pretty mundane. It started with a search for cool air.

It's summer and there's no air conditioning in my apartment. Buying a window unit and installing it and figuring out how to pay for the extra electricity—the very thoughts exhaust me. Planning has never been my strong suit. I like to take things one step at a time. It's why I'm still in the city with no job after college, trying to put off making that phone call to my parents about possibly moving back home. *You're right, Dad; it looks like that degree in literature and history really isn't so useful.*

So I go out for ice cream, for cold smoothies, for the cool air in discount stores where they sell everything you desire and nothing you need.

There's a family near the TVs with their color saturation turned up so high that the skin on the white actors look orange. The woman stands next to one of the 72-inch beasts, looking skeptical.

"I think it might be a bit too big," she says.

The man looks at her, and I see his face go through this weird transformation. It was a handsome face, but now it's not. It's like she has just insulted him in some unforgivable manner.

"I said I like this one," he says. I don't think I'm imagining that thing in his tone, the thing that makes the skin on the back of my neck cold, makes me want to cringe.

She must be hearing it, too. She tenses, straightens up. One of her hands goes to the TV, leaning on it for support; the other hand reaches down and grabs the hand of her little boy, who's maybe four and tries to shake her off but she refuses to let him go.

"Sorry," she says.

"You think our place is too small, is that it?" he asks.

"No," she says.

"You make ten dollars an hour and complain about not getting enough hours, but you think we should be in a bigger place."

"No," she says. Her voice gets smaller. The boy has stopped struggling and lets her hold his hand.

"I guess it must be my fault. I should be working more. That must be what you mean."

"No. Look, I'm sorry—"

"I tell you I like this TV and you start this again."

"I like the TV."

The man glares at her, and I can see his face grow redder and redder as if he's still figuring out all the ways she's insulted him. I realize what a big man he is, how this rage magnifies him, gives him that aura of power. Abruptly, he turns around and heads for the exit.

The woman lets out a held breath, as do I.

She takes her hand off the TV and starts to follow the man, the boy obediently trailing her. Our eyes meet for a moment and her face flushes, embarrassed.

I want to say something but don't. What am I supposed to say? *He's got a temper, doesn't he? You going to be okay? Is he hitting you?* What do I know about the lives of strangers? What do I know about the right thing to do?

So I watch as they leave the store, the fog from the air conditioning over the automatic doors enveloping her for a moment as she steps through.

I go up to the TV they had been looking at, and for some reason that I can't even explain, put my hand on the TV, put my hand where she put hers earlier. It's like I'm seeking the lingering trace of the warmth of her hand, some assuring sign that she'll be all right.

And it feels electric, feels like the moon opens up and the stars are singing to me.

An apartment a few tiny rooms the bed the table the kitchen the carpet a mess Damn you're lazy I'm sorry I was late Teddy was sick had to take him Damn you're lazy

A toy piano is like a window a handle on a polished shoe grinding mezzo soprano Daddy is angry He is he is my darling Let's be quiet

The link is with us woman with woman. Your eyes your face It's nothing Why do you not leave Because So Because

Why did you look at him?

19

I wasn't I wasn't I wasn't

Lets dance So tender sometimes I'm sorry I was angry forgive me but sometimes you push me

He can be so sweet

A girl is a woman because a woman is an omen Oh man a whole man a hole in a woman a wholesome woman.

An awl is a drill some sharply polished nail

Broken dish a wailing a crying a tantrum Get him to stop! I'm trying I'm trying Damn you're lazy I'm tired Talking back I told you not to push me Don't don't you're scaring him get away from me

A burst of crimson of red ink iron sweet

Screaming and screaming and screaming he's not stopping Call the police call

My first vision leaves me breathless and ill.

I ask myself questions in an attempt at persuasion: What have I seen? What am I supposed to do with these images? What is their epistemological status? What is the rational reaction?

So I plead ignorance and do nothing.

Then there she is in the news: on TV, on the web, in the stacks of papers they still put in the convenience stores.

She was getting ready to leave him. Already found an apartment.

He came at her with that awl while their son watched. I couldn't stop him, and I tried. I tried.

I show up to the funeral, where lots of strangers have gathered outside the chapel to lay flowers around a fountain. I watch the bubbling water and imagine the blood gushing out of her. Guilt gnaws at my insides like an iron file, but the rest of me feels numb. I catch sight of the boy once, and his stoic eyes stab at me like a pair of awls.

And then he swoops in like some butterfly, dressed in his flowing cape and skintight costume. With his hair slicked back, his square jaw steeled, and his arms akimbo—arms that could bend beams of titanium and hold up a falling airplane—he poses. The cameras flash. Despite my cynical nature, I feel my heart lift up. We all need a hero, especially a superhero.

He gives a speech in that familiar baritone. He declares war on domestic violence; he promises to keep his super eye out for signs of trouble; he asks neighbors and friends to see something and say something. "Women shouldn't have to fear the men in their lives."

He doesn't explain how he's going to accomplish this. Is he going to examine every family in the city? Ferret out the poison from the root of our fucked up culture? Maybe he thinks it's enough for him to pay attention to the problem, to muscle his way to victory the way he grabbed that burning plane out of the sky, set it down by the shore, and peeled it open like a banana so everyone inside tumbled out and said *oh thank you thank you.*

But really, what right do I have to mock him and his platitudes? I should have done something. I saw what was going to happen.

His eyes sweep over the crowd, and our gazes meet for a moment. His eyes linger on my face just a second too long, and I wonder what he sees.

The next time it happens I'm about to enter the convenience store.

The man comes barging out the door with his head down and eyes on the ground. He doesn't hold the door open for me and I have to duck out of the way before he runs me over. He gives me a quick glance as he passes by and I see something in his face that makes my heart stop—intense anger at the world, anger at everybody and everything, anger at me.

I pull the door open, unsettled; an old lady is trying to come out with a bag of bananas and crackers; I put my palm on the inside of the door to hold it open, put it on the spot where the man had slammed his hand a moment earlier.

A winter a splinter I'm a nice guy ice guy my life is not nice Why don't you why

You owe me you owe me you all owe me

The girl who said no the boy who laughed why does he He doesn't deserve it nobody does and they say I'm the weird one

A gun

Look at me look at me look at me you can't hear me screaming you don't know how much the silence and an island and a new land and it's the same the same nothing ever changes

Two guns

I can see you I see all of you cowering terrified shivering shaking trembling leaves that you are should I let you live Why

I'm a nice guy ice thrice bang bang bang yes oh yes now you wish you were nice

Three guns

You're supposed to get in touch with him by calling 911. He monitors that. If it's the kind of emergency that can use his help, he'll come.

This *is* an emergency, but the police will mock me if I call and maybe charge me for wasting their time. *Sure, officer, happy to repeat my story. I followed a man home and got his address because I saw a vision that he was going to go on a mass shooting.*

So I write to him at his fan club email. I try to keep it vague but promise him IMPORTANT URGENT INFORMATION. I try not to use any capital letters in the rest of the email. To get to the superhero I have to defeat the spam filter first.

It's afternoon and there's a thundershower. He hovers outside the window and taps the glass lightly. I rush over to open it.

"Thanks for coming," I say, as though it's perfectly normal to have a superhero step through my window. "You must be really busy."

He shrugs and gives me a smile that shows off his perfect teeth. "When it rains really hard, the crime rate goes down."

It has never occurred to me that villains, super or otherwise, might have plans derailed by the weather. I suppose it makes sense. Even henchmen don't like to get wet.

"I have a crime to report."

He listens to my story, nodding encouragingly from time to time. I tell him about my newfound power and dead Annie, whose funeral he attended, and angry Bobby, who's going to kill.

He looks at me with those eyes that exude practiced kindness. "I'll take care of it."

And he opens the window and leaps out, as smooth as a fish leaping back into the ocean. I run to the window, my heart so full of happiness that I'm half expecting to see a rainbow. I watch his figure shrink over the rooftops, a blue-and-red angel of justice, truth, and all that is good and worthy.

I pace around my apartment, unable to remain still for even a minute.

He comes back an hour later, tapping on my window. The rain hasn't let up, and he shakes himself off like a wet dog before alighting gently in my living room.

"Did you see him?" I ask.

He nods but says nothing. I scrutinize his face, and something in me wilts, dies.

"He's a perfectly nice young man," he says. "Away from home, living on his own for the first time. He's a bit shy, is all."

"But the guns!"

"He doesn't have any guns."

"Maybe they're just really well hidden."

"I have X-ray vision."

"Maybe he's going to get them." I realize that I don't know anything about the timing of my vision. Maybe Bobby will buy the gun tomorrow, maybe not until twenty years from now.

I think of Annie's picture and how she looked embarrassed the only time we looked at each other. *I knew something. And I did nothing.*

"You have to believe me. I saw Annie die."

He sighs and shakes his head. "Nobody knows the future."

"They used to think nobody could fly. Or dodge bullets. Or see through walls. Or pluck a burning airplane out of the sky before it crashed."

He looks at me, his face hardening. "Then tell me how I'm going to die."

I look at him, my mouth opening and closing wordlessly. Finally, I say, "I don't know. It doesn't work like that."

He nods. "Nobody knows the future."

I become obsessed with Bobby. I stalk him from a distance, watch his comings and goings, try to piece together his life. I buy directional microphones and long-range zoom lenses. I download manuals written by private detectives and read them late at night.

I find out just how good my tradecraft is one day on the subway. I follow him onto the platform and get into the same car, at the other end. The train starts to move. He turns, looks me straight in the eyes, and walks over.

"You've been following me around."

I try to deny it, but I don't even have a story ready.

"Why?"

His eyes are confused, but his tone is polite.

I mumble something about living in the same neighborhood and having the same schedule. He asks for my name. He seems ill at ease but not in a way that appears dangerous—though to be honest, how is he supposed to act when he thinks he's confronting a stalker? We shake hands and tell each other it's nice to meet you.

His hand is warm, damp. I don't get any visions.

I ask him to dinner.

Bobby doesn't know anything about guns. He's never gotten into a fight. He's lonely but likes to read and play video games. He's thinking about becoming vegan. This is the extent of what I find out about him by the end of dinner.

He's awkward but polite. Our conversation doesn't flow smoothly because he seems to try out everything he says in his head ten times before he says it. Not my type. But dangerous? I can't see it.

We walk back together from the restaurant and stop in front of my building.

I look at him. He's nervous and expectant. I comb through our conversation. *Nobody knows the future.*

Before he can ask for a hug or a kiss, I shake his hand and step back, "I'll see you around the neighborhood."

He looks dejected but not surprised. "Why did you follow me around if you aren't interested?"

I think about how to answer this in a way that is truthful but not too truthful. "Because I wanted to know if I'm special."

"Special how?"

Just then Showboat zooms over us in the evening sky, a patriotic-color-schemed comet. We stare up at him together.

"A bit like that," I say.

"I bet he gets all the girls," Bobby says. "I bet it's nice to have that kind of power."

"Maybe," I tell him. "I don't know. Good night."

I try to go on with my life. The visions come more frequently now, are more vivid. I don't see visions of happy strangers; my gift is for brutal, bloody futures.

I take to wearing gloves marketed for germaphobes, made of some space age material that's supposed to be able to breathe while killing germs—pure lies. In fact, they make my hands sweat and the germs probably think of them as Club Med.

But they do keep me safe, safe from myself.

Once in a while, when I must touch something that hold traces of other hands—a touch screen tablet repurposed for taking credit cards or a restroom faucet—the visions leave me with a headache and palpitating heart.

There is a silence in singing, a violence in wringing, a justice and a tenderness and a rustiness in anything sweet and needs no explaining

The path all knowing everywhere sharp objects regret dark and thick and tangy as undersea molasses

Here is your attempt at explication but listen to the sound of sweet sweet sweet wee wee wee like some foundation in a room full of inattention which is death miles and miles of death

There is a mention of a tension that is quite an extension of my intention. For a rose is a rose is a rose is a briar a poke at a nose a bloody nose a gory a glory the same as flag waving.

Then comes the shooting, the bodies, the note left behind by Bobby in which he recounts his years of rejection and rage. My name shows up near the end, the stuck-up girl who thinks she's special and is obsessed with guns and who comes on to him only to reject him like everyone else. He talks about the desire to experience power, like the man with the red cape and blue tights. He writes about guns and their ability to remake the meek into the mighty, into superheroes. He speaks in the language of vengeance and unstanched wounds bleeding for years.

"You're responsible for this," he says, his cape looking cheap in the fluorescent light of my apartment.

I hear in his voice the voice of easy accusation, the pinning of blame upon imagined proximate causes. It's disappointing to see your heroes fall.

"That's absurd. He has been building up this delusion of rejection and hatred for years. He was just good at hiding it. You should have listened to me. You're just as responsible."

"Sophistry," he says. "You made the future you claim you saw. That's your power."

"No," I tell him. "We make the future together."

I suppose I could have just kept the gloves on all the time or moved back to my parents' house and never emerged, never touched anything that might still hold the heat and sweat from someone else.

It's one thing to be ignorant, but another to refuse to know.

If I can see the future but decline to, how am I different from a man passing by a pond and averting his eyes from the drowning child?

So I learn to live with the visions, to interpret them, to do what I can to thwart fate. I learn how to filter out the noise and blur and shifting lights, to focus and make sense of what I see and turn it into a scene, a sequence, a narrative. I learn to pay attention to details in the fleeting images: to clocks, to newspapers, to the lengths of shadows and the density of crowds.

At the ATM I see money being hidden in a locker in a changing room, a bribe to a woman in charge of something or other. I go to the gym and wait until five minutes after she's gone. I go in, take the money, and leave.

I don't know if that did any good. Maybe she'll just go back and ask for more, or demand payment from someone else. Maybe whatever she's being bribed for, she ends up doing anyway. But at least I have money to live on and to devote to my new career.

The man emerging from the elevator holds the door open for me.

"Thanks."

He nods and leaves. I put my hand on the door where his hand had been. I'm compelled to know.

I see a street corner. A tourist couple with a little daughter.

"Carla!" the father calls out. "Don't run so far ahead."

She turns down a narrow alley, in which I'm hiding. The parents follow their daughter in, admonishing her.

I go up to them and demand their money. I speak in the voice of the man who had held the elevator door open. The father refuses, and I take out my gun. Instead of complying, he lunges at me, trying to disarm me. I squeeze the trigger and he crumples to the ground, his face fixed in disbelief. The woman tries to flee, pulling the little girl behind her, and I shoot her also. Then I stare at the little girl standing next to her dead mother. She doesn't understand what has happened. She looks back at me, confused.

Why not? I think. One more isn't going to make any difference now.

I glance down at my watch and make a note of the time.

I shake off the cold desolation of the killer's mind. I get into my car and drive, frantically looking for that street corner on the GPS. I have only a few minutes.

There he is, loping along on the sidewalk, heading for his destiny. What am I going to do? Tell him I've seen him kill? If he backs off today, what about tomorrow, and the day after that? Can fate be so easily averted?

I ram my car into him as he starts to climb up a hill. A jolt of adrenaline, the pure thrill of thwarting the future.

Then I spin the wheel and back up, and speed away with screeching tires and the smell of burnt rubber in my nose. As I crest the hill I think I see Carla and her parents, obliviously happy.

I drive. And drive.

That one is simple. Most futures are far more complicated. There's Alexander, for example, hard working and well meaning.

From a distance, I see him standing at the street corner and mashing the button for the crosswalk impatiently. By the time I arrive at the corner he's already dashed across and the light has changed.

I tap the button and am overwhelmed by what I see: he's working on machines that will massacre a village of old people and children. He doesn't know it yet and he doesn't intend to. But it will happen. Intent is not magic.

How do I stop him? Could I intervene along the way, use some gentler roadblock to divert him from this future? But there are a thousand visions screaming for my attention, a thousand future victims to save. If I devote all my time to diverting Alexander, I will have also made the choice to let Hal go through with his kidnapping or Liam succeed in strangling his ex-wife.

We know what we know. What we do with that knowledge makes the future.

In the end, I opt for killing Alexander also. He's at the corner again, oblivious, a creature of habit with a set routine. I have a new car, a guided missile of future vengeance, or anticipatory justice. I step on the gas.

I stay where I am.

I turn around, and he's there, the red cape whipping in the wind.

"I've been watching you," he says. "You aren't very good at this, repeating the same modus operandi. But then again, most villains don't know any better. I'm taking you in."

He rips the top of the car off for dramatic effect. People exclaim in the distance. I hear the sirens of police cars.

I don't try to resist. "If you don't stop him"—I lift my chin in the direction of Alexander—"you'll have the blood of dozens, maybe hundreds, on your hands." I sketch my vision for him in a few sentences. "You could claim ignorance before, but not any more. You know I'm right."

Alexander, some distance away, is still trying to recover from the shock of his near encounter with death. He looks like a mild-mannered bureaucrat, his lips moving like a fish's.

"I don't know any such thing," Showboat says.

"Wouldn't it be better," I plead, "to kill the man long before he got on the plane rather than having to rescue the plane as it plunges toward the ground?"

He shakes his head adamantly, confident in his faith, his liberty, his justice, his truth. "We're not going to live in a society of pre-crimes."

"We're not as free as we think. There are tendencies, inclinations, forces that compel us—what we call fate."

"But you think you're free," he says. "You think you're qualified to judge."

He has me in a bind. If I succeed in thwarting the future, then my vision was wrong. If I don't succeed, then I may be said to be a proximate cause. If I do nothing, I can't live with myself.

"Is it so hard to believe someone can look through time as easily as you can through solid walls? Do you really believe it a mere coincidence that what I spoke of came to pass, that I might have been its sole cause?"

For a moment, the face of our caped hero shows doubt, but it's fleeting, and the resolute expression quickly returns like a mask. "Even if you're right, what makes you think you have seen the *whole* future? Maybe he'll also save the lives of dozens of soldiers; maybe his machines will kill a kid who grows up to be a dictator. The future is not knowable until it has become the past. But I just stopped you from murder. I know that. It is enough."

I think about my fragmentary visions. What do I *really* know?

"And you can't stop what you think will happen by killing him," he tells me. "He's just one man out of many others working on the same thing. Fate, if it exists, is resilient."

He's not entirely wrong, I suppose. I am a time traveler in a sense, and stories about time travelers changing history are often frustratingly stupid. The larger trends of history are rarely dependent on a single individual. Who would you have had to kill to prevent the destruction of the native peoples of the Americas, of Australia, of Hawaii? To stop the Atlantic slave trade? To avoid the mass atrocities of the wars in Indochina and East Asia? You could have killed every named explorer and general and emperor and king in the history books and the currents of colonial conquest probably wouldn't have shifted by much.

But that way lies madness. We'll never have complete knowledge. I know what I know, but he refuses to learn what he can. That makes all the difference.

The police car screeches to a stop nearby. He reaches for my hand to pull me out of the wreck of my car. His hand is warm and dry; it doesn't feel like the hand of someone who kills by refusing to believe, who takes refuge in the assumed condition of our ignorance, secure in his knowledge.

A blur that resolves into flashing images. Clarity.

Through his eyes, I see him regretting not following me in the squad car to be sure I'm put away; I see him examining the drive-through window of the fast-food restaurant and the bank across the street, where the robbers had emerged, his super-vision picking out the bullet holes in the sidewalk and walls and calculating their trajectories; I see him taking in the site of the shoot-out and clench his jaws; I hear the officers apologizing for rushing to confront the robbers without having secured me properly.

His visions are as orderly and predictable as his clichés.

Our hands separate. "Goodbye," he says, that familiar smug smile on his face again. "The city is safer today with you out of the way."

I look out the back window. He can't resist the cameras. He's going to give another impromptu press conference. The city's criminals, say, bank robbers, like to wait until he's on TV before making their moves.

Perfect.

The car starts to move. "You hungry?" one of the officers asks the other.

"I can eat."

"What are you in the mood for?"

I pipe up, "There's a *Pollo Pollo* on Third Avenue, across from the Metropolitan Bank."

The one in the passenger seat turns to look at me.

I put on a hungry and pleading look. "I have a coupon if you also get me something. My treat."

The officers look at each other and shrug. "All right. You aren't going to get a chance to use that coupon for a while."

"My loss. Say, do you work out or is that a bullet-proof vest under the jacket?"

I train. I learn to shoot, to fight, to become the super villain he already thinks I am.

If killing one man is not enough stop all the abusers, to reverse the momentum of culture, to uninvent the machinery of death, to change the currents of history, then I have to kill more.

I move from the empty apartments of vacationing couples to houses that had just been moved out of and not yet moved in—a touch on the doorknob is enough to tell me the story. I get good and then better at my craft.

I kill violent boyfriends in their sleep, poison future gunmen over meals, plot the erasure and destruction of clean, dust-free laboratories where they design weapons that kill while minimizing guilt. Sometimes I succeed; sometimes he stops me. He becomes obsessed, the anticipation of my next move haunting him as my visions haunt me.

I know a little about many things: snippets from people's futures, paths that will cross and uncross. I can't see that far into the fog: every action has a consequence, and consequences have other consequences. It's true that only when the future has become the past can it be seen as a whole and understood, but to do nothing because you don't know everything is not a path I can follow. I know that a little girl named Carla is alive because of me. It is enough.

He and I are not so different, perhaps, just a matter of degrees.

So we dance across the city, he and I, antagonists locked in the eternal struggle between the scattered knowledge of fate and the ignorant certainty of free will.

Ken Liu is an author and translator of speculative fiction, as well as a lawyer and programmer. A winner of the Nebula, Hugo, and World Fantasy Awards, he has been published in *The Magazine of Fantasy & Science Fiction, Asimov's, Analog, Clarkesworld, Lightspeed,* and *Strange Horizons,* among other places. He lives with his family near Boston, Massachusetts.

Ken's debut novel, *The Grace of Kings,* the first in a silkpunk epic fantasy series, will be published by Saga Press, Simon & Schuster's new genre fiction imprint, in April 2015. Saga will also publish a collection of his short stories.

The Long Goodnight of Violet Wild (Part 2)

CATHERYNNE M. VALENTE

Part One appeared in issue #100, January 2015

.

3. Green

The place between the Blue Country and the Green Country is full of dinosaurs called stories, bubble-storms that make you think you're somebody else, and a sky and a ground that look almost exactly the same. And, for a little while, it was full of me. My sorrow and me and the Sparrowbone Mask of the Incarnadine Fisherwomen crossed the Blue Country where it gets all narrow and thirsty. I was also all narrow and thirsty, but between the two of us, I complained less than the Blue Country. I shut my eyes when we stepped over the border. I shut my eyes and tried to remember kissing Orchid Harm and knowing that we were both thinking about ice cream.

When I was little and my hair hadn't grown out yet but my piss-and-vinegar had, I asked my Papo:

"Papo, will I ever meet a story?"

My Papo took a long tug on his squirrel-bone pipe and blew smoky lilac rings onto my fingers.

"Maybe-so, funny bunny, maybe-not-so. But don't be sad if you don't. Stories are pretty dumb animals. And so aggressive!"

I clapped my hands. "Say three ways they're dumb!"

"Let's see." Papo counted them off on his fingers. "They're cold-blooded, they use big words when they ought to use small ones, and they have no natural defense against comets."

So that's what I was thinking about while my sorrow and me hammered a few tent stakes into the huge blue night. We made camp at the edge of a sparkling oasis where the water looked like liquid labradorite. The reason I thought about my Papo was because the oasis was already *occupado*. A herd of stories slurped up the water and munched up the blueberry brambles and cobalt cattails growing up all over the place out of the aquamarine desert. The other thing that slurped and munched and stomped about the oasis was the great electro-city of Lizard Tongue. The city limits stood a ways off, but clearly Lizard Tongue crept closer all the time. Little houses shaped like sailboats and parrot eggs spilled out of the metropolis, inching toward the water, inching, inching—nobody look at them or they'll stampede! I could hear the laughing and dancing of the city and I didn't want to laugh and I didn't want to dance and sleeping on the earth never troubled me so I stuck to my sorrow and the water like a flat blue stone.

It's pretty easy to make a camp with a sorrow as tall as a streetlamp, especially when you didn't pack anything from home. I did that on purpose. I hadn't decided yet if it was clever or stupid as sin. I didn't have matches or food or a toothbrush or a pocketknife. But the Ordinary Emperor couldn't come sneaking around impersonating my matches or my beef jerky or my toothbrush or my pocketknife, either. I was safe. I was Emperor-proof. I was not squirrel-proof. The mauve squirrels of time and/or space milled and tumbled behind us like a stupid furry wave of yesterpuke and all any of us could do was ignore them while they did weird rat-cartwheels and chittered at each other, which sounds like the ticks of an obnoxiously loud clock, and fucked with their tails held over their eyes like blindfolds in the blue-silver sunset.

My sorrow picked turquoise coconuts from the paisley palm trees with her furry lavender trunk and lined up the nuts neatly all in a row. Sorrows are very fastidious, as it turns out.

"A storm is coming at seven minutes past seven," the Sparrowbone Mask of the Incarnadine Fisherwomen said. "I do not like to get wet."

I collected brambles and crunched them up for kindling. In order to crunch up brambles, I had to creep and sneak among the stories, and that made me nervous, because of what Papo said when my hair was short.

A story's scales are every which shade of blue you can think of and four new ones, too. I tiptoed between them, which was like tiptoeing between trolley-cars. I tried to avoid the poison spikes on their periwinkle tails and the furious horns on their navy blue heads and the crystal sapphire plates on their backs. The setting sun shone through their sapphire plates and burned up my eyeballs with blue.

"Heyo, guignol-girl!" One story swung round his dinosaur-head at me and smacked his chompers. "Why so skulk and slither? Have you scrofulous aims on our supper?"

"Nope, I only want to make a fire," I said. "We'll be gone in the morning."

"Ah, conflagration," the herd nodded sagely all together. "The best of all the -ations."

"And whither do you peregrinate, young sapiens sapiens?" said one of the girl-dinosaurs. You can tell girl-stories apart from boy-stories because girl-stories have webbed feet and two tongues.

I was so excited I could have chewed rocks for bubblegum. Me, Violet Wild, talking to several real live stories all at once. "I'm going to the Red Country," I said. "I'm going to the place where death is a red dress and love is a kind of longing and maybe a boy named Orchid didn't get his throat ripped out by squirrels."

"We never voyage to the Red Country. We find no affinity there. We are allowed no autarchy of spirit."

"We cannot live freely," explained the webfooted girl-story, even though I knew what autarchy meant. What was I, a baby eating paint? "They pen us up in scarlet corrals and force us to say exactly what we mean. It's deplorable."

"Abhorrent."

"Iniquitous!"

The stories were working themselves up into a big blue fury. I took a chance. I grew up a Nowgirl on the purple pampas, I'm careful as a crook on a balcony when it comes to animals. I wouldn't like to spook a story. When your business is wildness and the creatures who own it, you gotta be cool, you gotta be able to act like a creature, talk like a creature, make a creature feel like you're their home and the door's wide open.

"Heyo, Brobdingnagian bunnies," I said with all the sweetness I knew how to make with my mouth. "No quisquoses or querulous tristiloquies." I started to sweat and the stars started to come out. I was already almost out of good words. "Nobody's going to . . . uh . . . ravish you off to Red and rapine. Pull on your tranquilities one leg at a time. Listen to the . . . um . . . psithurisma? The psithurisma of the . . . vespertine . . . trees rustling, eat your comestibles, get down with dormition."

The stories milled around me, purring, rubbing their flanks on me, getting their musk all over my clothes. And then I had to go lie down because those words tired me right out. I don't even know if all of them were really words but I remembered Mummery saying all of them at one point or another to this and that pretty person with a pretty name.

My sorrow lay down in the moonlight. I leaned against her furry indigo chest. She spat on the brambles and cattails I crunched up and they blazed up purple and white. I didn't know a sorrow could set things on fire.

"I love you," my sorrow said.

In the Blue Country, when you say you love someone it means you want to eat them. I knew that because when I thought about Orchid Harm on the edge of the oasis with water like labradorite all I could think of was how good his skin tasted when I kissed it; how sweet and savory his mouth had always been, how even his bones would probably taste like sugar, how even his blood would taste like hot cocoa. I didn't like those thoughts but they were in my head and I couldn't not have them. That was what happened to my desire in the Blue Country. The blue leaked out all over it and I wanted to swallow Orchid. He would be okay inside me. He could live in my liver. I would take care of him. I would always be full.

But Orchid wasn't with me which is probably good for him as I have never been good at controlling myself when I have an ardor. My belly growled but I didn't bring anything to eat on account of not wanting an Emperor-steak, medium-rare, so it was coconut delight on a starlit night with the bubbles coming in. In the Blue Country, the bubbles gleam almost black. They roll in like dark dust, an iridescent wall of go-fuck-yourself, a soft, ticklish tsunami of heart-killing gases. I didn't know that then but I know it now. The bubble-storm covered the blue plains and wherever a bubble popped something invisible leaked out, something to do with memory and the organs that make you feel things even when you would rather play croquet with a plutonium mallet than feel one more drop of anything at all. The blue-bruise-black-bloody bubbles tumbled and popped and burst and glittered under the ultramarine stars and I felt my sorrow's trunk around my ankle which was good because otherwise I think I would probably have floated off or disappeared.

People came out of the houses shaped like sailboats and the houses shaped like parrot eggs. They held up their hands like little kids in the bubble-monsoon. Bubbles got stuck in their hair like flowers, on their fingers like rings. I'd never seen a person who looked like those people. They had hair the color of tropical fish and skin the color of a spring sky and the ladies wore cerulean dresses with blue butterflies all over them and the boys wore midnight waistcoats and my heart turned blue just looking at them.

"Heyo, girlie!" The blue people called, waggling their blue fingers in the bubbly night. "Heyo, elephant and mask! Come dance with us! Cornflower Leap and Pavonine Up are getting married! You don't even have any blueberry schnapps!"

Because of the bubbles popping all over me I stopped being sure who I was. The bubbles smelled like a skull covered in moss and tourmalines. Their gasses tasted like coffee with too much milk and sugar left by an Emperor on a kitchen counter inside a wine bottle.

"Cornflower Leap and Pavonine Up are dead, dummies," I said, but I said it wrong somehow because I wasn't Violet Wild anymore but rather a bubble and inside the bubble of me I was turning into a box of matchsticks. Or Orchid Harm. Or Mummery. I heard clarinets playing the blues. I heard my bones getting older. "They got dead two hundred years ago, you're just too drunk to remember when their wedding grew traffic laws and sporting teams and turned into a city."

One of the blue ladies opened her mouth right up and ate a bubble out of the air on purpose and I decided she was the worst because who would do that? "So what?" she giggled. "They're still getting married! Don't be such a drip. How did a girlie as young as you get to be a drip as droopy as you?"

People who are not purple are baffling.

You better not laugh but I danced with the blue people. Their butterflies landed on me. When they landed on me they turned violet like my body and my name but they didn't seem upset about it. The whole world looked like a black rainbow bubble. It was the opposite of drinking the sun that Orchid's family brewed down in their slipstills. When I drink the sun, I feel soft and edgeless. When the bubbles rained down on me I felt like I was made of edges all slicing themselves up and the lights of Lizard Tongue burned up my whole brain and while I was burning I was dancing and while I was dancing I was the Queen of the Six-Legged squirrels. They climbed up over me in between the black bubbles. Some of them touched the turquoise butterflies and when they did that they turned blue and after I could always tell which of the squirrels had been with me that night because their fur never got purple again, not even a little.

I fell down dancing and burning. I fell down on the cracked cobalt desert. A blue lady in a periwinkle flapper dress whose hair was the color of the whole damn ocean tried to get me to sit up like I was some sad sack of nothing at Mummery's parties who couldn't hold her schnapps.

"Have you ever met anyone who stopped being dead?" I asked her.

"Nobody blue," she said.

I felt something underneath me. A mushy, creamy, silky something. A something like custard with a crystal heart. I rolled over and my face made a purple print in the blue earth and when I rolled over I saw Jellyfish looking shamefaced, which she should have done because stowaways should not look proudfaced, ever.

"I ate a bunch of bleu cheese at the wedding buffet in the town square and now my tummy hates me," the watercolor unicorn mourned.

One time Orchid Harm told me a story about getting married and having kids and getting a job somewhere with no squirrels or prohibited substances. It seemed pretty unrealistic to me. Jellyfish and I breathed in so much blackish-brackish bubble-smoke that we threw up together, behind a little royal blue dune full of night-blooming lobelia flowers. When we threw up, that story came out and soaked into the ground. My sorrow picked us both up in her trunk and carried us back to the fire.

The last thing I said before I fell asleep was: "What's inside your cabinet?"

The only answer I got was the sound of a lock latching itself and a squirrel screeching because sorrow stepped on it.

When I woke up the Blue Country had run off. The beautiful baffling blue buffoons and the black bubbles and the pompous stories had legged it, too.

Green snow fell on my hair. It sparkled in my lap and there was a poisonous barb from the tail of a story stuck to the bottom of my shoe. I pulled it off very carefully and hung it from my belt. My hand turned blue where I'd held it and it was always blue forever and so I never again really thought of it as my hand.

4. Yellow

Sometimes I get so mad at Mummery. She never told me anything important. Oh, sure, she taught me how to fly a clarinet and how much a lie weighs and how to shoot her stained-glass Nonegun like a champ. *Of course, you can plot any course you like on a clarinet, darlingest, but the swiftest and most fuel efficient is Première Rhapsodie by Debussy in A Major.* Ugh! Who needs to know the fuel efficiency of Debussy? Mummery toot-tooted her long glass horn all over the world and she never fed me one little spoonful of it when I was starving to death for anything other than our old awful wine bottle in Plum Pudding. What did Mummery have to share about the Green Country? *I enjoyed the saunas in Verdigris, but Absinthe is simply lousy with loyalty. It's a serious problem.* That's nothing! That's rubbish, is what. Especially if you know that in the Green Country, loyalty is a type of street mime.

The Green Country is frozen solid. Mummery, if only you'd said one useful thing, I'd have brought a thicker coat. Hill after hill of green snow under a chartreuse sky. But trees still grew and they still gave fruit—apples and almonds and mangoes and limes and avocados shut up in crystal ice pods, hanging from branches like party lanterns. People with eyes the color of mint jelly and hair the color of unripe bananas, wearing knit olive caps with sage poms on the ends zoomed on jade toboggans, up and down and everywhere, or else they skate on green glass rivers, ever so many more than in the Blue Country. Green people never stop moving or shivering. My sorrow slipped and slid and stumbled on the lime-green ice. Jellyfish and I held on for dear life. The Sparrowbone Mask of the Incarnadine Fisherwomen clung to my face, which I was happy about because otherwise I'd have had green frost growing on my teeth.

One time Orchid Harm and I went up to the skull socket of the opera house and read out loud to each other from a book about how to play the guitar. It never mattered what we read about really, when we read out loud to each other. We just liked to hear our voices go back and forth like a seesaw. *Most popular songs are made up of three or four or even two simple chords,* whispered Orchid seductively. *Let us begin with the D chord, which is produced by holding the fingers thusly.* And he put his fingers on my throat like mine was the neck of a guitar. And suddenly a terror happened inside me, a terror that Orchid must be so cold, so cold in my memory of the skull socket and the D chord and cold wherever he might be and nothing mattered at all but that I had to warm him up, wrap him in fur or wool or lay next to him skin to skin, build a fire, the biggest fire that ever wrecked a hearth, anything if it would get him warm again. Hot. Panic went zigzagging through all my veins. We had to go faster.

"We'll go to Absinthe," I said shakily, even though I didn't know where Absinthe was because I had a useless Mummery. I told the panic to sit down and shut up. "We need food and camping will be a stupid experience here."

"I love you," said my sorrow, and her legs grew like the legs of a telescope, longer even than they had already. The bottoms of her fuzzy hippo-feet flattened out like pancakes frying in butter until they got as wide as snowshoes. A sorrow is a resourceful beast. Nothing stops sorrow, not really. She took the snowy glittering emerald hills two at a stride. Behind us the army of squirrels flowed like the train of a long violet gown. Before us, toboggan-commuters ran and hid.

"In the Green Country, when you say you love somebody, it means you will keep them warm even if you have to bathe them in your own blood," Jellyfish purred. Watercolor unicorns can purr, even though real unicorns can't. Jellyfish rubbed her velvety peach and puce horn against my sorrow's spine.

"How do you know that?"

"Ocherous Wince, the drunken dog-lover who painted me, also painted a picture more famous than me. Even your Mummery couldn't afford it. It's called *When I Am In Love My Heart Turns Green.* A watercolor lady with watercolor wings washes a watercolor salamander with the blood pouring out of her wrists and her elbows. The salamander lies in a bathtub that is a sawn-open lightbulb with icicles instead of clawfeet. It's the most romantic thing I ever saw. I know a lot of things because of Ocherous Wince, but I never like to say because I don't want you to think I'm a know-it-all even though I really *want* to say because knowing things is nicer when somebody else knows you know them."

Absinthe sits so close to the border of the Yellow Country that half the day is gold and half the day is green. Three brothers sculpted the whole city—houses, pubs, war monuments—out of jellybean-colored ice with only a little bit of wormwood for stability and character. I didn't learn that from Jellyfish or Mummery, but from a malachite sign on the highway leading into the city. The brothers were named Peapod. They were each missing their pinky fingers but not for the same reason.

It turns out everybody notices you when you ride into town on a purple woolly mammoth with snowshoes for feet with a unicorn in your lap and a bone mask on your face. I couldn't decide if I liked being invisible better or being watched by everybody all at once. They both hurt. Loyalties scattered before us like pigeons, their pale green greasepainted faces miming despair or delight or umbrage, depending on their schtick. They mimed tripping over each other, and then some actually did trip, and soon we'd cause a mime-jam and I had to leave my sorrow parked in the street. I was so hungry I could barely shiver in the cold. Jellyfish knew a cafe called O Tannenbaum but I didn't have any money.

"That's all right," said the watercolor unicorn. "In the Green Country, money means grief."

So I paid for a pine-green leather booth at O Tannenbaum, a stein of creme de menthe, a mugwort cake and parakeet pie with tears. The waiter wore a waistcoat of clover with moldavite buttons. He held out his hands politely. I didn't think I could do it. You can't just grieve because the bill wants 15% agony on top of the prix fixe. But my grief happened to me like a back alley mugging and I put my face into his hands so no one would see my sobbing; I put my face into his hands like a bone mask so no one could see what I looked like on the inside.

"I'm so lonely," I wept. "I'm nobody but a wound walking around." I lifted my head—my head felt heavier than a planet. "Did you ever meet anyone who fucked up and put it all right again, put it all back the way it was?"

"Nobody green," said the waiter, but he walked away looking very pleased with his tip.

It's a hard damn thing when you're feeling lowly to sit in a leather booth with nobody but a unicorn across from you. Lucky for me, a squirrel hopped up on the bamboo table. She sat back on her hind two legs and rubbed her humongous paradox-pregnant belly with the other four paws. Her bushy mauve tail stood at attention behind her, bristling so hard you could hear it crackling.

"Pink and green feel good on my eyes," the time-squirrel said in Orchid Harm's voice.

"Oh, go drown yourself in a hole," I spat at it, and drank my creme de menthe, which gave me a creme de menthe mustache that completely undermined much of what I said later.

The squirrel tried again. She opened her mouth and my voice came out.

"No quisquoses or querulous tristiloquies," she said soothingly. But I had no use for a squirrel's soothe.

"Eat shit," I hissed.

But that little squirrel was the squirrel who would not quit. She rubbed her cheeks and stretched her jaw and out came a voice I did not know, a man's voice, with a very expensive accent.

"The Red Country is the only country with walls. It stands to reason something precious lives there. But short of all-out war, which I think we can all agree is at least inconvenient, if not irresponsible, we cannot know what those walls conceal. I would suggest espionage, if we can find a suitable candidate."

Now, I don't listen to chronosquirrels. They're worse than toddlers. They babble out things that got themselves said a thousand months ago or will be said seventy years from now or were only said by a preying mantis wearing suspenders in a universe that's already burned itself out. When I was little I used to listen, but my Papo spanked me and told me the worst thing in the world was for a Nowboy to listen to his herd. *It'll drive you madder than a plate of snakes*, he said. He never spanked me for anything else and that's how I know he meant serious business. But this dopey doe also meant serious business. I could tell by her tail. And I probably would have gotten into it with her, which may or may not have done me a lick of good, except that I'd made a mistake without even thinking about it, without even brushing off a worry or a grain of dread, and just at that moment when I was about to tilt face first into Papo's plate of snakes, the jade pepper grinder turned into a jade Emperor with black peppercorn lips and a squat silver crown.

"Salutations, young Violet," said the Ordinary Emperor in a voice like a hot cocktail. "What's a nice purple girl like you doing in a bad old green place like this?"

Jellyfish shrieked. When a unicorn shrieks, it sounds like sighing. I just stared. I'd been so careful. The Emperor of Peppercorns hopped across the table on his grinder. The mauve squirrel patted his crown with one of her hands. They were about the same height. I shook my head and declined to say several swear words.

"Don't feel bad, Miss V," he said. "It's not possible to live without objects. Why do you think I do things this way? Because I enjoy being hand brooms and cheese-knives?"

"Leave me alone," I moaned.

"Now, I just heard you say you were lonely! You don't have to be lonely. None of my subjects have to be lonely! It was one of my campaign promises, you know."

"Go back to Mummery. Mind your own business."

The Ordinary Emperor stroked his jade beard. "I think you liked me better when I was naked in your kitchen. I can do it again, if you like. I want you to like me. That is the cornerstone of my administration."

"No. Be a pepper grinder. Be a broom."

"Your Papo cannot handle the herd by himself, señorita," clucked the Ordinary Emperor. "You've abandoned him. Midnight comes at 3 p.m. in Plum Pudding. Every day is Thursday. Your Mummery has had her clarinet out day and night looking for you."

"Papo managed before I was born, he can manage now. And you could have told Mums I was fine."

"I could have. I know what you're doing. It's a silly, old-fashioned thing, but it's just so *you*. I've written a song about it, you know. I called it *My Baby Done Gone to Red*. It's proved very popular on the radio, but then, most of my songs do."

"I've been gone for three days!"

"Culture moves very quickly when it needs to, funny bunny. Don't you like having a song with you in it?"

I thought about Mummery and all the people who thought she was fine as a sack of bees and drank her up like champagne. She lived for that drinking-up kind of love. Maybe I would, too, if I ever got it. The yellow half of Absinthe's day came barreling through the cafe window like a bandit in a barfight. Gold, gorgeous, impossible gold, on my hands and my shoulders and my unicorn and my mouth, the color of the slat under my bed, the color of the secret I showed Orchid before I loved him. Sitting in that puddle of suddenly gold light felt like wearing a tiger's fur.

"Well, I haven't heard the song," I allowed. Maybe I wanted a little of that champagne-love, too.

Then the Ordinary Emperor wasn't a pepper grinder anymore because he was that beautiful man in doublet and hose and a thousand hundred colors who stood in my kitchen smelling like sex and power and eleven kinds of orange and white. He put his hands over mine.

"Didn't you ever wonder why the clarinauts are the only ones who travel between countries? Why they're so famous and why everyone wants to hear what they say?"

"I never thought about it even one time." That was a lie; I thought about it all the time the whole year I was eleven but that was long enough ago that it didn't feel like much of a lie.

He wiped away my creme de menthe mustache. I didn't know it yet, but my lips stayed green and they always would. "A clarinaut is born with a reed in her heart through which the world can pass and make a song. For everyone else, leaving home is poison. They just get so lost. Sometimes they spiral down the drain and end up Red. Most of the time they just wash away. It's because of the war. Bombs are so unpredictable. I'm sure everyone feels very embarrassed now."

I didn't want to talk about the specialness of Mummery. I didn't want to cry, either, but I was, and my tears splashed down onto the table in big, showy drops of gold. The Ordinary Emperor knuckled under my chin.

"*Mon petite biche*, it is natural to want to kill yourself when you have bitten off a hurt so big you can't swallow it. I once threw myself off Split Salmon Bridge in the Orange Country. But the Marmalade Sea spit me back. The Marmalade Sea thinks suicide is for cowards and she won't be a part of it. But you and I know better."

"I don't want to kill myself!"

"It doesn't matter what death means in the Red Country, Violet. Orchid didn't die in the Red Country. And you won't make it halfway across the Tangerine Tundra. You're already bleeding." He turned over my blue palm, tracing tracks in my golden tears. "You'll ride your sorrow into a red brick wall."

41

"It does matter. It does. You don't matter. My sorrow loves me."

"And what kind of love would that be? The love that means killing? Or eating? Or keeping warm? Do you know what 'I love you' means in the Yellow Country?"

"It means 'I cannot stand the sight of you,'" whinnied Jellyfish, flicking her apricot and daffodil tail. "Ocherous Wince said it to all her paintings every day."

The waiter appeared to take the Ordinary Emperor's order. He trembled slightly, his clovers quivering. "The pea soup and a glass of green apple gin with a dash of melon syrup, my good man," his Majesty said without glancing at the help. "I shall tell you a secret if you like, Violet. It's better than a swipe of gold paint, I promise."

"I don't care." My face got all hot and plum-dark even through the freezing lemony air. I didn't want him to talk about my slat. "Why do you bother with me? Go be a government by yourself."

"I like you. Isn't that enough? I like how much you look like your Mummery. I like how hard you rode Stopwatch across the Past Perfect Plains. I like how you looked at me when you caught me making coffee. I like that you painted the underside of your bed and I especially like how you showed it to Orchid. I'm going to tell you anyway. Before I came to the throne, during the reign of the Extraordinary Emperor, I hunted sorrows. Professionally. In fact, it was I who hunted them to extinction."

"What the hell did you do that for?" The waiter set down his royal meal and fled which I would also have liked to do but could not because I did not work in food service.

"Because I am from the Orange Country, and in the Orange Country, a sorrow is not a mammoth with a cabinet in its stomach, it is a kind of melancholic dread, a bitter, heartsick gloom. It feels as though you can never get free of a sorrow once you have one, as though you become allergic to happiness. It was because of a certain sorrow that I leapt from the Split Salmon Bridge. My parents died of a housefire and then my wife died of being my wife." The Ordinary Emperor's voice stopped working quite right and he sipped his gin. "All this having happened before the war, we could all hop freely from Orange to Yellow to Purple to Blue to Green—through Red was always a suspicious nation, their immigration policies never sensible, even then, even then when no one else knew what a lock was or a key. When I was a young man I did as young men do—I traveled, I tried to find women to travel with me, I ate foreign food and pretended to like it. And I saw that everywhere else, sorrows roamed like buffalo, and they were not distresses nor dolors nor disconsolations, but animals who could bleed. Parasites drinking from us like fountains. I did not set out for politics, but to rid the world of sorrows. I thought if I could kill them in the other countries, the Orange Country sort of sorrow would perish, too. I rode the ranges on a quagga with indigestion. I invented the Nonegun myself—I'll tell you that secret, too, if you like, and then you will know something your Mums doesn't, which I think is just about the best gift I could give you. To make the little engine inside a Nonegun you have to feel nothing for anyone. Your heart has to look like the vacuum of space. Not coincidentally, that is also how you make the engine inside an Emperor. I shot all the sorrows between the eyes. I murdered them. I rode them down. I was merciless."

"Did it work?" I asked softly.

"No. When I go home I still want to die. But it made a good campaign slogan. I have told you this for two reasons. The first is that when you pass into the Orange Country you will want to cut yourself open from throat to navel. Your sorrow has gotten big and fat. It will sit on you and you will not get up again. Believe me, I know. When I saw you come home with a sorrow following you like a homeless kitten I almost shot it right there and I should have. They have no good parts. Perhaps that is why I like you, really. Because I bleached sorrow from the universe and you found one anyway."

The Ordinary Emperor took my face in his hands. He kissed me. I started to not like it but it turned into a different kind of kiss, not like the kisses I made with Orchid, but a kiss that made me wonder what it meant to kiss someone in the Orange Country, a kiss half full of apology and half full of nostalgia and a third half full of do what I say or else. So in the end I came round again to not liking it. I didn't know what he was thinking when he kissed me. I guess that's not a thing that always happens.

"The second reason I told you about the sorrows, Violet Wild, is so that you will know that I can do anything. I am the man who murdered sorrow. It said that on my election posters. You were too young to vote, but your Mummery wasn't, and you won't be too young when I come up for re-election."

"So?"

"So if you run as my Vice-Emperor, which is another way of saying Empress, which is another way of saying wife, I will kill time for you, just like I killed sorrow. Squirrels will be no trouble after all those woolly monsters. Then everything can happen at once and you will both have Orchid and not have him at the same time because the part where you showed him the slat under your bed and the part where his body disappeared on the edge of the Blue Country will not have to happen in that order, or any order. It will be the same for my wife and my parents and only in the Red Country will time still mean passing."

The squirrel still squatted on the table with her belly full of baby futures in her greedy hands. She glared at the Ordinary Emperor with unpasteurized hate in her milky eyes. I looked out the great ice picture window of the restaurant that wasn't called O Tannenbaum anymore, but The Jonquil Julep, the hoppingest nightspot in the Yellow Country. Only the farthest fuzz on the horizon still looked green. Chic blonde howdy-dos started to crowd in wearing daffodil dresses and butterscotch tuxedos. Some of them looked sallow and waxy; some of them coughed.

"There is always a spot of cholera in the Yellow Country," admitted the Ordinary Emperor with some chagrin. Through the glass I saw my sorrow hunched over, peering in at the Emperor, weeping soundlessly, wiping her eyes with her trunk. "But the light here is so good for painting."

Everything looked like the underside of my bed. The six-legged squirrel said:

"Show me something your parents don't know about."

And love went pinballing through me but it was a Yellow kind of love and suddenly my creme de menthe was banana schnapps and suddenly my mugwort cake was lemon meringue and suddenly I hated Orchid Harm. I hated him for making me have an ardor for something that wasn't a pony or a Papo or a color of paint, I hated him for being a Sunslinger all over town even though everybody knew that shit would hollow you out and fill you back up with nothing if you stuck with it. I hated him for making friends with my unicorn and I hated him for hanging around Papo and me till he got dead from it and I hated him for bleeding out under me and making everything that happened happen. I didn't want to see his horrible handsome face ever again. I didn't want alive-Orchid and dead-Orchid at the same time, which is a pretty colossally unpleasant idea when you think about it. My love was the sourest thing I'd ever had. If Orchid had sidled up and ordered a cantaloupe whiskey, I would have turned my face away. I had to swallow all that back to talk again.

"But killing sorrow didn't work," I said, but I kept looking at my sorrow on the other side of the window.

"I obviously missed one," he said grimly. "I will be more thorough."

And the Ordinary Emperor, quick as a rainbow coming on, snatched up the squirrel of time and whipped her little body against the lemonwood table so that it broke her neck right in half. She didn't even get a chance to squeak.

Sometimes it takes me a long time to think through things, to set them up just right in my head so I can see how they'd break if I had a hammer. But sometimes I have a hammer. So I said:

"No, that sounds terrible. You are terrible. I am a Nowgirl and a Nowgirl doesn't lead her herd to slaughter. Bring them home, bring them in, my Papo always said that and that's what I will always say, too. Go away. Go be dried pasta. Go be sad and orange. Go jump off your bridge again. I'm going to the Red Country on my sorrow's back."

The Ordinary Emperor held up his hand. He stood to leave as though he were a regular person who was going to walk out the door and not just turn into a bar of Blue Country soap. He looked almost completely white in the loud yellow sunshine. The light burned my eyes.

"It's dangerous in the Red Country, Violet. You'll have to say what you mean. Even your Mummery never flew so far. "

He dropped the corpse of the mauve space-time squirrel next to his butter knife by way of paying his tab because in the Yellow Country, money means time.

"You are not a romantic man," said Jellyfish through clenched pistachio-colored teeth. That's the worst insult a watercolor unicorn knows.

"There's a shortcut to the Orange Country in the ladies' room. Turn the right tap three times, the left tap once, and pull the stopper out of the basin." That was how the Ordinary Emperor said goodbye. I'm pretty sure he told Mummery I was a no-good whore who would never make good even if I lived to a hundred. That's probably even true. But that wasn't why I ran after him and stabbed him in the neck with the poisonous prong of the story hanging from my belt. I did that because, no matter what, a Nowgirl looks after her herd.

5. Orange

This is what happened to me in the Orange Country: I didn't see any cities even though there are really nice cities there, or drink any alcohol even though I've always heard clementine schnapps is really great, or talk to any animals even though in the Orange Country a poem means a kind of tiger that can't talk but can sing, or people, even though there were probably some decent ones making a big bright orange life somewhere.

I came out of the door in the basin of The Jonquil Julep and I lay down on floor of a carrot-colored autumn jungle and cried until I didn't have anything wet left to lose. Then I crawled under a papaya tree and clawed the orange clay until I made a hole big enough to climb inside if I curled up my whole body like a circle you draw with one smooth motion. The clay smelled like fire.

"I love you," said my sorrow. She didn't look well. Her fur was threadbare, translucent, her trunk dried out.

"I don't know what 'I love you' means in the Orange Country," sighed Jellyfish.

"I do," said the Sparrowbone Mask of the Incarnadine Fisherwomen, who hadn't had a damn thing to say in ages. "Here, if you love someone, you mean to keep them prisoner and never let them see the sun."

"But then they'd be safe," I whispered.

"I love you," said my sorrow. She got down on her giant woolly knees beside my hole. "I love you. Your eyes are yellow."

I began to claw into the orange clay my hole. I peeled it away and crammed it into my mouth. My teeth went through it easy as anything. It didn't taste like dirt. It tasted like a lot of words, one after the other, with conflict and resolution and a beginning, middle, but no end. It tasted like Mummery showing me how to play the clarinet. It tasted like an Emperor who wasn't an Emperor anymore. The earth stained my tongue orange forever.

"I love you," said my sorrow.

"I heard you, dammit," I said between bright mouthfuls.

Like she was putting an exclamation point on her favorite phrase, my sorrow opened up her cabinet doors in the sienna shadows of the orange jungle. Toucans and orioles and birds of paradise crowed and called and their crowing and calling caromed off the titian trunks until my ears hated birdsong more than any other thing. My sorrow opened up her cabinet doors and the wind whistled through the space inside her and it sounded like Première Rhapsodie in A Major through the holes of a fuel-efficient crystal clarinet.

Inside my sorrow hung a dress the color of garnets, with a long train trailing behind it and a neckline that plunged to the navel. It looked like it would be very hard to dance in.

6. Red

In the Red Country, love is love, loyalty is loyalty, a story is a story, and death is a long red dress. The Red Country is the only country with walls.

I slept my way into the Red Country.

I lay down inside the red dress called death; I lay down inside my sorrow and a bone mask crawled onto my face; I lay down and didn't dream and my sorrow smuggled me out of the orange jungles where sorrow is sadness. I don't remember that part so I can't say anything about it. The inside of my sorrow was cool and dim; there wasn't any furniture in there, or any candles. She seemed all right again, once we'd lumbered on out of the jungle. Strong and solid like she'd been in the beginning. I didn't throw up even though I ate all that dirt. Jellyfish told me later that the place where the Orange Country turns into the Red Country is a marshland full of flamingos and ruby otters fighting for supremacy. I would have liked to have seen that.

I pulled it together by the time we reached the riverbanks. The Incarnadine River flows like blood out of the marshes, through six locks and four sluice gates in the body of a red brick wall as tall as clouds. Then it joins the greater rushing rapids and pools of the Claret, the only river in seven kingdoms with dolphins living in it, and all together, the rivers and the magenta dolphins, roar and tumble down the valleys and into the heart of the city of Cranberry-on-Claret.

Crimson boats choked up the Incarnadine. A thousand fishing lines stuck up into the pink dawn like pony-poles on the pampas. The fisherwomen all wore masks like mine, masks like mine and burgundy swimming costumes that covered them from neck to toe and all I could think was how I'd hate to swim in one of those things, but they probably never had to because if you fell out of your boat you'd just land in another boat. The fisherwomen cried out when they saw me. I suppose I looked frightening, wearing that revealing, low-cut death and the bone mask and riding a mammoth with a unicorn in my arms. They called me some name that wasn't Violet Wild and the ones nearest to shore climbed out of their boats, shaking and laughing and holding out their arms. I don't think anyone should get stuck holding their arms out to nothing and no one, so I shimmied down my sorrow's fur and they clung on for dear live, touching the Sparrowbone Mask of the Incarnadine Fisherwomen, stroking its cheeks, its red spiral mouth, telling it how it had scared them, vanishing like that.

"I love you," the Sparrowbone Mask of the Incarnadine Fisherwomen kept saying over and over. It felt strange when the mask on my face spoke but I didn't speak. "I love you. Sometimes you can't help vanishing. I love you. I can't stay."

My mask and I said both together: "We are afraid of the wall."

"Don't be doltish," an Incarnadine Fisherwoman said. She must have been a good fisherwoman as she had eight vermillion catfish hanging off her belt and some of them were still opening and closing their mouths, trying to breathe water that had vanished like a mask. "You're one of us."

So my sorrow swam through the wall. She got into the scarlet water which rose all the way up to her eyeballs but she didn't mind. I rode her like sailing a boat and the red water soaked the train of my red death dress and magenta dolphins followed along with us, jumping out of the water and echolocating like a bunch of maniacs and the Sparrowbone Mask of the Incarnadine Fisherwomen said:

"I am beginning to remember who I am now that everything is red again. Why is anything unred in the world? It's madness."

Jellyfish hid her lavender face in her watermelon-colored hooves and whispered:

"Please don't forget about me, I am water soluble!"

I wondered, when the river crashed into the longest wall in the world, a red brick wall that went on forever side to side and also up and down, if the wall had a name. Everything has a name, even if that name is in Latin and nobody knows it but one person who doesn't live nearby. Somebody had tried to blow up the wall several times. Jagged chunks were missing; bullets had gouged out rock and mortar long ago, but no one had ever made a hole. The Incarnadine River slushed in through a cherry-colored sluice gate. Rosy sunlight lit up its prongs. I glided on in with all the other fisherwomen like there never was a wall in the first place. I looked behind us—the river swarmed with squirrels, gasping, half drowning, paddling their little feet for dear life. They squirmed through the sluice gate like plague rats.

"If you didn't have that mask on, you would have had to pay the toll," whispered Jellyfish.

"What's the toll?"

"A hundred years as a fisherwoman."

Cranberry-on-Claret is a city of carnelian and lacquerwork and carbuncle streetlamps glowing with red gas flames because the cities of the Red Country are not electrified like Plum Pudding and Lizard Tongue and Absinthe. People with hair the color of raspberries and eyes the color of wood embers play ruby bassoons and chalcedony hurdy-gurdies and cinnamon-stick violins on the long, wide streets and they never stop even when they sleep; they just switch to nocturnes and keep playing through their dreaming. When they saw me coming, they started up *My Baby Done Gone to Red*, which, it turns out, is only middling as far as radio hits go.

Some folks wore deaths like mine. Some didn't. The Ordinary Emperor said that sometimes the dead go to the Red Country but nobody looked dead. They looked busy like city people always look. It was warm in Cranberry-on-Claret, an autumnal kind of warm, the kind that's having a serious think about turning to cold. The clouds glowed primrose and carmine.

"Where are we going?" asked my watercolor unicorn.

"The opera house," I answered.

I guess maybe all opera houses are skulls because the one in the Red Country looked just like the one back home except, of course, as scarlet as the spiral mouth of a mask. It just wasn't a human skull. Out of a cinnabar piazza hunched up a squirrel skull bigger than a cathedral and twice as fancy. Its great long teeth opened anc closed like proper doors and prickled with scrimshaw carving like my Papo used to do on pony-bones. All over the wine-colored skull grew bright hibiscus flowers and devil's hat mushrooms and red velvet lichen and fire opals.

Below the opera house and behind they kept the corrals. Blue stories milled miserably in pens, their sapphire plates drooping, their eyes all gooey with cataracts. I took off the Sparrowbone Mask of the Incarnadine Fisherwomen and climbed down my sorrow.

"Heyo, beastie-blues," I said, holding my hands out for them to sniff through the copper wire and redwood of their paddock. "No lachrymose quadrupeds on my watch. Be not down in the mouth. Woe-be-gone, not woe-be-come."

"That's blue talk," a boy-story whispered. "You gotta talk red or you get no cud."

"Say what you mean," grumbled a girl-story with three missing scales over her left eye. "It's the law."

"I always said what I meant. I just meant something very fancy," sniffed a grandfather-story lying in the mud to stay cool.

"Okay. I came from the Purple Country to find a boy named Orchid Harm."

"Nope, that's not what you mean," the blue grandpa dinosaur growled, but he didn't seem upset about it. Stories mostly growl unless they're sick.

"Sure it is!"

"I'm just a simple story, what do I know?" He turned his cerulean rump to me.

"You're just old and rude. I'm pretty sure Orchid is up there in the eye of that skull, it's only that I was going to let you out of your pen before I went climbing but maybe I won't now."

"How's about we tell you what you mean and then you let us out and nobody owes nobody nothing?" said the girl-story with the missing scales. It made me sad to hear a story talking like that, with no grammar at all.

"I came from the Purple Country to find Orchid," I repeated because I was afraid.

"Are you sure you're not an allegory for depression or the agrarian revolution or the afterlife?"

"I'm not an allegory for anything! You're an allegory! And you stink!"

"If you say so."

"What do *you* mean then?"

"I mean a blue dinosaur. I mean a story about a girl who lost somebody and couldn't get over it. I can mean both at the same time. That's allowed."

"This isn't any better than when you were saying *autarchy* and *peregrinate*."

"So peregrinate with autarchy, girlie. That's how you're supposed to act around stories, anyway. Who raised you?"

I kicked out the lock on their paddock and let the reptilian stories loose. They bolted like blue lightning into the cinnabar piazza. Jellyfish ran joyfully among them, jumping and wriggling and whinnying, giddy to be in a herd again, making a mess of a color scheme.

"I love you," said my sorrow. She had shrunk up small again, no taller than a good dog, and she was wearing the Sparrowbone Mask of the Incarnadine Fisherwomen. By the time I'd gotten half way up the opera-skull, she was gone.

"Let us begin by practicing the chromatic scale, beginning with E major."

That is what the voice coming out of the eye socket of a giant operatic squirrel said and it was Orchid's voice and it had a laugh hidden inside it like it always did. I pulled myself up and over the lip of the socket and curled up next to Orchid Harm and his seven books, of which he'd already read four. I curled up next to him like nothing bad had ever happened. I fit into the line of his body and he fit into mine. I didn't say anything for a long, long time. He stroked my hair and read to me about basic strumming technique but after awhile he stopped talking, too and we just sat there quietly and he smelled like sunlight and booze and everything purple in the world.

"I killed the Ordinary Emperor with a story's tail," I confessed at last.

"I missed you, too."

"Are you dead?"

"The squirrels won't tell me. Something about collapsing a waveform. But I'm not the one wearing a red dress."

I looked down. Deep red silky satin death flowed out over the bone floor. A lot of my skin showed in the slits of that dress. It felt nice.

"The squirrels ate you, though."

"You never know with squirrels. I think I ate some of them, too. It's kind of the same thing, with time travel, whether you eat the squirrel or the squirrel eats you. I remember it hurt. I remember you kissed me till it was over. I remember Early-to-Tea and Stopwatch screaming. Sometimes you can't help vanishing. Anyway, the squirrels felt bad about it. Because we'd taken care of them so well and they had to do it anyway. They apologized for ages. I fell asleep once in the middle of them going on and on about how timelines taste."

"Am I dead?"

"I don't know, did you die?"

"Maybe the bubbles got me. The Emperor said I'd get sick if I traveled without a clarinet. And parts of me aren't my own parts anymore." I stretched out my legs. They were the color of rooster feathers. "But I don't think so. What do you mean the squirrels had to do it?"

"Self-defense, is what they said about a million times."

"What? We never so much as kicked one!"

"You have to think like a six-legged mauve squirrel of infinite time. The Ordinary Emperor was going to hunt them all down one by one and set the chronology of everything possible and impossible on fire. They set a contraption in motion so that he couldn't touch them, a contraption involving you and me and a blue story and a Red Country where nobody dies, they just change clothes. They're very tidy creatures. Don't worry, we're safe in the Red Country. There'll probably be another war. The squirrels can't fix that. They're only little. But everyone always wants to conquer the Red Country and nobody ever has. We have a wall and it's a really good one."

I twisted my head up to look at him, his plum-colored hair, his amethyst eyes, his stubborn chin. "You have to say what you mean here."

"I mean I love you. And I mean the infinite squirrels of space and time devoured me to save themselves from annihilation at the hands of a pepper grinder. I can mean both. It's allowed."

I kissed Orchid Harm inside the skull of a giant rodent and we knew that we were both thinking about ice cream. The ruby bassoons hooted up from the piazza and scarlet tanagers scattered from the rooftops and a watercolor unicorn told a joke about the way tubas are way down the road but the echoes carried her voice up and up and everywhere. Orchid stopped the kiss first. He pointed to the smooth crimson roof of the eye socket.

A long stripe of gold paint gleamed there.

THE END

All Original Brightness
MIKE BUCKLEY

Gonzo arrived in an assault of brass music and spilling banners rippling the pelt of cannon smoke where her feet would've been, taking up the hotel entrance in all its marble and chrome—its expensive anachronisms and the people paid to stand next to them in red vests—filling it up as I probably had, Mitchum thought. Funny; from the inside, none of us feel so big.

But then PFC Evelyn "Gonzo" Gonzalez's immerso read the space it had available and shrunk. The smoke recoiled as if some great lungs within had inhaled, banners withdrew, the brass march quieted. A hovering face clarified in the nano swarm of the immerso, shifting features, for a moment not quite this person or that, then Gonzo's still-beautiful voice came out of it.

"Mitchum, you goat rapist."

"Gonzo, you short bus rock star."

Medals blinked into existence on Gonzo's immerso, and Mitchum watched the floating pictures next to them—images that expressed her state of mind: Gonzo pretending to ride a broken surfboard, or standing in the sun at high school graduation. And here, with a boy. Mitchum felt his weight shift among the suspension gel in his tank—or maybe it was his imagination. Seeing Gonzo now, he wondered if she could feel her weight in the gel, if she sometimes felt the tug of the jack that ran from the inside of the tank and bolted to her forehead just like Mitchum's did, between his two vanished eyes, the jack that carried images from the cameras on the outside of the tank and landed them in his brain, in what the AIs called the V2 portion of the gray matter. The AIs had a separate language altogether. Multisensory Projective Identity Display is what they called the nanites that clouded around the tank and formed images to express the tanked Marine's emotional state. The Marines just knew them as immersos.

They stood apart from each other, as soldiers do, looking at and thinking about the other.

Gonzo broke the silence.

"What are we waiting for?" she said. "Let's drink, man."

A year ago, Mexico City, following the purchase of the Mexican capital by the Morninglory Corporation

For the first two months it had been DF, Distrito Federal, but then the Marines changed it. DF, USA. Then just DFUS, Distrito Federal United States, they told the officers, but it really meant something nastier. The 5th was billeted in a church close to the city center. Pews had been yanked out to accommodate the rows of Marines. During the day the middle of the church was a sort of communal space. Mitchum left it alone as much as he could and spent time in one of the draped-off naves, reading the books his mother sent him. Gonzo got them after he was done.

"I think your mom's a lonely woman," Gonzo said one day.

"Huh?"

"All she sends you are romances."

"It's what she reads."

"Which is why I said she was lonely, Brainstein."

Every night they suited up and met the patrol convoy out front. Fat bellied med robos, carrying gallons of compressed stabilization gel, passed the thinner, lethal firing platforms. The boss robo, the thing that had taken the place of the officer corps in the field, wasn't even within sight. It floated a mile above DF, staring down at the squad and reading the nano-spread in their blood. These patrols were meant to hit the Narkys, gangsters from all over the world hired by Morninglory, brought in to cause mayhem, just before they bought DF—to drive the price down, of course. The Narkys were too dumb to know that once the deal was done Morninglory would turn its attention to killing them off. They'd hired the USMC to do it.

"Good evening, Squad six," the boss robo said into their earpieces as they stepped out into the night. No one answered. Humvees moved up the block, patched in scrap metal. Small black globes floated over them, anti-ballistic nano swarms. Once on the road they'd disperse around the vehicle.

Their ritual: Before every patrol Gonzo smacked Mitchum's back hard.

"Tip of the spear," she said.

Gonzo and Mitchum walked farther into the hotel, their immersos expanding from the joy they felt at seeing each other.

"Where you been," Gonzo said.

"Been home."

"So I was right about the goats?"

They floated into the Marine Corps Ball.

Mitchum and Gonzo ordered drinks, and red-suited waiters reached in to the multicolored boil of the immersos. The bottles of beer were gripped by the nano swarms in the immersos, which could act like hands. Around them other Marines started arriving, grouping up, formal but just barely containing their joy and rage. Mitchum had felt this before. Get a bunch of Marines in a room and you can almost hear the whir of life. What other people were like this? Mitchum's mom had been a teacher. Get twenty-five teachers in a room and the bitterness and disappointment they put off was like scalded coffee.

"God," Gonzo sighed, sipping through the oral port in her tank. "Beer tastes like God."

"You're a heathen, Gonzo."

"You can't tell me you still believe in that shit you used to talk about."

"What?"

"Jesus. God. The holy toast."

Mitchum twitched. To calm himself, he watched Gonzo's medals turn. He had the same medals: campaign ribbons, Mexico and Panama; meritorious service award; Purple Heart.

Mitchum didn't believe in God anymore. Not even close.

But because it was Gonzo, he lied. "Of course I do. Now more than ever."

"Ain't that special," she said.

Mitchum drank.

"There's something I have to tell you," he said to Gonzo. "It's important."

"What?"

Mitchum thought about what he needed to say to Gonzo. He formed the words but didn't release them. And then he lost his nerve.

"I'm going to the head," he said.

"You're right, that is important. Thanks for keeping me in the loop," Gonzo answered as he moved away.

This was Mitchum's first MC Ball. They always happened in hotels like this one, expensive enough to have marble and soft carpets, but cheap enough to have rooms available to Marines that would trash half of them. Every Marine brought a date, which they ditched when they arrived so drinking could begin. The Dump tonight was a bar adjacent to the main ballroom. The abandoned dates were standing in groups, mostly women but a few men. They weren't excited to be here, but seeing women dressed in their gowns calmed Mitchum, reminding him of pictures of his mother, and rose petals fell around him in a drifting snow—a reflection in the immerso of the change in his heart rate.

"Ah, womanhood," a monotone voice next to him said. It was Mandell, his immerso part dress blues and part mind-bending mirror labyrinth.

"Yes," Mitchum said.

"They possess many pleasing features. Their neck. Their asscrack."

Mandell had gone down in a helicopter crash over DF, broke his neck and got total body burns and a TBI so bad that his eyes popped out and gray matter leaked from his ears. When they were done putting him back together again, Mandell had become all interface, an AI that connected to hyped-up receptors in his brain. It put together the Marine's thoughts as best it could and spoke them for him, usually in its own halting lingo, so the Marine could have a version of a social life. The more messed up your brain was, the more the interface scrapped together neural impulses, adding its own halting lingo when it needed to. It made him creepy to talk to.

"The pleasing tractability of their flesh," Mandell said.

"I live with my mom," Mitchum answered. "Ain't had no pleasing tractability in awhile. Not like I could feel it anyway through this tank."

And of course among the things I lost in DF were my hands, my arms, my shoulders. Eyes. Jaw. Face. Who would want to be with me?

Beer traveled through the sip port. Had he wanted to drink?

The women in the bar shifted closer together. Some of them tilted their heads and smiled at Mandell and Mitchum. Others pursed their lips and looked away. The male dates talked loudly about sports.

"We're making them uncomfortable," Mitchum said. Unbidden came the image of his legs, balls, dick—where they'd been. He ended in a tucked abdomen now. Fourteen robo surgeries. Every inch of his flesh mapped out in constructs, mulled over day and night by med AIs trying to think up new surgeries.

Again beer in the sip port.

I know I didn't want to drink this time, Mitchum thought. I've got to keep a clear head.

"Their pre-orgasmic sighs," Mandell said.

One of the women split away from her group, glaring at Mandell and Mitchum as she crossed the floor, pure disgust and hatred.

That expression hooked into such a lovely, delicate face made Mitchum boil in his gel.

DF

Despite the rumors, nothing had ever happened between them. Mitchum spent down time with Gonzo, slept next to her, played cards with her. Sometimes he helped her trim her toenails, taking each toe gently and carving the excess half-moon nail away with a blade. As he cut she told him all of the different things about him that made him impossible to love. His melon head. His pale, disconcerting eyes. The *smell*.

At night they talked.

"What do you do back in Fresno?" she asked. They were on the roof of the church, DF stretched out around them, light spread like shells upon the cathedrals.

"My mom has goats. I help out."

"How many goats?"

"Thirty-six." He thought back to the last letter he'd read. "Thirty-five."

"Your mom is an animal hoarder," she said, and flicked his ear hard enough to make him duck.

"Ow. What?"

"She collects animals 'cause she's lonely."

"No."

"Clever refutation. I take it back."

Gonzo was from West Long Beach, the Morninglory part, which had been bought out by the corp when she was eight. Ten story tall Panopticon towers stood in the neighborhood. She lived near the one closest to Santa Fe Street. People in her neighborhood called it The Dick. All night Morninglory agents watched the houses from The Dick, shining spotlights up and down the streets. Once in awhile they caught somebody breaking the law, usually boys, and they made examples of them. Frank Andrades was crucified just before Gonzo signed up with the Marines, right on Santa Fe, near the food complex.

"Which is why it's a very bad time to be a male," she said. Gonzo's argument was that the young male's in-built desire to peacock all over the place had outlived its genetic usefulness. Frank's body hung there for a month, she'd heard, The Dick shining a spot on it all night to make sure no one cut it down. Finally the ligaments in the arms gave, and he fell to the sidewalk.

Gonzo was a scholar. She read everything, and spent high school lunch periods in the school's library touring the world via holo and even reading the old, tagged-in books. When she learned that the university allotments for West Long Beach had been filled, she snuck out and joined the Marines instead of going to work for the corp.

The night before they got hit they'd played Threes. Scholar though she was, Gonzo was a dunce with cardplay. Mitchum destroyed her game after game. It got boring, and only because the option of straight conversation was worse, they played and talked.

First the future.

"I'll finish here. Go back to Fresno. Live with my mom," Mitchum said.

"Which is the only thing that could possibly make you more attractive to the ladies."

He ignored that. "I'll raise goats. When my mom gets old I'll take care of her."

"Me—I'm gonna take the GI bill and go to school, somewhere still in the US, not bought up by Morninglory yet. Maybe Seattle."

Then they talked about the past.

"It's because of my dad," Mitchum said, answering a question from Gonzo. "Mom was all messed up after he left. So when I think about, you know, standing in the door, about to leave, I can't do it. It was hard enough joining the MC."

Gonzo answered a version of her own question. "My mom would've sold us for cigarettes. But I don't hate her for it." She went on to tell Mitchum what it was like after the US sold West Long Beach to Morninglory. The Panopticon going up. The city cops walking off the streets for the last time. Everyone in the city being drafted to work in the corp's factories. "If you stay in that city you learn to see people as money on legs: you spend them. Which is why I'm getting the fuck out."

Then, obliquely, they discussed each other.

"Something I learned here," Gonzo said, "is that most of these Marines are all talk. They're so brave smoking cigarettes in the church. But Narkys start shooting and you can see it in their eyes that they're afraid. And that they're somewhere in their minds weighing whether you're worth saving. Like they see you as currency too."

Mitchum shrugged.

"But you, Mitchum," Gonzo set her cards down in a small fan around her left knee. "I look in your eyes and I know. You'd do anything for someone you love."

Mitchum stared and gulped and tried to think of something to say. Gonzo beat him to it.

"You dumb motherfucker you."

Da Fuck Us, the Marines called Mexico City. Like this: the Morninglory agents da fuck us, the Narkys da fuck us, we're living in a church da fuck us.

When they got back from patrols Gonzo would sit and smoke cigarettes and re-read letters. She told Mitchum everything going on back home. West Long Beach was locked down. A street gang had sprung up, something that Morninglory had promised to abolish when it bought the city. The corp had a couple gun battles, burned down half a block of houses. Snipers were assigned to The Dick.

"And how's mom and the goats?" she asked one day.

"Good."

Sometimes it dizzied Mitchum to compare Gonzo to his mother. Gonzo was strong. You could see it when she moved, light and precise on her feet like they were blades. She had the kind of presence that could make even the biggest Marines shut up. These same guys would dog Mitchum out day and night when they first got to the church, but Gonzo had stopped it. One day in the common area of the church the Marines were calling Mitchum slow, stupid-quiet, and doing impressions of him staring at things. All he could think was—is that really me? Do I stare at stuff like I'm slow?

Gonzo was cleaning her weapon and cut in.

"Why do you think Mitchum don't say much?" she asked.

That shut the room up in a way that Mitchum hadn't expected. Then she answered her own question.

" 'Cause he *ain't gotta* say shit. You all . . . " Gonzo moved her hand like a talking mouth. Then she pointed to Mitchum. "Dude just does his job, no hype. That's what a hero looks like."

Mitchum thought about that every night. He didn't feel like a hero. They'd been in a few firefights and he'd done all right, but nothing special. Gonzo had tied him to her in a kind of charity, and he wasn't sure why.

But there were the rumors.

"People say we love each other, you know that, right Mitchum?" Gonzo said to him one afternoon. They were checking each other's gear for the night patrol.

He shook his head. Gonzo waited; she was beautiful in the way that frightening things sometimes were, appreciation mixed up with mortality.

"Do you love me, Mitchum?"

What did she want him to say? Mitchum thought, his eyes on her boots. He wanted to say yes, yes, yes, but he couldn't even bring himself to look at her.

Mitchum traveled back through the lobby, the immerso around him full of eagles and footage of squads moving down ruined streets. A march played softly, laced through with snippets of famous Marine Corps speeches. Holographic children followed the immerso, barefoot and filthy and starving, vanishing once out of projector range, expressions of liberated glee on their faces. Gonzo was in the middle of the dance floor, shooting off lightning bolts and banging street grind. Regular Marines around her did something like dancing.

Marines parted as Mitchum crossed the dance floor. Somehow Gonzo didn't see him coming. Mitchum passed through the projective area of Gonzo's immerso until their tanks clunked together.

"Shit," Gonzo said. "Mitchum."

"Evelyn Gonzalez," Mitchum said, to get her attention.

"Since when do you call me that?"

"This is what I wanted to tell you: They're taking my immerso."

The street grind raged around them.

Finally: "How?"

"I was at the VA a week ago. DF's gone way longer than anybody expected. There aren't enough immersos. They told me about a guy from a mech unit that got burned in his tank. No skin, barely any muscle left. He's lying in a bed, can't say shit, probably crazy from the pain. They told me all about his wife and kids."

Imagine that he's your father, the med AI had said, trying to be casual—but that, a flayed tortured speck of life, was Mitchum too.

"I don't care whose father it is," Mitchum had answered.

But that was it. An up-and-running immerso cost as much as two drone-swarm networks. And what would happen to Mitchum? The casual AI answered: you are stable, private.

It's not like he'd die.

"They'll let me stay in the tank. Everything else they'll take. The interface, the V2 jack. Everything. I won't be able to talk, see anything, hear. They'll feed me, those fuckers, through a gastro-drip."

Gonzo was quiet. But he knew what she was going to ask next.

"Shit. Will they take mine?"

Mitchum stared at Gonzo—*stare*—that was the word he had to use, although it wasn't accurate. Nano-swarms were networking visual data about Gonzo's tank, her own projections and nano-swarm, the dancing Marines, the disco lights hung high in the room, and firing it back to a pinpoint receiver on Mitchum's tank, which piped it through his V2 jack. His thoughts were on Gonzo's future, alone in the tank when someone else needed her immerso, in the dark of West Long Beach, the spotlights from the Morninglory tower dragging back and forth across the barred windows of her house.

"There are enough of *us*," Mitchum said, "and enough tanks to keep us alive, in the dark, forever. Everything else is going away. I'd rather be dead than be locked in the dark alone. I'm going to . . . "

Mitchum thought of what he had decided to do. Of Mandell. And then he turned and moved away.

DF

In DFUS, just before the sun came up, there was this quality to the air. Clean, a little cold. Mitchum and Gonzo used to sit on the roof of the church, watching the robos float over the city, and not even talk, just breathe. The lights below winked out one by one as the sun came up, a dog barked somewhere, sometimes there was gunfire. But in between the sounds was silence. A perfect tension of being.

Mitchum and Gonzo had been hit on the same block.

It was a day patrol, around three o'clock. Mitchum was standing on a corner, shoulder against a building, watching Marines move up the street ahead. He wasn't nervous. The days were usually peaceful in DF. Network implants were part of the contract the Narkys got from Morninglory and they turned them into fast-eyed psychos for twelve hours at a time and crashed them the rest.

That day, on the corner, Mitchum watched Gonzo step out into the empty street and look from one building to another. A Humvee idled behind him. The driver called out Mitchum's name. At that moment, while his name coursed its sonic wash through the air to his ear and through that into his understanding, into his self-told-history, into the synaptic constellation that was the memory of the awful thing that was about to happen; at that moment while Gonzo squinted into the sun, while Mitchum registered the kneeling point-man's back as a brown loaf shape a hundred yards away, Mitchum's thought was of the church they were billeted in, his thought was that the city itself was also a church, as was the Humvee behind him and the robos slipping through the air and of course Gonzo too, there in the sun.

He turned. The driver was already looking past him.

The EMP rocket hit Gonzo first. It was the Narky's way of coun-teracting the defensive nanite swarms that every Marine had—EMPs were RPG shells emptied of their explosive and loaded with a one-time, short-range pulse that killed any computer tech. Mitchum heard the EMP rocket hit the defensive swarm then heard the swarm hit the street like a bucket of uncooked rice. He didn't see the second rocket hit Gonzo, but he felt the explosion in the soles of his feet. The med robo fell toward the smoke. Gonzo was crumpled there on the street, and Mitchum broke into a run, firing his mod gun at the roof of the near building. The med robo disgorged its suspension gel over Gonzo in a loud splat.

Mitchum ran.

When he got to her he kneeled, firing his mod gun. Shapes dropped out of sight on the roof. He looked down and saw the gel over Gonzo. She was raw beneath it, her limbs ruined, her face occluded as she bled into the gel.

A firing platform hit the building to his left, peppering glass and stone across him, and Mitchum looked back in the direction he'd come from. The Humvee had been hit—flames licked up behind the cracked windshield. The Marine who had called his name a few seconds ago was slumped on the dash.

A sound like a reversing thunderclap hit him. Another EMP. Mitchum's nanite swarm fell useless around him.

Thoughts came fast: I'm naked here, a perfect target. But I can't leave Gonzo. They'll pick her apart.

Mitchum fired at the roofs on both sides of him. Then he reached down, through the gel, and grasped Gonzo under her arms. Her skin was hot mush.

He stood and began to pull her to safety.

The next thing Mitchum remembered was darkness.

They told him later that the second rocket had landed right behind him, and although he was mangled, his body had shielded Gonzo from most of the blast.

Mitchum found Mandell still by the Dump, his projections whorling spirals of cloud and garbage, staring at the women. They'd forgotten about him, it seemed, and were drinking champagne.

Mitchum focused his attention into a fist and the nano cloud obeyed; he slammed it into Mandell's tank, aiming through the projection cloud as best he could to hit the seam, the weakest spot. It busted under the nano fist and Mitchum felt the raw, shameful glee that came with hurting someone.

Mandell roared and turned, his projections enflaming and turning the room incandescent. Mitchum's tank rocked as Mandell struck back and then the two tanks collided and fell, their projections intermingling into swirling light and smoke, faces, eagles in panicked flight, refugee children dragging bleeding American flags across the floor . . .

"Conflict is sexually gratifying . . . " Mandell growled through the overly formal interface, and Mitchum hit him again, feeling another section of the tank burst under the nanite fist. And Mitchum decided maybe it was exciting. There were such fine degrees between stroking and hitting. Either way the flesh is there, that dumb, wonderful moment of contact.

In DFUS he used to think about Gonzo's stomach, just above her hips. How smooth it would be. He'd never seen it, of course, and now her skin, like his, was gone.

Mitchum felt a strange agony grip him: the stabilization gel was leaking out of his tank. What was left of his body was settling against the inner wall. He experienced an intense thirst for air, the empty space where his lungs had been throbbing in some involuntary spasm, and then the nanite clouds lost power and fell to the floor.

As his consciousness narrowed, Mitchum listened to Mandell scream about the gel leaking out of his own tank, about the uncomfortable sensation of weight upon him, about women and how in all their beauty he wanted to smash them to shards.

Weight. Blackness. And then gone.

Slowly the darkness coned away until there was a small point of dim light.

The presence in the darkness thought. It realized it was Mitchum, a grievously injured Marine, what was left of a man. He remembered Gonzo and the MC Ball and what he'd done to Mandell, but he couldn't see the outside world or hear anything or feel his body. His interface was off. He was alone in the suspension gel.

So what is this light? I don't have eyes . . . How is this light getting into my brain?

Don't start singing, a voice said. *It ain't Heaven.*

Gonzo?

Tip of the spear.

Where are we?

In the same tank. There's a jack cable going between our heads.

How did we get in the same tank?

After you hit Mandell—and he's OK by the way, nice of you to ask, at this moment he's probably telling a nurse that she has pleasingly tractable flesh— they were gonna take your interface gear and leave you in your tank, just like you said they would. I made a deal.

What?

I told them they could have all of my interface gear too, and even my immerso tank, if they just put me in here with you and connected us.

It was hard to explain, but Mitchum could feel Gonzo's presence. It might've been a degree of warmth in the gel. It might've been that they were touching; perhaps their ruined skulls were forehead to forehead. Perhaps the V2 jack was unneeded.

Gonzo laughed.

Two bodies, one coffin.

Mitchum watched the light in front of him. Slowly it clarified. He was back in DF, on the roof of the church. But it wasn't. This roof had a forest of statues. Saints towered over him, ribboning the sun across his face, and there were statues of killers and con men and mothers and children too. There were statues of soldiers rushing through the other statues, panic and bravery mixed on their faces like lightning in full sunlight.

Her voice echoed out from within the stone shapes.

Mitchum? Find me, she said. *I'm here.*

ABOUT THE AUTHOR

Mike Buckley's work has appeared in *The Best American Non-Required Reading, 2003, The Southern California Review,* and numerous times in *The Alaska Quarterly Review.* He has been nominated for various awards, and his debut short story collection, *Miniature Men,* was released in 2011. He is a practicing Creative Futurist, using science fiction storytelling to improve corporate and government policy.

Coming of the Light
CHEN QIUFAN
TRANSLATED BY KEN LIU

0.

My mother told me about a Buddhist monk she and I met while shopping on my first birthday.

The monk caressed my head—back then as bald as his—and chanted a few lines that sounded like poetry.

After we returned home, my mom recited a few fragments to my father. Dad, who had had a few more years of schooling than my mom and completed middle school, told her that the lines weren't poetry, but from a Buddhist koan. Only by consulting the village schoolmaster did he finally discover the origin of those fragments, words which would come to determine my life.

As clouds drift across the sky, so Master in the Void is seen.
Dust clings to everything but what is true.
Over and over the monk queries: "What does your visit mean?"
Master points to cypress which in courtyard has taken root.

They thought these lines must contain some deep meaning, and so they renamed me Zhou Chongbo, which means "Repeat-Cypress."

1.

I'm sitting in a steamer. I'm a dumpling being steamed.

Everyone keeps on inhaling and exhaling and then staring at the white smoke coming out of everyone else's mouths, like cartoon characters with thought bubbles drifting over their heads containing logical musings, naked women, or frozen obscenicons. Then the smoke dissipates, revealing coarse, swollen faces. The air purifier screams as though it's gone mad, and the young women sitting in chairs along the wall silently put on their face masks, slide their fingers across the screens of their phones, and frown.

I don't need to look at the time to know it's past midnight. My wife won't even respond to my WeChat messages anymore.

I was dragged here at the last minute. My wife and I were on our way home after taking a stroll when we encountered a man dressed in an army coat on the pedestrian overpass. With a booming voice that startled both of us, he said, "The Quadrantid meteor shower will come on January 4. Don't miss it—"

I waited for him to finish with what is known to us marketing professionals as the "call to action"—e.g., "Join the Haidian Astrology Club," "Call this number now!", or even pulling out a portable telescope from his pocket and telling me "Now for only eighty-eight yuan"—which would have made this a reasonably well executed bit of street peddling.

But like a stuck answering machine, he started again from the beginning: "The Quadrantid meteor shower will come on January 4 . . . "

Mission failed.

Disappointed, we left him. That was when my phone rang.

It was Lao Xu. I glanced apologetically at my wife, who gave me her usual unhappy look when my work intruded on our time together—this was certainly not the first time. I answered the call, and that was how I ended up here, sitting in this room.

The last thing my wife said to me was: "Tell your mother to quit pestering me about a grandchild. Her son is such a pushover he might as well be a baby."

"Chongbo!" Lao Xu's voice drags me back to this room filled with cancer-inducing smoke. "You're in charge of strategy. Contribute!"

Peering through the obscure haze, I struggle to make sense of the confusing notes on the whiteboard: user insights, key selling points, market research . . . dry erase marker lines in various colors connect the words like the trails left by the finger on some mobile picture-matching game: triangle, pentagon, hexagram, the seven Dragon Balls . . .

It's all bullshit. Meaningless bullshit.

The pressure in the steamer is rising. Beads of sweat form on my forehead, slide down my face, drip.

"Is it too hot in here?" Lao Xu hands me a wrinkled paper napkin whose color is rather suspect. "Wipe yourself!"

I obey, too terrified to object.

"Mr. Wan wasn't happy with the marketing plan last time and wanted to switch agencies. I begged and pleaded to get him to stay. If we don't succeed this time, I think you all understand what that means."

The cheap napkin comes apart in my hand and bits of paper are stuck to my sweaty face.

Mr. Wan is our god, the CEO of an Internet company. Out of any ten random people who accost strangers in the streets of Zhongguancun—"China's Silicon Valley"—one would be engaged in "network marketing," two would be trying to hook you on pyramid schemes, three would be trying to talk to you about Jesus, and the rest would all be founders or C-whatever-Os of some startup.

But if you got these individuals to engage in one-on-one conversion bouts—time limited to three minutes—I'm sure the last group would achieve complete victory. They're not interested in selling you a mere *product*, but an *idea* that would change the world. They're not there to speak for some deity; they're gods already.

Mr. Wan is just such a god.

Due to Lao Xu's persistence and luck, our little agency managed to land Mr. Wan as a client. We are supposed to spend the euros, dollars, yen, and yuan flowing in from angel investors, from private equity funds, from rounds A-B-C-D, and help Mr. Wan's company expand the market for their mobile app, raise product awareness, and improve daily engagement levels so that Mr. Wan could then use the new numbers to attract even more investment.

The flywheel goes round and round.

So where is the sticking point?

"Where is the sticking point?" Lao Xu's dry and thin voice screeches like a subway train shrieking through a tunnel, and an invisible force presses against me until I'm about to blackout. Trembling, I stand up, avoiding the gazes of others on purpose. I'm like some two-dimensional inhabitant of a mathematical plane: my body is made up of points, but I can't see any.

"It's . . . a problem with the product." I lower my head shamefully, prepared for an angry tirade from Lao Xu.

"This is your fucking insight?"

I hold my tongue.

Mr. Wan's co-founder—let's call him Y—is a former classmate from USTC who had worked in America for many years. Mr. Wan convinced him to return to China, bringing with him valuable key patent rights to build a business. Y's patent covers a digital watermarking technology, which, because it involves information theory and complex mathematics, is a bit hard to explain.

I'll use a simple example. Let's say you take a picture and use the patented technology to add a watermark invisible to the naked eye; then, no matter how this photograph is subsequently modified or edited—even if 80 percent of the image were cropped—you would still be able to apply a special algorithm to recover the original image. The secret is that the invisible watermark itself carries all the information in the photo at the time it's applied.

This is, of course, only the most basic application for the technology. It could become an authentication/anti-tampering mechanism with many uses in fields such as media, finance, forensics, military security, and medicine—the possibilities are endless.

However, after Y returned to China, the two co-founders discovered that all the core industries they were interested in had barriers to entry—the difficulty wasn't so much that the fences were high, but that they couldn't even tell where they were. After bumping into walls multiple times, they decided that they had to make an end run around the difficulties by starting with entertainment, hoping to popularize the technology first through grassroots consumer acceptance before gradually infiltrating enterprise business use cases.

Mr. Wan is always emphasizing the word "sexy," as though this is the only yardstick by which everything should be judged. But their product rather resembles a punctured, crumpled blowup doll left to dry in the shade.

"Why don't you use our client's product?" Lao Xu screams at the young women sitting along the wall. Blood drains from their faces as they pretend to be busy taking notes.

Mr. Wan's mobile app is called "Truthgram," and it automatically applies the special digital watermark to every picture the user takes. No matter how many times the image is transmitted, photoshopped, or otherwise altered beyond recognition, a simple button press would restore the original image. At first, the marketing angle focused on safety: *as long as you stick to Truthgram, Mom will never have to worry about your face showing up in some photoshopped pornographic image.*

Besides priming the sales channels, we also planned a web marketing event called "The Big Reveal." We recruited a hundred women and helped them take selfies with Truthgram, which we then retouched until everyone looked like a supermodel. We posted the photos on the web along with an animated GIF explaining how to use Mr. Wan's app to reveal the truth: "Turn Beauty to Beast in less than one second!"

Male users—maybe *losers* would be more accurate—responded to the gimmick with extraordinary exuberance, recommending the app to each other and coming up with a veritable flood of variations that fulfilled the promise of user-generated content. Women, on the other hand, detested the marketing trick. They filled the forums with negative commentary about the company, arguing that the app vilified and insulted women by playing up the hoary trope of treating women's right to pursue beauty as a twisted form of narcissistic deceit. The marketing event became a PR crisis.

If it were up to me, I would have declared victory. Developing a market is all about pressing the key point, like plunging a sharp needle into the hypothalamus, the emotional center of the brain. If you don't see some blood spill, it probably means your needle is too dull or maybe you haven't stabbed at the right spot.

But Mr. Wan thought our little exercise could only grab some eyeballs temporarily at the cost of damaging the long-term brand value. As it turned out, the data proved him right. After a brief spike, the number of downloads went down and stayed down, and the losers we managed to attract eventually stopped using the app because we couldn't keep them stimulated with a constant stream of new content.

"I'm more interested in whether others see me from the most beautiful angle than in the security of my photos," a perfectly ordinary girl stated in an interview we conducted with our customers. Her phone's photo album was filled with selfies that showed signs of excessive retouching, all of them similar and none resembling her. Still, every half hour or so, she would hold her phone overhead at a 45-degree angle, pout her lips like a duck, and snap a shot.

If a tower's foundations are built on the shifting sands of a beach, how can you expect it to stay standing until the tides come in?

Lao Xu stares at me; I stare at the whiteboard; the whiteboard stares at everyone; everyone stares at their phone. We are like a flock of birds lost in fog, constantly drawn to flashing screens until we've forgotten the direction we were headed in. Yet, cold night has fallen, and hungry predators are approaching in the dark.

My phone beeps, indicating that it's nearly out of battery. My instinctive reaction is not to conserve, but to rush to look through WeChat Moments posted in my network. Every last drop of juice must be used to its fullest extent and not be wasted with invisible background processes. Now you get a glimpse of my values, my philosophy.

I see the latest posts by Mr. Wan. All of a sudden, the dumpling skin has burst, and the fillings spill out.

"I've got it!" I slam my hand down on the table. Everyone jerks awake from their somnambulant state.

I hold my phone under Lao Xu's nose.

Under Mr. Wan's profile, he has posted a new photo, accompanied by the following caption:

On Saturday, the fifteenth of the month under the lunar calendar, I'm going to perform the Buddhist good deed of freeing captive animals on the shore of Wenyu River. I'll purchase and free river snails laden with eggs, birds, reptiles, fish, and other animals. By this compassionate deed, I hope the Buddha brings blessings to everyone so that the aged may live longer, the middle-aged may have harmonious families, and children may gain wisdom and health! Happy Saturday! (Donations to help purchase more animals to free gratefully accepted: more animals = more good karma for all! Funds may be sent to this account: XXXXXXX. Sharing and reposting this message will also gain you blessings.)

"Err—I hadn't realized that they were running so low on funds." Lao Xu's eyes are wide as teacups. "They haven't paid us our last invoice yet!"

"Keep on reading," I say. I continue to slide my finger up the screen. Mr. Wan's dynamic timeline is woven from high-tech news and pop-Buddhism, a mixture of concentrated caffeine pills and chicken soup for the soul. "I think we've discovered his other passion."

"So what?"

"Let's think about why, every day, so many people share and forward these posts about how to do good deeds to build up merit and gain the Buddha's protection. Are they really that faithful? I doubt it. Maybe preventing their photographs from being tempered with isn't a core need for people, but the anxious contemporary Chinese are obsessed with personal security, especially the psychological sense of being safe. We have to connect Mr. Wan's product with this psychological need."

"Be specific!"

"Everyone, what kind of posts would you share to feel more secure?" I ask.

"Powerful mantras!" "Pictures of buddhas!" "The Birthday of the Buddha, and other festival birthdays!" "Wise sayings by famous master monks!"

"What sort of posts would make you believe and willingly hand over money?"

There's a pause as everyone in the room ponders my question. Then, one of the girls timidly speaks up, "Something that's been con . . . consecrated . . . um, you know, when the light has been—"

"Bingo!"

The room falls silent. Lao Xu gets up, and, poker-faced, walks behind me. I hear a loud slam, and a chill wind pours into the back of my shirt as though a bucket of ice has been emptied into it. The haze in the room instantly dissipates.

"Awake now?" Lao Xu closes the window. "Explain what you mean again, but stop being so damned mystical."

I hold his gaze and speak slowly. "Let's find a famous and respected monk to consecrate this app—'bring light into it'—so that every picture it takes becomes a charm to ward off evil. We'll create a sharing economy of blessings."

Everyone shifts their gaze from the phone screen to me; I gaze at Lao Xu; Lao Xu says nothing but gazes at the phone.

After a while, he lets out a held breath. "You know, all those rinpoches in Chaoyang District are going to get you for this."

I have no idea what's in store for me.

10.

My wife is a Neo-Luddite.

Once, she had been a heavy gamer. She spent so much time on the computer that her parents sent her to a summer camp that specialized in curing Internet addiction. The experience caused her attitude toward technology to turn a hundred and eighty degrees.

Many times I asked her, what really happened in that campground located on Phoenix Mountain called "The Nirvana Plan"?

She never answered me directly.

This was the biggest philosophical difference between us. She believed that despite the appearance of unprecedented novelty, the high-tech industry was ultimately no different from another ancient trade: they both took advantage of the weaknesses of ordinary men and women, and, under the guise of words like "progress," "uplift," and "salvation," manipulated their emotions. Whether you put your hand on a Bible or an iPad, in the end you were praying to the same god.

We only give the people what they want. They desire comfort, joy, a sense of security. They want to improve themselves, to see themselves stand out in the crowd. We can't take such desires away from them. That was how I always argued back at her.

Oh, please! Don't give me that. You're just playing a game to satisfy your own yearning for control, she said.

Come on, give people a little credit! I said. *Everyone's got a brain. How can anyone "control" anyone else?*

71

There are always NPCs.

What are you talking about?

Non-Player Characters. What if everything is controlled from behind the scenes by some invisible background process? Then every action you take will affect the game logic. The system will react with NPCs and they will carry out their predetermined programming.

I stared at her face as though I'd never really known her. I even wondered whether she had just joined some new cult.

You don't really believe that, do you?

I'm going to walk the dog. There shouldn't be much dog poop in the streets this early in the morning.

11.

Every day, as the temple bell tolls five, I have to get up to sweep the grounds. I sweep the wooden floor of the gallery from the new library to the stone steps, and thence to the temple gates, where the ancient pagoda tree grows, its gnarled branches spread like the talons of a rampant beast.

As for whether I will be quietly reciting the *Surangama Sutra*, the *Lotus Sutra*, or the *Diamond Sutra* as I sweep, that depends on the day's PM2.5 air quality index. My throat hurts when I breathe the polluted air; I don't need the distraction.

Any of the faithful coming to the temple to make offerings can see that I haven't been truly called by the Buddha. Just like all the other "disciples" flocking here on weekends to study Buddhist doctrine, I'm here to hide from the real world.

In a way, I'm not too different from the throngs of shoppers at the Buddhist shop outside Yonghe Lamasery vying to buy electronic "Buddha boxes." They bring the box home, push a button, and the box starts chanting sutras. On the hour (or at designated times), the box will even emit a tranquil, meditative *duannnnng*, like the ringing of the bell in a temple. The purchasers apparently think this will bring them blessings and cleanse bad karma. I often imagine all the passengers squeezed like canned sardines into the number 2 subway train leaving from the lamasery station, all of their Buddha boxes ringing harmoniously together on the hour. Perhaps the so-called *Chan* state of mind refers to the detachment of such a moment from real life.

And now that I have to commit to a Buddhist vegetarian diet, I miss the restaurant at Beixinqiao where they serve chitterlings soup made from ancient stock that has supposedly been accumulating flavor for years.

I've canceled my mobile number and deleted all my accounts on social media; my wife has left me and returned to her hometown; I've even been given a Dharma name: "Chenwu"—"Free of Worldly Dust." All I want is for those crazy people to never find me again.

I've had enough.

Everything began that night with the crazy marketing scheme that seemed to make no sense.

Mr. Wan bought my idea. Overnight he summoned the engineers to develop the new product. Lao Xu laid out the marketing plan and strategy. The most important piece of the project, of course, was assigned to me, the originator.

I had to go find a respected master monk willing to consecrate our app, to bring it light.

Lao Xu demanded that the entire process be filmed and turned loose online to go viral. I ran through every excuse I could think of: *my family have been Christians for three generations; my wife is pregnant and can't come in contact with raw foods, animal fur, or anything having to do with spirits . . .*

Lao Xu responded with only one line: *This is your baby. If you don't want to see it through, get out and don't come back, you get me?*

I visited every temple in Beijing, begging and pleading with the master monks, and I sought out every lama secluded in spiritual solitude in the city's various nooks and crannies. Each time, however, even after having come to an agreement on the price, as soon as I brought out my camera, the monks' faces turned stony, and after a few *Amitabha*s, they would cover their faces and escape my presence.

We tried using hidden cameras a few times, but the combination of incense haze and camera shake made the results unwatchable.

As the deadline approached, I could no longer sleep, but tossed and turned all night. My wife asked me what I was doing.

"Rolling dough for pancakes," I said.

She kicked me. "If you want to do that, get on the floor. Don't pretend you're a rolling pin in bed. I'm trying to sleep."

The kick managed to free my clogged neural pathways. Instantly, I was inspired.

Mr. Wan's new app went on sale on time. Lao Xu, energized like his Land Rover, shifted into high gear and whipped us into a frenzy. Videos, new concepts, and new campaigns were released one after another. Soon, a video depicting a master monk consecrating a mobile phone went viral, and Buddhagrams began to conquer Weibo and WeChat. The number of downloads and daily engagement level rose exponentially like rockets heading for the clouds at escape velocity.

Don't ask me the impact of such growth on the long-term brand value; don't ask me what this meant for the subsequent development and application of the digital watermark technology. Those are problems Mr. Wan had to solve. I was only a strategist for a third-rate marketing company who had some crazy ideas. I could only work on problems that I was capable of solving with my own methods.

In the end, we underestimated the creativity of users. It turned out that Buddhagram pictures, due to the presence of the watermark, could be recovered from even low-resolution copies or cropped fragments. This meant they could be shared and forwarded without taking up much bandwidth or time. Trying to take advantage of the situation, we released a series of new ads touting this newly discovered advantage.

Downloads spiked again, but no one anticipated what happened next.

It started with a picture of an apple taken with Buddhagram. A week later, the poster shared a second picture of the same apple: it was apparently rotting at a much slower rate than other apples.

Next came the various pictures of pets that miraculously recovered their health after having had their pictures taken with Buddhagram.

Then, an old lady claimed that after she had taken a Buddhaselfie, she managed to survive a deadly car accident.

Rumors multiplied. Taken individually, each seemed some preposterous April Fool's joke, but behind every story stood a witness who swore it was true, and the number of believers snowballed.

The posts grew stranger. Patients with terminal cancer posted selfies showing their tumors diminishing daily; couples who had trouble conceiving took nude selfies and became pregnant; migrant laborers took group selfies and won the lottery. The kind of news that one would normally expect to find only on tabloids on the subway filled every social media platform. All the pictures had the Buddhagram watermark, and all of us thought they were from astroturfers hired by the company.

We thought wrong.

Supposedly, Mr. Wan's phone was ringing nonstop with calls from interested investors. Other than asking about a chance to invest, the next most popular question was: *Who is the master monk who brought light to the app?*

The logic was simple: if a consecrated mobile app could have such magical effects, then asking the monk himself to perform some rite would surely result in earthshaking miracles. The investors thought of this, and so did millions and millions of users.

In this age, truth was as rare as virtue. Even more tragic, when faced with the truth, most people preferred to doubt its veracity because they would rather believe the truthy mirage created by their own minds.

Soon, my contact details were leaked. Email, phone, text . . . everyone screamed the same question at me: *Who is the master monk???*

I refused to answer. I knew they would figure it out sooner or later.

Crowdsourcing the search, they finally managed to locate the master monk and the disciples in the viral video—a bunch of actors my friend had found for me among the crowd of extras congregated at Hengdian World Studios, hoping to get a role. They were supposed to portray commoners during the Qing Dynasty, which meant they were already shaved bald—just like Buddhist monks. This made negotiations rather easy. The extras who harbored dreams of making it big in the movies were especially diligent, and the lead even argued with the makeup artist over the correct placement of the burn marks over his head to indicate his ordained status. Watching the scene, I grew concerned.

They were all good people. The fault was entirely mine.

The poor actors who had been located by the "human flesh search engine" could no longer live in peace. The enraged netizens hounded them and their families using the vilest language, forcing them to acknowledge what was obviously true: they were mere extras hired by the company to portray the master monk and his disciples.

Except that the crowd still wasn't quite on the same page as me: they continued to believe that my company—or more precisely, I—was hiding the real master monk. Out of greed or selfishness, I was refusing to disclose his identity to the public so that everyone could benefit from the master's powers.

I really wasn't.

Lao Xu closed the company temporarily. Every day, groups of middle-aged women congregated at the foot of the building, holding up protest banners. Even if we could endure the pressure, the building's property manager couldn't. Lao Xu put us all on paid leave, hoping that the storm would quickly blow over. Kindly, he told me that it was best for me to leave the city and return to my parents' home for a few days. It was just a matter of time before one of the netizens who was terminally ill might arrive at my door with his family, pleading with me to give up the master monk's WeChat ID.

I realized that Lao Xu was right. I couldn't put my family at risk.

And so, after I settled my affairs, I came to this ancient temple to become a grounds sweeper.

The bell tolls nine times, indicating the end of morning lessons. The staff of the temple, including me, assume our positions. The temple is open to the public today, and the abbot, Master Deta, will be greeting a group of VIP faithful from the Internet industry and conducting a salon to discuss the connections between Buddhist doctrine and the Web.

My assigned job is to hand out the visitor's badges. On the list of VIPs, I see more than a few familiar names, including Mr. Wan.

Though it's thirty-eight degrees Celsius, I put on my cotton medical face mask. Sweat pours off me as though I'm drenched by rain.

100.

The faithful, now dressed in the yellow robes and yellow shoes normally reserved for monks, stream in one after another, their colorful badges swaying on lanyards before their chests. For a moment I suffer the illusion of having returned to my old life from a few months ago: the China National Convention Center, JW Marriott Beijing, 798 D Park . . . I was either at meetings or on my way to meetings, handing out my business card, adding people's WeChat IDs, puffing up our clients, sketching incredible visions, peppering my speech with "Internet thinking" buzzwords—like some updated version of a Red Guard clutching his Little Red Book.

The faces before me are still the same, but now their badges have been stripped of the eye-catching titles. "CXO," "Co-Founder," and "VP of Investment" have been replaced by "Householder," "Believer," and "Benefactor." At least for the moment, they've retracted their typical arrogance and protruding bellies. Mumbling mantras, they take their seats, and piously hand their phones, iPads, Google Glasses, smart wristbands, and so on to the waiting novice monks in exchange for a numbered ticket.

I see Mr. Wan. His face looks pallid and thin, but his gaze is steady and his steps airy. Placidly, he places the palms of his hands together and bows to the guests on either side of him, showing no trace of his former domineering air. As he passes me, I lower my head, and he lowers his in turn to acknowledge my greeting.

Many things must have happened in the intervening months.

Supposedly, Master Deta had once been a promising student at the Computer Science Department of Tsinghua University. However, as a result of his enlightenment, he gave up offers for graduate study at Stanford, Yale, UC Berkley and other ivy-clad campuses, took up vows, and became ordained as a monk. With him as an example, a group of other graduates of elite colleges also joined our temple and began to spread the teachings of Buddhism online, bringing relief to all mortal beings with methods adapted to the Internet age.

The master's lecture today roams over many subjects—so many that I barely remember any of them. I do see Mr. Wan holding a pious pose and nodding frequently. When the master discusses how big data techniques could be used to help locate the young reincarnations of tulkus, his eyes even grow tearful.

I'm trying to hide from him, but I also can't suppress the urge to go up to him and ask if the storm has finally blown over. I don't miss my old life, but I miss my family.

Here, only monks who have achieved a certain status have the right to use the Internet. The layered green branches of the ancient cypress grove, like a firewall, separate us from the noise and dust of the secular world. My daily life, however, is not boring at all: sweeping, working, chanting, debating, and copying. Uncluttered by material possessions, I've been sleeping without trouble for the first time in years, and no longer live in constant dread of sudden vibrations from my phone—though occasionally my right quadriceps still suffers phantom pulses. But my teacher tells me that if I count my prayer beads—all one thousand and eight hundred of them—every day for a hundred eighty days, I shall be fully cured.

I think it's because we want too much, more than what our bodies and minds are designed to withstand.

My old job was all about creating need, encouraging people to pursue things that didn't matter for their lives, and then I used the money they gave in exchange to purchase illusions others had created for me. Round after round, we never seemed to tire of the game.

I think about my wife's words: *Her son is such a pushover he might as well be a baby.* Fuck, I'm even more useless than a baby.

This is my sin, my bad karma, the blockage I need to clear for my progress.

I'm starting to understand Mr. Wan.

After the lecture, Mr. Wan and a few others surround Master Deta, apparently because they have many questions that need his insight. Master Deta beckons to me. I gird myself and walk over.

"Would you bring these honored guests to meditation room three? I'll be over in a moment."

I nod, and lead the group to the room in the back reserved for VIPs.

I ask them to sit, and I pour tea for everyone. They nod and smile at each other, but their conversation is restricted to small talk. I'm guessing that they are competitors outside the temple.

Mr. Wan doesn't look at me directly. He sips his tea and closes his eyes, meditating. His lips move as he silently recites some mantra, and his hands are busy with a string of rosewood prayer beads. After the forty-ninth time through the beads, I can't hold myself back any longer. I walk up to him, bend down, and whisper next to his ear, "Do you remember me?"

Mr. Wan opens his eyes and scrutinizes me for half a minute. "You are Zhou . . . "

"Zhou Chongbo. You have excellent memory, sir."

Mr. Wan grimaces and lunges at me, wrapping the string of prayer beads about my neck and pushing me to the floor.

"You fucking idiot!" He curses and strikes me. The two guests next to him stand up, startled, but they don't dare to intervene. "Amitabha. Amitabha," they murmur.

I protect my face with my hands, but I don't know what to say. "Mercy!" I cry. "Mercy!"

"Stop!" Master Deta's voice booms. "This is a sanctified place! Such violence has no place here."

Mr. Wan's fist, suspended in midair, stops. He stares at me, and tears suddenly spill from them and fall onto my face, as though he's the one wronged.

"All gone . . . I've lost everything . . . " he murmurs. Then he falls back into his seat.

I get up. I guess someone who's lost everything can't even strike very hard. My body isn't hurting at all.

"Amitabha." I put my palms together and bow to him. I know he's not feeling much better compared to me. Just as I'm about to leave the meditation room, the abbot stops me, and strikes me with his ferule: twice on the left shoulder, once on the right.

"Don't discuss what happened today with others. You still have too much worldly arrogance about you and cannot handle important tasks. You must study harder and reflect on your actions."

I'm about to argue the point but then remember that I once tolerated much worse from Lao Xu and Mr. Wan. Master Deta is basically the temple's CEO. I have to swallow my pride.

I bow to him and back out.

I lean against the wall of the gallery and watch the woods in the setting sun. Smog glistens above the city like the piled layers of a sari. The bell tolls on the hour, and startled birds take to the air.

A thought flashes through my mind. I am reminded of how Master Subhuti once struck Monkey three times on the head with a ferule and then walked away with his hands held behind him, which was a message for Monkey to come to the backdoor of the master's bedroom at the hour of the third watch for special lessons.

But how am I supposed to interpret two strikes on the left shoulder and one on the right?

101.

At around nine o'clock at night—that's when first watch turns to second watch under the ancient time system—I head for the abbot's chambers via backwoods trails. My journey through the dark woods is accompanied only by the gentle susurration of pines, with not even a chirp from a bird.

I knock twice on the door, and then once. Someone seems to be stirring inside. I knock again. The door opens automatically.

Abbot Deta is sitting with his back to the door. Before him is a giant screen, completely dark. I seem to hear the low-frequency buzzing of electronics. He sighs loudly.

"Teacher! Your student is here!" I fall to my knees and prepare to kowtow.

"I think you've read *Journey to the West* too many times." The abbot gets up, and I can see that his expression isn't one of joy. "I told you to come at one minute past ten o'clock."

I'm stumped for words. Apparently the master was using binary notation.

I hurry to hide my embarrassment. "Um . . . this afternoon—"

"It wasn't your fault; I know what happened. As soon as you stepped into this temple, I learned everything about you."

" . . . then why did you accept me?"

"Though your heart wasn't directed towards the Buddha, you have within you the root of wisdom. If I didn't take you in, I'm afraid you might have sought refuge in suicide."

"Master is indeed merciful." I'm still completely as a loss.

"I know you don't understand." Master Deta isn't actually that old. He's barely in his forties. As he laughs with his glasses perched on his nose, he resembles a college professor.

"Forgive your foolish student, master. Please enlighten me."

Master Deta waves his hand. The giant screen, apparently controlled by body motion, lights up. The image on the screen is difficult to describe: a gigantic, compressed oval whose background is various shades of blue, studded with irregular patches of orange-red dots. Or maybe it's the other way around. I think the image resembles the false-color version of some planet's topographic map, or maybe a slide full of multiplying mold seen through a microscope.

"What is this?"

"The universe. Or more precisely, the cosmic microwave background. This is the image of the universe about 380,000 years after the Big Bang. You're looking at the most precise photograph of it so far." His enthusiastic admiration contrasts sharply with his humble monk's garb.

"Um . . . "

"This was made by computation based on the data gathered by the European Space Agency's Planck space observatory. Look here, and here—do you see how the pattern is a bit odd? . . . "

Other than patches of orange-red or cobalt mold, I can't see what's so special.

"Are you saying that . . . um . . . the Buddha doesn't exist?" I ask tentatively.

"The Buddha teaches that the great trichiliocosm consists of a billion worlds." He glares at me, as though forcing me to retract my words. "This picture proves that multiple universes once existed. After so many years of effort, humanity finally proved, through technology, the Buddhist cosmology."

I should have realized this would happen. The abbot is just like the pyramid schemers in Zhongguancun—anything, no matter how unrelated, could be seen by them as powerful proof for their point of view. I try to imagine how a Christian might interpret this picture.

"Amitabha." I put my palms together to show piety.

"The question is: why has the Buddha chosen now to reveal the truth to all of humanity?" He speaks slowly and forcefully. "I pondered this question for a long time, but then I saw your scheme."

"Buddhagram?"

Master Deta nods. "I can't say I approve of your methods. However, since you ended up coming here, that proves that my guesses were correct."

Cold sweat seeps onto the skin at my back, not unlike that night so long ago that it seems unreal.

"This world is no longer the same as its original form. Put it another way: its creator, the Buddha, God, Deity—no matter what name you give it, has changed the rules by which the world operates. Do you really believe that the consecration was what allowed Buddhagram to perform miracles?"

I hold my breath.

"Suppose the universe is a program. Everything that we can observe is the result of the machine-executable code. But the cosmic microwave background can be understood as the record of some earlier version of the source code. We can invoke this code via computation, which means that we can also use algorithmic processing to change the version of the code that's currently running."

"You're saying that Mr. Wan's algorithm really caused all of this?"

"I dare not jump to conclusions. But if you forced me to guess, that would be it."

"I'm pretty science-illiterate, master. Please don't joke with me."

"Amitabha. I am a Technologist-Buddhist. I believe in the words of Arthur C. Clarke: 'Any sufficiently advanced technology is indistinguishable at first glance from Buddhist magic.'"

I know there's something not quite right here, but I don't know how to debate him. "But . . . but that project failed. Look at what a sad state Mr. Wan is in. I don't think I have anything more to do with this."

"What is not real? That which form possesses.
The Tathagata will be seen
When mind past form progresses."

"Master, please allow me to leave the temple and return to the secular world. I miss my wife." A nameless fear suddenly seizes me like a bottomless pit rising out of the screen on the wall, trying to pull me in.

Master Deta sighs and smiles wryly, as though he has long since predicted all this.

"I was hoping that by studying Buddhist doctrine with me, you would be sufficiently calmed to stay here and wait out the catastrophe. But . . . you and I are both caught in the wheel of samsara, so how can we escape our destinies? All right. Take this as a memento of our time together."

He hands over a gold-colored Buddha card. On the back is a toll-free number as well as a VIP account number and security code.

"Teacher, what is this?"

"Don't lose it! The resale value of this card is 8888 yuan. If anything happens, you can give me a call."

Master Deta turns and waves his hand, and the moldy image on the screen is replaced by regular TV programming. An American quantum physicist has been killed by gunshot. Bizarrely, the shooter claims that it was an accident because he thought the victim was someone else.

110.

Half a year passes. I meet Lao Xu at Guanji Chiba, a popular barbecue restaurant in Zhongguancun.

Lao Xu hasn't changed much. He's still pathologically in love with barbecued lamb kidneys. Like a stereotypical Northeasterner, after a few bottles of beer, his face glowing with grease and jittering with emotion, Lao Xu begins to say what's really on his mind.

"Chongbo, why don't you come and join me again? You know I'll take care of you."

Animatedly, Lao Xu tells me what's been going on with him, spewing flecks of spittle through the smoky haze. After he hid and rested for a while at home, another phone call drew him back into the IT world. This time, he didn't start a marketing company with no future, but became an "angel investor." With all the contacts he made among entrepreneurs, now he gets to spend other people's money—the faster the better.

He thinks I have potential.

"What's going on with Mr. Wan?" I change the subject. My wife has just found out that she's pregnant. Although my current job is boring, it's stable. Lao Xu, on the other hand, isn't.

"I haven't heard from him for a while . . . " Lao Xu's eyes dimmed, and he took a long drag on his cigarette. "Fortune is so fickle. Back when Buddhagram was on fire, a whole bunch of companies wanted to invest. An American company even wanted to talk about purchasing the whole company. But at the last minute, an American man showed up claiming that Y's core algorithm was stolen from one of his graduate school research labmates. The American sued, and he just wouldn't let it go. So the patent rights had to be temporarily frozen. All the investors scattered to the wind, and Lao Wan had to sell everything he owned . . . but in the end, it still wasn't enough."

I drain my cup.

"It wasn't your fault," Lao Xu said. "Honestly, if you hadn't come up with that idea, I bet Lao Wan would have failed even earlier."

"But if they hadn't made Buddhagram, maybe the Americans wouldn't have found out about the stolen algorithm."

"I've finally got it figured out. If what happened hadn't happened, something else would have. That's what fate means. Later, I heard that the labmate Y stole from was shot and killed in America. So now the patent case is in limbo."

Lao Xu's voice seems to drone on while time stands frozen. My gaze penetrates the slight crack between his cigarette-holding fingers, and the background of noisy, smoky, shouting, drinking patrons of the restaurant fades into the distance. I remember something, something so important that I've managed to forget it completely until now.

I thought everything was over, but it's only starting.

After saying goodbye to Lao Xu, I return home and begin to search, turning everything in the house upside down. My wife, her belly protruding, asks me if I've had too much to drink.

"Have you seen a golden card with a picture of the Buddha on there?" I ask her. "There's a toll-free number on the back."

She looks at me pitifully, as though gazing at an abandoned Siberian husky, a breed known for its stupidity and difficulty in being trained. She turns away to continue her pregnancy yoga exercises.

In the end, I find it tucked away inside a fashion magazine in the bathroom. The page I open to happens to be the picture of a Vaseline-covered, nude starlet lounging amongst a pile of electronics. Each screen in the image reflects a part of her glistening body.

I dial the number and enter the VIP account number and security code. A familiar voice, sounding slightly tired, answers.

"Master Deta, it's me! Chenwu!"

"Who?"

"Chenwu! Secular name Zhou Chongbo! Remember how you struck my shoulders three times and told me to go to your room at ten-oh-one to view the picture of the cosmic microwave background?"

"Er . . . you make it sound so odd. Yes, I do remember you. How've you been?"

"You were right! The problem is with the algorithm!" I take a deep breath and quickly recount the story as well as give him my guess. Someone is working really hard to prevent this algorithm from being put into wide application, even to the point of killing people.

The earpiece of the phone is silent for a long while, and then I hear another long sigh.

"You still don't get it. Do you play games?"

"A long time ago. Do you mean arcade, handheld, or consoles?"

"Whatever. If your character attacks a big boss, the game's algorithms usually summons all available forces to its defense, right?"

"You mean the NPCs?"

"That's right."

"But I didn't do anything! All I did was to suggest a stupid fucking marketing plan!"

"You misunderstand." Master Deta's voice becomes low and somber, as though he's about to lose his patience. "You're not the player who's attacking the boss. You're just an NPC."

"Wait a second! You are saying . . . " Suddenly my thoughts turned jumbled and slow, like a bowl of sticky rice porridge.

"I know it's hard to accept, but it's the truth. Someone, or maybe some group, has done things that threaten the entire program—the stability of our universe. And so the system, following designated routines, has invoked the NPCs to carry out its order to eliminate the threat and maintain the consistency of the universe."

"But I did everything on my own! I just wanted to do my job and earn a living. I thought I was helping him."

"All NPCs think like that."

"So what should I do? Lao Xu wants me to go work for him. How do I know if this is . . . Are you there?"

Strange noises are coming out of the earpiece, as though a thousand insect legs are scrabbling against the microphone.

"When you are confused . . . *hiss* . . . the teacher helps . . . Enlightened . . . *hiss* . . . help yourself. All you have to do . . . *hiss* . . . and that's it . . . *hiss* . . . Sorry, your VIP account balance is insufficient. Please refill your account and dial again. Sorry, . . . "

"Fuck!" I hang up angrily.

"What's wrong with you, screaming like that? If you frighten me and cause me to miscarry, are you going to assume the responsibility?" My wife's voice drifts to me slowly from the bedroom.

In three seconds, I sort though my thoughts and decide to tell her everything. Of course, I do have to limit it to the parts she can understand.

"Tell Lao Xu that your wife is worried about earning good karma for the baby. She doesn't want you to follow him and continue to do unethical work."

I'm just about to argue with her when the phone rings again. Lao Xu.

"Have you made up your mind? USTC's quantum lab is making rapid progress! Their machine is tackling the NP-completeness problem now. Once they've proved that P=NP, do you realize what that means?"

I look at my wife. She places the edge of her palm against her throat and makes a slicing motion, and then she sticks her tongue out.

"Hello? You there? Do you know what that means—" I hang up, and Lao Xu's voice lingers in my ear.

Every program has bugs. In this universe, I'm pretty sure that my wife is one of them. Possible the most fatal one.

I still remember the day when Lailai was born: rose-colored skin, his whole body smelling of milk. He's the most beautiful baby I've ever seen.

My wife, still weak from labor, asked me to come up with a good name. I agreed. But really, I was thinking: *It really makes no difference what he's named.*

I'm no hero. I'm just an NPC. To tell the truth, I've never believed that all this was my fault. I didn't join Lao Xu; I didn't come up with some outrageous idea that would have caused the whole project to fail; I didn't prevent that stupid quantum computer from proving that P=NP—even now I still don't know what that fucking means.

If this is the reason that the universe is collapsing, then all I can say is that the Programmer is incompetent. Why regret destroying such a shitty world?

But I'm holding my baby son, his tiny fist enclosed in my hand, and all I want is for time to stop forever, right now.

I regret everything I've done, or maybe everything I haven't done.

In these last few minutes, a scene from long ago appears in my mind: that guy wearing the army coat on the pedestrian overpass.

He's staring at me and my wife, and like some stuck answering machine, he says, "The Quadrantid meteor shower will come on January 4. Don't miss it . . . "

No one is going to miss this grand ceremony for going offline.

I play with my son, trying to make him laugh, or make any sort of expression. Suddenly, I see a reflection in his eyes, rapidly growing in size.

It's the light coming from behind me.

First published in Chinese in *Offline Magazine,* February 2015.

Translated and published in partnership with Storycom.

ABOUT THE AUTHOR

Chen Qiufan was born in 1981, in Shantou, China. (In accordance with Chinese custom, Mr. Chen's surname is written first. He sometimes uses the English name Stanley Chan.) He is a graduate of Peking University and published his first short story in 1997 in *Science Fiction World*, China's largest science fiction magazine. Since 2004, he has published over 30 stories in *Science Fiction World*, *Esquire*, *Chutzpah* and other magazines. His first novel, *The Abyss of Vision*, came out in 2006. He won Taiwan's Dragon Fantasy Award in 2006 with "A Record of the Cave of Ning Mountain," a work written in Classical Chinese. His story, "The Tomb," was translated into English and Italian and can be found in *The Apex Book of World SF II* and *Alias 6*. He now lives in Beijing and works for Google China.

The Clear Blue Seas of Luna
GREGORY BENFORD

You know many things, but what he knows is both less and more than what I tell to us.

Or especially, what we all tell to all those others—those simple humans, who are like him in their limits.

I cannot be what you are, you the larger.

Not that we are not somehow also the same, wedded to our memories of the centuries we have been wedded and grown together.

For we are like you and him and I, a life form that evolution could not produce on the rich loam of Earth. To birth forth and then burst forth a thing—a great, sprawling metallo-bio-cyber-thing such as we and you—takes grander musics, such as I know.

Only by shrinking down to the narrow chasms of the single view can you know the intricate slick fineness, the reek and tingle and chime of this silky symphony of self.

But bigness blunders, thumb-fingered.

Smallness can enchant. So let us to go an oddment of him, and me, and you:

He saw:

A long thin hard room, fluorescent white, without shadows.

Metal on ceramo-glass on fake wood on woven nylon rug.

A granite desk. A man whose name he could not recall.

A neat uniform, so familiar he looked beyond it by reflex.

He felt: light gravity (Mars? the moon?); rough cloth at a cuff of his work shirt; a chill dry air-conditioned breeze along his neck. A red flash of anger.

Benjan smiled slightly. He had just seen what he must do.

"Gray was free when we began work, centuries ago," Benjan said, his black eyes fixed steadily on the man across the desk. Katonji, that was the man's name. His commander, once, a very long time ago.

"It had been planned that way, yes," his superior said haltingly, begrudging the words.

"That was the only reason I took the assignment," Benjan said.

"I know. Unfortunately—"

"I have spent many decades on it."

"Fleet Control certainly appreciates—"

"World-scaping isn't just a job, damn it! It's an art, a discipline, a craft that saps a man's energies."

"And you have done quite well. Personally, I—"

"When you asked me to do this I wanted to know what Fleet Control planned for Gray."

"You can recall an ancient conversation?"

A verbal maneuver, no more. Katonji was an amplified human and already well over two centuries old, but the Earthside social convention was to pretend that the past faded away, leaving a young psyche. "A 'grand experiment in human society,' I remember your words."

"True, that was the original plan—"

"But now you tell me a single faction needs it? The whole moon?"

"The Council has reconsidered."

"Reconsidered, hell." Benjan's bronze face crinkled with disdain. "Somebody pressured them and they gave in. Who was it?"

"I would not put it that way," Katonji said coldly.

"I know you wouldn't. Far easier to hide behind words." He smiled wryly and compressed his thin lips. The view-screen near him looked out on a cold silver landscape and he studied it, smouldering inside. An artificial viewscape from Gray itself. Earth, a crescent concerto in blue and white, hung in a creamy sky over the insect working of robotractors and men. Gray's air was unusually clear today, the normal haze swept away by a front blowing in from the equator near Mare Chrisum.

The milling minions were hollowing out another cavern for Fleet Control to fill with cubicles and screens and memos. Great Gray above, mere gray below. Earth swam above high fleecy cirrus and for a moment Benjan dreamed of the day when birds, easily adapted to the light gravity and high atmospheric density, would flap lazily across such views.

"Officer Tozenji—"

"I am no longer an officer. I resigned before you were born."

"By your leave, I meant it solely as an honorific. Surely you still have some loyalty to the Fleet."

Benjan laughed. The deep bass notes echoed from the office walls with a curious emptiness. "So it's an appeal to the honor of the crest, is it? I see I spent too long on Gray. Back here you have forgotten what I am like,'" Benjan said. *But where is "here"? I could not take Earth full gravity any more, so this must be an orbiting Fleet cylinder, spinning gravity.*

A frown. "I had hoped that working once more with Fleet officers would change you, even though you remained a civilian on Gray. A man isn't—"

"A man is what he is," Benjan said.

Katonji leaned back in his shiftchair and made a tent of his fingers. "You . . . played the Sabal Game during those years?" he asked slowly.

Benjan's eyes narrowed. "Yes, I did." The Game was ancient, revered, simplicity itself. It taught that the greater gain lay in working with others, rather than in self-seeking. He had always enjoyed it, but only a fool believed that such moral lessons extended to the cut and thrust of Fleet matters.

"It did not . . . bring you to community?"

"I got on well enough with the members of my team," Benjan said evenly.

"I hoped such isolation with a small group would calm your . . . spirit. Fleet is a community of men and women seeking enlightenment in the missions, just as you do. You are an exceptional person, anchored as you are in the Station, using linkages we have not used—"

"Permitted, you mean."

"Those old techniques were deemed . . . too risky."

Benjan felt his many links like a background hum, in concert and warm. What could this man know of such methods time-savored by those who lived them? "And not easy to direct from above."

The man fastidiously raise a finger and persisted: "We still sit at the Game, and while you are here would welcome your—

"Can we leave my spiritual progress aside?"

"Of course, if you desire."

"Fine. Now tell me who is getting my planet."

"Gray is not your planet."

"I speak for the Station and all the intelligences who link with it. We made Gray. Through many decades, we hammered the crust, released the gases, planted the spores, damped the winds."

"With help."

"Three hundred of us at the start, and eleven heavy spacecraft. A puny beginning that blossomed into millions."

"Helped by the entire staff of Earthside—"

"They were Fleet men. They take orders, I don't. I work by contract."

"A contract spanning centuries?"

"It is still valid, though those who wrote it are dust."

"Let us treat this in a gentlemanly fashion, sir. Any contract can be renegotiated."

"The paper I—we, but I am here to speak for all—signed for Gray said it was to be an open colony. That's the only reason I worked on it," he said sharply.

"I would not advise you to pursue that point," Katonji said. He turned and studied the viewscreen, his broad, southern Chinese nose flaring at the nostrils. But the rest of his face remained an impassive mask. For a long moment there was only the thin whine of air circulation in the room.

"Sir," the other man said abruptly, "I can only tell you what the Council has granted. Men of your talents are rare. We know that, had you undertaken the formation of Gray for a, uh, private interest, you would have demanded more payment."

"Wrong. I wouldn't have done it at all."

"Nonetheless, the Council is willing to pay you a double fee. The Majiken Clan, who have been invested with Primacy Rights to Gray—"

"What!"

"—have seen fit to contribute the amount necessary to reimburse you—"

"So that's who—"

"—and all others of the Station, to whom I have been authorized to release funds immediately."

Benjan stared blankly ahead for a short moment. "I believe I'll do a bit of releasing myself," he murmured, almost to himself.

"What?"

"Oh, nothing. Information?"

"Infor—. Oh."

"The Clans have a stranglehold on the Council, but not the 3D. People might be interested to know how it came about that a new planet—a rich one, too—was handed over—"

"Officer Tozenji—"

Best to pause. Think. He shrugged, tried on a thin smile. "I was only jesting. Even idealists are not always stupid."

"Um. I am glad of that."

"Lodge the Majiken draft in my account. I want to wash my hands of this."

The other man said something, but Benjan was not listening. He made the ritual of leaving. They exchanged only perfunctory hand gestures. He turned to go, and wondered at the naked, flat room this man had chosen to work in: It carried no soft tones, no humanity, none of the feel of a room that is used, a place where men do work that interests them, so that they embody it with something of themselves. This office was empty in the most profound sense. It was a room for men who lived by taking orders. He hoped never to see such a place again.

Benjan turned. Stepped—the slow slide of falling, then catching himself, stepped—

You fall over Gray.

Skating down the steep banks of young clouds, searching, driving.

Luna you know as Gray, as all in Station know it, because pearly clouds deck high in its thick air. It had been gray long before, as well—the aged pewter of rock hard-hammered for billions of years by the relentless sun. Now its air was like soft slate, cloaking the greatest of human handiworks.

You raise a hand, gaze at it. So much could come from so small an instrument. You marvel. A small tool, five-fingered slab, working over great stretches of centuries. Seen against the canopy of your craft, it seems an unlikely tool to heft worlds with—

And the thought alone sends you plunging—

Luna was born small, too small.

So the sun had readily stripped it of its early shroud of gas. Luna came from the collision of a Mars-sized world into the primordial Earth. From that colossal crunch—how you wish you could have seen that!—spun a disk, and from that churn Luna condensed redly. The heat of that birth stripped away the moon's water and gases, leaving it bare to the sun's glower.

So amend that:

You steer a comet from the chilly freezer beyond Pluto, swing it around Jupiter, and smacked it into the bleak fields of Mare Chrisium. In bits.

For a century, all hell breaks loose. You wait, patient in your Station. It is a craft of fractions: Luna is smaller, so needs less to build an atmosphere.

There was always some scrap of gas on the moon—trapped from the solar wind, baked from its dust, perhaps even belched from the early, now long-dead volcanoes. When Apollo descended, bringing the first men, its tiny exhaust plume doubled the mass of the frail atmosphere.

Still, such a wan world could hold gases for tens of thousands of years; physics said so. Its lesser gravity tugs at a mere sixth of Earth's hefty grip. So, to begin, you sling inward a comet bearing a third the mass of all Earth's ample air, a chunk of mountain-sized grimy ice.

Sol's heat had robbed this world, but mother-massive Earth herself had slowly stolen away its spin. It became a submissive partner in a rigid gavotte, forever tide-locked with one face always smiling at its partner.

Here you use the iceteroid to double effect. By hooking the comet adroitly around Jupiter, in a reverse swingby, you loop it into an orbit opposite to the customary, docile way that worlds loop around the sun. Go opposite! Retro! Coming in on Luna, the iceball then has ten times the impact energy.

Mere days before it strikes, you blow it apart with meticulous brutality. Smashed to shards, chunks come gliding in all around Luna's equator, small enough that they cannot muster momentum enough to splatter free of gravity's grip. Huge cannonballs slam into gray rock, but at angles that prevent them from getting away again.

Earth admin was picky about this: no debris was to be flung free, to rain down as celestial buckshot on that favored world.

Within hours, Luna had air—of a crude sort. You mixed and salted and worked your chemical magicks upon roiling clouds that sported forked lightning. Gravity's grind provoked fevers, molecular riots.

More: as the pellets pelted down, Luna spun up. Its crust echoed with myriad slams and bangs. The old world creaked as it yielded, spinning faster from the hammering. From its lazy cycle of twenty-eight days it sped up to sixty hours—close enough to Earth-like, as they say, for government work. A day still lazy enough.

Even here, you orchestrated a nuanced performance, coaxed from dynamics. Luna's axial tilt had been a dull zero. Dutifully it had spun at right angles to the orbital plane of the solar system, robbed it of summers and winters.

But you wanted otherwise. Angled just so, the incoming ice nuggets tilted the poles. From such simple mechanics you conjured seasons. And as the gases cooled, icy caps crowned your work.

You were democratic, at first: allowing both water and carbon dioxide, with smidgens of methane and ammonia. Here you called upon the appetites of bacteria, sprites you sowed as soon as the winds calmed after bombardment. They basked in sunlight, broke up the methane. The greenhouse blanket quickly warmed the old gray rocks, coveting the heat from the infalls, and soon algae covered them.

You watched with pride as the first rain fell. For centuries the dark plains had carried humanity's imposed, watery names: Tranquility, Serenity, Crises, Clouds, Storms. Now these lowlands of aged lava caught the rains and made muds and fattened into ponds, lakes, true seas. You made the ancient names come true.

Through your servant machines, you marched across these suddenly murky lands, bristling with an earned arrogance. They—*yourself!*— plowed and dug, sampled and salted. Through their eyes and tongues and ears you sat in your high Station and heard the sad baby sigh of the first winds awakening.

The Station was becoming more than a bristling canister of metal, by then. Its agents grew, as did you.

You smiled down upon the gathering Gray with your quartz eyes and microwave antennas. For you knew what was coming. A mere sidewise glance at rich Earth told you what to expect.

Like Earth's tropics now, at Luna's equator heat drove moist gases aloft. Cooler gas flowed from the poles to fill in. The high wet clouds skated poleward, cooled—and rained down riches.

On Earth, such currents are robbed of their water about a third of the way to the poles, and so descend, their dry rasp making a world-wide belt of deserts. Not so on Luna.

You had judged the streams of newborn air rightly. Thicker airs than Earth's took longer to exhaust, and so did not fall until they reached the poles. Thus the new world had no chains of deserts, and one simple circulating air cell ground away in each hemisphere. Moisture worked its magicks.

You smiled to see your labors come right. Though anchored in your mammoth Station, you felt the first pinpricks of awareness in the crawlers, flyers and diggers who probed the freshening moon.

You tasted their flavors, the brimming possibilities. Northerly winds swept the upper half of the globe, bearing poleward, then swerving toward the west to make mild the occasional mild tornado. (Not all weather should be boring.)

Clouds patroled the air, still fretting over their uneasy births. Day and night came in their slow rhythm, stirring the biological lab that worked below. You sometimes took a moment from running all this, just to watch.

Lunascapes. Great Grayworld.

Where day yielded to dark, valleys sank into smoldering blackness. Already a chain of snowy peaks shone where they caught the sun's dimming rays, and lit the plains with slanting colors like live coals.

Sharp mountains cleaved the cloud banks, leaving a wake like that of a huge ship. At the fat equator, straining still to adjust to the new spin, tropical thunderheads glowered, lit by orange lightning that seemed to be looking for a way to spark life among the drifting molecules.

All that you did, in a mere decade. You had made "the lesser light that rules the night" now shine five times brighter, casting sharp shadows on Earth. Sunrays glinted by day from the young oceans, dazzling the eyes on Earth. And the mother world itself reflected in those muddy seas, so that when the alignment was right, people on Earth's night side gazed up into their own mirrored selves. Viewed at just the right angle, Earth's image was rimmed with ruddy sunlight, refracting through Earth's air.

You knew it could not last, but were pleased to find the new air stick around. It would bleed away in ten thousand years, but by that time other measures could come into play. You had plans for a monolayer membrane to cap your work, resting atop the whole atmosphere, the largest balloon ever conceived.

Later? No, act in the moment—and so you did.

You wove it with membrane skill, cast it wide, let it fall—to rest easy on the thick airs below. Great holes in it let ships glide through and fro, but the losses from those would be trivial.

Not that all was perfect. Luna had no soil, only the damaged dust left from four billion years beneath the solar wind's anvil.

After a mere momentary decade (nothing, to you), fresh wonders bloomed.

Making soil from gritty grime was work best left to the micro-beasts who loved such stuff. To do great works on a global scale took tiny assistants. You fashioned them in your own labs, which poked outward from the Station's many-armed skin.

Gray grew a crust. Earth is in essence a tissue of microbial organisms living off the sun's fires. Gray would do the same, in fast-forward. You cooked up not mere primordial broths, but endless chains of regulatory messages, intricate feedback loops, organic gavottes.

Earth hung above, an example of life ornamented by eleborate decorations, structures of forest and grass and skin and blood—living quarters, like seagrass and zebras and eucalyptus and primates.

Do the same, you told yourself. *Only better.*

These tasks you loved. Their conjuring consumed more decades, stacked end on end. You were sucked into the romance of tiny turf wars, chemical assaults, microbial murders and invasive incests. But you had to play upon the stellar stage, as well.

You had not thought about the tides. Even you had not found a way around those outcomes of gravity's gradient. Earth raised bulges in Gray's seas a full twenty meters tall. That made for a dim future for coastal property, even once the air became breathable.

Luckily, even such colossal tides were not a great bother to the lakes you shaped in crater beds. These you made as breeding farms for the bioengineered minions who ceaselessly tilled the dirts, massaged the gases, filtered the tinkling streams that cut swift ways through rock.

Indeed, here and there you even found a use for the tides. There were more watts lurking there, in kinetic energy. You fashioned push-plates to tap some of it, to run your sub-stations. Thrifty gods do not have to suck up to (and from) Earthside.

And so the sphere that, when you began, had been the realm of strip miners amd mass-driver camps, of rugged, suited loners . . . became a place where, someday, humans might walk and breathe free.

That time is about to come. You yearn for it. For you, too, can then manifest yourself, your Station, as a mere mortal . . . and set foot upon a world that you would name Selene.

You were both Station and more, by then. How much more few knew. But some sliver of you clung to the name of Benjan—

—Benjan nodded slightly, ears ringing for some reason.

The smooth, sure interviewer gave a short introduction. "Man . . . or manifestation? This we must all wonder as we greet an embodiment of humanity's greatest—and now ancient—construction project. One you and I can see every evening in the sky—for those who are still surface dwellers."

3D cameras moved in smooth arcs through the studio darkness beyond. The two men sat in a pool of light. The interviewer spoke toward the directional mike as he gave the background on Benjan's charges against the Council.

Smiles galore. Platitudes aplenty. That done, came the attack.

"But isn't this a rather abstract, distant point to bring at this time?" the man said, turning to Benjan.

Benjan blinked, uncertain, edgy. He was a private man, used to working alone. Now that he was moving against the Council he had to bear these public appearances, these . . . manifestations . . . of a dwindled self. "To, ah, the people of the next generation, Gray will not be an abstraction—"

"You mean the moon?"

"Uh, yes, Gray is my name for it. That's the way it lookled when I—uh, we all—started work on it centuries ago."

"Yet you were there all along, in fact."

"Well, yes. But when I'm—we're—done." Benjan leaned forward, and his interviewer leaned back, as if not wanting to be too close. "it will be a real place, not just an idea—where you all can live and start a planned ecology. It will be a frontier."

"We understand that romantic tradition, but—"

"No, you don't. Gray isn't just an idea, it's something I've—we've— worked on for everyone, whatever shape or genetype they might favor."

"Yes yes, and such ideas are touching in their, well, customary way, but—"

"But the only ones who will ever enjoy it, if the Council gets away with this, is the Majiken Clan."

The interviewer pursed his lips. Or was this a *he* at all? In the current style, the bulging muscles and thick neck might just be fashion statements. "Well, the Majiken are a very large, important segment of the—"

"No more important than the rest of humanity, in my estimation."

"But to cause this much stir over a world which will not even be habitable for at least decades more—"

"We of the Station are there now."

"You've been modified, adapted."

"Well, yes. I couldn't do this interview on Earth. I'm grav-adapted."

"Frankly, that's why many feel that we need to put Earthside people on the ground on Luna as soon as possible. To represent our point of view."

"Look, Gray's not just any world. Not just a gas giant, useful for raw gas and nothing else. Not a Mercury type; there are millions of those littered out among the stars. Gray is going to be fully Earthlike. The astronomers tell us there are only four semiterrestrials outside the home system that humans can ever live on, around other stars, and those are pretty terrible. I—"

"You forget the Outer Colonies," the interviewer broke in smoothly, smiling at the 3D.

"Yeah—iceballs." He could not hide his contempt. What he wanted to say, but knew it was terribly old fashioned, was: *Damn it, Gray is happening now, we've got to plan for it. Photosynthesis is going on. I've seen it myself—hell, I caused it myself—carbon dioxide and water converting into organics and oxygen, gases fresh as a breeze. Currents carry the algae down through the cloud layers into the warm areas, where they work just fine. That gives off simple carbon compounds, raw carbon and water. This keeps the water content of the atmosphere constant, but converts carbon dioxide—we've got too much right now—into carbon and oxygen. It's going well, the rate itself is exponentiating—*

Benjan shook his fist, just now realizing that he *was* saying all this out loud, after all. Probably not a smart move, but he couldn't stop himself. "Look, there's enough water in Gray's deep rock to make an ocean a meter deep all the way around the planet. That's enough to resupply the atmosopheric loss, easy, even without breaking up the rocks. Our designer plants are doing their jobs."

"We have heard of these routine miracles—"

"—and there can be belts of jungle—soon! We've got mountains for climbing, rivers that snake, polar caps, programmed animals coming up, beautiful sunsets, soft summer storms—anything the human race wants. That's the vision we had when we started Gray. And I'm damned if I'm going to let the Majiken—"

"But the Majiken can defend Gray," the interviewer said mildly.

Benjan paused. "Oh, you mean—"

"Yes, the ever-hungry Outer Colonies. Surely if Gray proves as extraordinary as you think, the rebellious colonies will attempt to take it." The man gave Benjan a broad, insincere smile. *Dummy*, it said. *Don't know the real-politic of this time, do you?*

He could see the logic. Earth had gotten soft, fed by a tougher empire that now stretched to the chilly preserve beyond Pluto. To keep their manicured lands clean and "original" Earthers had burrowed underground, built deep cities there, and sent most manufacturing off-world. The real economic muscle now lay in the hands of ther suppliers of fine rocks and volatiles, shipped on long orbits from the Outers and the Belt. These realities were hard to remember when your attention was focused on the details of making a fresh world. One forgot that appetites ruled, not reason.

Benjan grimaced. "The Majiken fight well, they are the backbone of the Fleet, yes. Still, to give them a *world*—"

"Surely in time there will be others," the man said reasonably.

"Oh? Why should there be? We can't possibly make Venus work, and Mars will take thousands of years more—"

"No, I meant built worlds—stations."

He snorted. "Live inside a can?"

"That's what you do," the man shot back.

"I'm . . . different."

"Ah yes." The interviewer bore in, lips compressed to a white line, and the 3Ds followed him, snouts peering. Benjan felt hopelessly outmatched. "And just how so?"

"I'm . . . a man chosen to represent . . . "

"The Shaping Station, correct?"

"I'm of the breed who have always lived in and for the Station."

"Now, that's what I'm sure our audience really wants to get into. After all, the moon won't be ready for a long time. But you—an ancient artifact, practically—are more interesting."

"I don't want to talk about that." Stony, frozen.

"Why not." Not really a question.

"It's personal."

"You're here as a public figure!"

"Only because you require it. Nobody wants to talk to the Station directly."

"We do not converse with such strange machines."

"It's not just a machine."

"Then what is it?"

"An . . . idea," he finished lamely. "An . . . ancient one." How to tell them? Suddenly, he longed to be back doing a solid, worthy job—flying a jet in Gray's skies, pushing along the organic chemistry—

The interviewer looked uneasy. "Well, since you won't go there . . . Our time's almost up and—"

Again, I am falling over Gray.

Misty auburn clouds, so thin they might be only illusion, spread below the ship. They caught red as dusk fell. The thick air refracted six times more than Earth's, so sunsets had a slow-motion grandeur, the full pallet of pinks and crimsons and rouge-reds.

I am in a ramjet—the throttled growl is unmistakable—lancing cleanly into the upper atmosphere. Straps tug and pinch me as the craft banks and sweeps, the smoothly wrenching way I like it, the stubby snout sipping precisely enough for the air's growing oxygen fraction to keep the engine thrusting forward.

I probably should not have come on this flight; it is an uncharacteristic self-indulgence. But I could not sit forever in the Station to plot and plan and calculate and check. I had to see my handiwork, get the feel of it. To use my body in the way it longed for.

I make the ramjet arc toward Gray's night side. The horizon curves away, clean hard blue-white, and—*chungl*—I take a jolt as the first canister blows off the underbelly below my feet. Through a rearview camera I watch it tumble away into ruddy oblivion. The canister carries more organic cutures, a new matrix I selected carefully back on Station, in my expanded mode. I watch the shiny morsel explode below, yellow flash. It showers intricate, tailored algae through the clouds.

Gray is at a crucial stage. Since the centuries-ago slamming by the air-giving comets, the conspiracy of spin, water and heat (great gifts of astro-engineering) had done their deep work. Volcanoes now simmered, percolating more moisture from deep within, kindling, kindling. Some heat climbed to the high cloud decks and froze into thin crystals.

There, I conjure fresh life—tinkering, endlessly.

Life, yes. Carefully engineered cells, to breathe carbon dioxide and live off the traces of other gases this high from the surface. In time. Photosynthesis in the buoyant forms—gas-bag trees, spindly but graceful in the top layer of Gray's dense air—conjure carbon dioxide into oxygen.

I glance up, encased in the tight flight jacket, yet feeling utterly free, naked. *Incoming meteors.* Brown clouds of dust I had summoned to orbit about Gray were cutting off some sunlight.

Added spice, these—ingredients sent from the asteroids to pepper the soil, prick the air, speed chemical matters along. The surface was cooling, the Gray greenhouse winding down. Losing the heat from the atmosphere's birth took centuries. *Patience, prudence.*

Now chemical concerts in the rocks slowed. I felt those, too, as a distant sampler hailed me with its accountant's chattering details. Part of the song. Other chem chores, more subtle, would soon become energetically possible. Fluids could seep and run. In the clotted air below, crystals and cells would make their slow work. All in time . . .

In time, the first puddle had become a lake. How I had rejoiced then!

Centuries ago I wanted to go swimming in the clear blue seas of luna, I remember. Tropical waters at the equator, under Earthshine . . .

What joy it had been, to fertilize those early, still waters with minutely programmed bacteria, stir and season their primordial soup—and wait.

What sweet mother Earth did in a billion years I did to Gray in fifty. Joyfully! Singing the song of the molecules, in concert with them.

My steps were many, the methods subtle. To shape the mountain ranges I needed further infalls from small asteroids, taking a century— ferrying rough-cut stone to polish a jewel.

Memories . . . of a man and more. Fashioned from the tick of time, ironed out by the swift passage of mere puny years, of decades, of the ringing centuries. Worlds take *time.*

My ramjet leaps into night, smelling of hot iron and —*chung!*— discharging its burden.

I glance down at wisps of yellow-pearl. Sulphuric and carbolic acid streamers, drifting far below. There algae feed and prosper. Murky mists below pale, darken, vanish. *Go!*

Yet I felt a sudden sadness as the jet took me up again. I had watched every small change in the atmosphere, played shepherd to newborn cloud banks, raised fresh chains of volcanoes with fusion triggers that burrowed like moles—and all this might come to naught, if it became another private preserve for some Earthside power games.

I could not shake off the depression. Should I have that worry pruned away? It could hamper my work, and I could easily be rid of it for a while, when I returned to the sleeping vaults. Most in the Station spent about one month per year working;. Their other days passed in dreamless chilled sleep, waiting for the slow metabolism of Gray to quicken and change.

Not I. I slept seldom, and did not want the stacks of years washed away.

I run my tongue over fuzzy teeth. I am getting stale, worn. Even a ramjet ride did not revive my spirit.

And the Station did not want slackers. Not only memories could be pruned.

Ancient urges arise, needs . . .

A warm shower and rest await me above, in orbit, inside the mother-skin. Time to go.

I touch the controls, cutting in extra ballastic computer capacity and—

—suddenly I am there again, with *her*.
She is around me and beneath me, slick with ruby sweat.
And the power of it soars up through me. I reach out and her breast blossoms in my eager hand, her soft cries unfurl in puffs of green steam. *Aye!*
She is a splash of purple across the cool lunar stones, her breath ringing in me—
as she licks my rasping ear with a tiny jagged fork of puckered laughter,
most joyful and triumphant, yea verity.
The Station knows you need this now.
Yes, and the Station is right. I need to be consumed, digested, spat back out a new and fresh man, so that I may work well again.
—so she coils and swirls like a fine tinkling gas around me, her mouth wraps me like a vortex. I slide my shaft into her gratefully as she sobs great wracking orange gaudiness through me,
her, again, *her,*
gift of the strumming vast blue Station that guides us all down

centuries of dense, oily time.
You need this, take, eat, this is the body and blood of the Station, eat,
savor, take fully.
I had known her once—redly, sweet and loud—and now I know her
again,
my senses all piling up and waiting to be eaten from her.
I glide back and forth, moisture chimes between us, *she* is coiled
tight, too.
We all are, we creatures of the Station.
It knows this, releases us when we must be gone.
I slam myself into *her* because *she* is both that woman—known so
long ago,
delicious in her whirlwind passions, supple in colors of the mind,
singing in rubs and heats
I knew across the centuries. So the Station came to know *her*, too,
and duly recorded her—
so that I can now bury my coal-black, sweaty troubles in her, *aye!*
and thus in the Shaping Station,
as was and ever shall be, Grayworld without end, amen.

Resting. Compiling himself again, letting the rivulets of self knit up
into remembrance.

Of course the Station had to be more vast and able than anything
Humanity had yet known.

At the time the Great Shaping began, it was colossal. By then,
humanity had gone on to grander projects.

Mars brimmed nicely with vapors and lichen, but would take millennia
more before anyone could walk its surface with only a compressor to take
and thicken oxygen from the swirling airs.

Mammoth works now cruised at the outer rim of the solar system,
vast ice castles inhabited by beings only dimly related to the humans
of Earth.

He did not know those constructions. But he had been there, in
inherited memory, when the Station was born. For part of him and you
and me and us had voyaged forth at the very beginning . . .

The numbers were simple, their implications known to school
children.

(Let's remember that the future belongs to the engineers.)

Take an asteroid, say, and slice it sidewise, allowing four meters of
head room for each level—about what a human takes to live in. This

dwelling, then, has floor space that expands as the cube of the asteroid size. How big an asteroid could provide the living room equal to the entire surface of the Earth? Simple: about two hundred kilometers.

Nothing, in other words. For Ceres, the largest asteroid in the inner belt, was 380 kilometers across, before humans began to work her.

But room was not the essence of the Station. For after all, he had made the Station, yes? Information was her essence, the truth of that blossomed in him, the past as prologue—

He ambled along a corridor a hundred meters below Gray's slag and muds, gazing down on the frothy air-fountains in the foyer. *Day's work done.*

Even manifestations need a rest, and the interview with the smug Earther had put him off, sapping his resolve. Inhaling the crisp, cold air (a bit high on the oxy, he thought; have to check that) he let himself concentrate wholly on the clear scent of the splashing. The blue water was the very best, fresh from the growing poles, not the recycled stuff he endured on flights. He breathed in the tingling spray and a man grabbed him.

"I present formal secure-lock," the man growled, his third knuckle biting into Benjan's elbow port.

A cold, brittle *thunk.* His systems froze. Before he could move, whole command linkages went dead in her inboards. The Station's hovering presence, always humming in the distance, telescoped away. It felt like a wrenching fall that never ends, head over heels—

He got a grip. *Focus. Regain your links. The loss!*—It was like having fingers chopped away, whole pieces of himself amputated. *Bloody neural stumps—*

He sent quick, darting questions down his lines, and met . . . *dark.* Silent. Dead.

His entire aura of presence was gone. He sucked in the cold air, letting a fresh anger bubble up but keeping it tightly bound.

His attacker was the sort who blended into the background. Perfect for this job. A nobody out of nowhere, complete surprise. Clipping on a hand-restraint, the mousy man stepped back. "They ordered me to do it fast." A mousy voice, too.

Benjan resisted the impulse to deck him. He looked Lunar, thin and pale. One of the Earther families who had come to deal with the Station a century ago? Maybe with more kilos than Benjan, but a fair match. And it would feel *good.*

But that would just bring more of them, in the end. "Damn it, I have immunity from casual arrest. I—"

"No matter now, they said." The cop shrugged apologetically, but his jaw set. He was used to this.

Benjan vaguely recognized him, from some bar near the Apex of the crater's dome. There weren't more than a thousand people on Gray, mostly like him, manifestations of the Station. But not all. More of the others all the time . . . "You're Majiken."

"Yeah. So?"

"At least you people do your own work."

"We have plenty on the inside here. You don't think Gray's gonna be neglected, eh?"

In his elbow he felt injected programs spread, *clunk*, consolidating their blocks. A seeping ache. Benjan fought it all through his neuro-musculars, but the disease was strong.

Keep your voice level, wait for a chance. Only one of them—my God, they're sure of themselves! Okay, make yourself seem like a doormat.

"I don't suppose I can get a few things from my office?"

"'Fraid not."

"Mighty decent."

The man shrugged, letting the sarcasm pass. "They want you locked down good before they . . . "

"They what?"

"Make their next move, I'd guess."

"I'm just a step, eh?"

"Sure, chop off the hands and feet first." A smirking thug with a gift for metaphor.

Well, these hands and feet can still work. Benjan began walking toward his apartment. "I'll stay in your lock-down, but at home."

"Hey, nobody said—"

"But what's the harm? I'm deadened now." He kept walking.

"Uh, uh—" The man paused, obviously consulting with his superiors on an in-link.

He should have known it was coming. The Majikens were ferret-eyed, canny, unoriginal and always dangerous. He had forgotten that. In the rush to get ores sifted, grayscapes planed right to control the constant rains, a system of streams and rivers snaking through the fresh-cut valleys . . . a man could get distracted, yes. Forget how people were. *Careless.*

Not completely, though. Agents like this Luny usually nailed their prey at home, not in a hallway. Benjan kept a stunner in the apartment, right beside the door, convenient.

Distract him. "I want to file a protest."

"Take it to Kalespon." Clipped, efficient, probably had a dozen other slices of bad news to deliver today. To other manifestations. Busy man.

"No, with your boss."

"Mine?" His rock-steady jaw went slack.

"For—" he sharply turned the corner to his apartment, using the time to reach for some mumbo-jumbo—"felonious interrogation of inboards."

"Hey, I didn't touch your—"

"I felt it. Slimy little gropes—yeccch!" Might as well ham it up a little, have some fun.

The Majiken looked offended. "I never violate protocols. The integrity of your nexus is intact. You can ask for a scope-through when we take you in—"

"I'll get my overnight kit." Only now did he hurry toward the apartment portal and popped it by an inboard command. As he stepped through he felt the cop, three steps behind.

Here goes. One foot over the lip, turn to the right, snatch the stunner out of its grip mount—

—and it wasn't there. They'd laundered the place already. "Damn!"

"Thought it'd be waitin', huh?"

In the first second. When the Majiken was pretty sure of himself, *act*—

Benjan took a step back and kicked. A satisfying soft *thuuunk.*

In the low gravity the man rose a meter and his *uungh!* was strangely satisfying. The Majiken were warriors, after all, by heritage. Easier for them to take physical damage than life trauma.

The Majiken came up fast and nailed Benjan with a hand feint and slam. Benjan fell back in the slow gravity—and at a 45-degree tilt, sprang backward, away, toward the wall—

Which he hit, completing his turn in air, heels coming hard into the wall so that he could absorb the recoil—

—and spring off, head-height—

—into the Majiken's throat as the man rushed forward, shaped hands ready for the put-away blow. Benjan caught him with both hand-edges, slamming the throat from both sides. The punch cut off blood to the head and the Majiken crumbled.

Benjan tied him with his own belt. Killed the link on the screen. Bound him further to the furniture. Even on Gray, inertia was inertia. The Majiken would not find it easy to get out from under a couch he was firmly tied to.

The apartment would figure out that something was wrong about its occupant in a hour or two, and call for help. Time enough to run?

Benjan was unsure, but part of him liked this, felt a surge of adrenaline joy arc redly through his systems.

Five minutes of work and he got the interlocks off. His connections sprang back to life. Colors and images sang in his aura.

He was out the door, away—

The cramped corridors seemed to shrink, dropping down and away from him, weaving and collapsing. Something came toward him—chalk-white hills, yawning craters.

A hurricane breath whipped by him as it swept down from the jutting, fresh-carved mountains. His body strained.

He was running, that much seeped throcugh to him. He breathed brown murk that seared but his lungs sucked it in eagerly.

Plunging hard and heavy across the swampy flesh of Gray.

He moved easily, bouncing with each stride in the light gravity, down an infinite straight line between rows of enormous trees. Vegetable trees, these were, soft tubers and floppy leaves in the wan glow of a filtered sun. There should be no men here, only machines to tend the crops. Then he noticed that he was not a man at all. A robo-hauler, yes—and his legs were in fact wheels, his arms the working grapplers. Yet he read all this as his running body. Somehow it was pleasant.

And *she* ran with him.

He saw beside him a miner-bot, speeding down the slope. Yet he knew it was *she*, Martine, and he loved her.

He whirred, clicked—and sent a hail.

You are fair, my sweet.

Back from the lumbering miner came, *This body will not work well at games of lust.*

No reason we can't shed them in time.

To what end? she demanded. Always imperious, that girl.

To slide silky skin again.

You seem to forget that we are fleeing. That cop, someone will find him.

In fact, he had forgotten. *Uh . . . update me?*

Ah! How exasperating! You've been off, romping through your imputs again, right?

Worse than that. He had only a slippery hold on the jiggling, surging lands of mud and murk that funneled past. Best not to alarm her, though. *My sensations seem to have become a bit scrambled, yes. I know there is some reason to run—*

They are right behind us!

Who?

*The Majiken Clan! They want to seize you as a primary manifestation!
Damn! I'm fragmenting.*

You mean they're reaching into your associative cortex?

Must be, my love. Which is why you're running with me.

What do you mean?

How to tell her the truth but shade it so that she does not guess . . .
the Truth? *Suppose I tell you something that is more useful than accurate?*

Why would you do that, m'love?

Why do doctors slant a diagnosis?

Because no good diagnostic gives a solid prediction.

Exactly. Not what he had meant, but it got them by an awkward fact.

Come on, she sent. *Let's scamper down this canyon. The topo maps
say it's a short cut.*

Can't trust 'em, the rains slice up the land so fast. He felt his legs
springing like pistons in the mad buoyance of adrenaline.

They surged together down slippery sheets that festered with life—
spreading algae, some of the many-leaved slim-trees Benjan had himself
helped design. Rank growths festooned the banks of dripping slime,
biology run wild and woolly at a fevered pace, irked by infusions of
smart bugs. A landscape on fast forward.

What do you fear so much? she said suddenly

The sharpness of it stalls his mind. He was afraid for her more than
himself, but how to tell her? This apparition of her was so firm and
heartbreakingly warm, her whole presence welling through to him on
his sensorium . . . Time to tell another truth that conceals a deeper truth.

They'll blot out every central feature of me, all those they can find.

If they catch you. Us.

Yup. Keep it to monosyllables, so the tremor of his voice does not
give itself away. If they got to her, she would face final, total erasure.
Even of a fragment self.

Save your breath for the run, shesent. So he did, gratefully.

If there were no omni-sensors lurking along this approach to the
launch fields, they might get through. Probably Fleet expected him to
stay indoors, hiding, working his way to some help. But there would be
no aid there. The Majikan were thorough and would capture all human
manifestations, timing the arrests simultaneously to prevent anyone
sending a warning. That was why they had sent a lone cop to grab him;
they were stretched thin. Reassuring, but not much.

It was only three days past the 3D interview, yet they had decided to
act and put together a sweep. What would they be doing to the Station
itself? He ached at the thought. After all, *she* resided there . . .

And *she* was here. He was talking to a manifestation that was remarkable, because he had opened his inputs in a way that only a crisis can spur.

Benjan grimaced. Decades working over Gray had aged him, taught him things Fleet could not imagine. The Sabal Game still hummed in his mind, still guided his thoughts, but these men of the Fleet had betrayed all that. They thought, quite probably, that they could recall him to full officer status,and he would not guess that they would then silence him, quite legally.

Did they think him so slow? Benjan allowed himself a thin, dry chuckle as he ran.

They entered the last short canyon before the launch fields. Tall blades like scimitar grasses poked up, making him dart among them. She growled and spun her tracks and plowed them under. She did not speak. None of them liked to destroy the life so precariously remaking Gray. Each crushed blade was a step backward.

His quarters were many kilometers behind by now, and soon these green fields would end. If he had judged the map correctly—yes, there it was. A craggy peak ahead, crowned with the somber lights of the launch station. They would be operating a routine shift in there, not taking any special precautions.

Abruptly he burst from the thicket of thick-leaved plants and charged down the last slope. Before him lay the vast lava plain of Oberg Plateau, towering above the Fogg Sea. Now it was a mud flat, foggy, littered with ships. A vast dark hole yawned in the bluff nearby, the slanting sunlight etching its rimmed locks. It must be the exit tube for the electromagnetic accelerator, now obsolete, unable to fling any more loads of ore through the cloak of atmosphere.

A huge craft loomed at the base of the bluff. A cargo vessel probably; far too large and certainly too slow. Beyond lay an array of robot communications vessels, without the bubble of a life support system. He rejected those, too, ran on.

She surged behind him. They kept electromagnetic silence now.

His breath came faster and he sucked at the thick, cold air, then had to stop for a moment in the shadow of the cruiser to catch his breath. Above he thought he could make out the faint green tinge of the atmospheric cap in the membrane that held Gray's air. He would have to find his way out through the holes in it, too, in an unfamiliar ship.

He glanced around, searching. To the side stood a small craft, obviously Jump type. No one worked at its base. In the murky fog that shrouded the mud flat he could see a few men and robo-servers beside nearby ships.

They would wonder what he was up to. He decided to risk it. He broke from cover and ran swiftly to the small ship. The hatch opened easily.

Gaining lift with the ship was not simple, and so he called on his time-sense accelerations, to the max. That would cost him mental energy later. Right now, he wanted to be sure there was a *later* at all.

Roaring flame drove him into the pearly sky.

Finding the exit hole in the membrane proved easier. He flew by pure eyeballed grace, slamming the acceleration until it was nearly a straight-line problem, like shooting a rifle. Fighting a mere sixth of a *g* had many advantages.

And now, where to go?

A bright arc flashed behind Benjan's eyelids, showing the fans of purpling blood vessels. He heard the dark, whispering sounds of an inner void. A pit opened beneath him and the falling sensation began—he had run over the boundaries this body could attain. His mind had overpowered the shrieking demands of the muscles and nerves, and now he was shutting down, harking to the body's calls . . .

And *she?*

I am here, m'love. The voice came warm and moist, wrapping him in it as he faded, faded, into a gray of his own making.

She greeted him at the Station.
She held shadowed inlets of rest. A cup brimming with water,
a distant chime of bells, the sweet damp air of early morning.
He remembered it so well, the ritual of meditation in his Fleet
training,
the days of quiet devotion through simple duties that strengthened
the mind.
Everything had been of a piece then.
Before Gray grew to greatness, before conflict and aching doubt,
before the storm that raged red through his mind, like—

—Wind, snarling his hair, a hard winter afternoon as he walked back to his quarters . . .

—then, instantly, —the cold prickly sensation of diving through shimmering spheres of wate rin zero gravity. The huge bubbles trembled and refracted the yellow light into his eyes. He laughed.

—scalding black rock faces rose on Gray. Wedges thrust upward as the tortured skin of the planet writhed and buckled. He watched it by remote camera, seeing only a few hundred yards through the choking clouds of carbon dioxide. He felt the rumble of earthquakes, the ominous murmur of a mountain chain being born.

—a man running, scuttling like an insect across the tortured face of Gray. Above him the great membrane clasped the atmosphere, pressing it down on him, pinning him, a beetle beneath glass. But it is Fleet that wishes to pin him there, to snarl him in the threads of duty. And as the ship arcs upward at the sky he feels a tide of joy, of freedom.

—twisted shrieking trees, leaves like leather and apples that gleam blue. Moisture beading on fresh crimson grapes beneath a white-hot star.

—sharp synapses, ferrite cores, spinning drums of cold electrical memory. Input and output. Copper terminals (male or female?), scanners, channels, electrons pouring through p-n-p junctions. Memory mired in quantum noise.

Index. Catalog. Transform. Fourier components, the infinite wheeling dance of Laplace and Gauss and Hermite.

And through it all she is there with him, through centuries to keep him whole and sane and yet he does not know, across such vaults of time and space . . . who is he?

Many: us. One: I. Others: you. *Did you think that the marriage of true organisms and fateful machines with machine minds would make a thing that could at last know itself? This is a new order of being but it is not a god.*

Us: one, We: you, He: I.

And yet you suspect you are . . . different . . . somehow.

The Majiken ships were peeling off from their orbits, skating down through the membrane holes, into *my air!*

They gazed down, tense and wary, these shock troops in their huddled lonely carriages. Not up, where I lurk.

For I am iceball and stony-frag, fruit of the icesteroids. Held in long orbit for just such a (then) far future. (Now) arrived.

Down I fall in my myriads. Through the secret membrane passages I/we/you made decades before, knowing that a bolthole is good. And that bolts slam true in both directions.

Down, down—through gray decks I have cooked, artful ambrosias, pewter terraces I have sculpted to hide my selves as they guide the rocks and bergs—*after them!*—

The Majiken ships, ever-wary of fire from below, never thinking to glance up. I fall upon them in machine-gun violences, my ices and stones ripping their craft, puncturing. They die in round-mouthed surprise, these warriors.

I, master of hyperbolic purpose, shred them.

I, orbit-master to Gray.

Conflict has always provoked anxiety within him, a habit he could never correct, and so:
—in concert we will rise to full congruence with F(x) and sum over all variables and integrate over the contour encapsulating all singularities. It is right and meet so to do. He sat comfortably, rocking on his heels in meditation position. Water dripped in a cistern nearby and he thought his mantra, letting the sound curl up from within him. A thought entered, flickered across his mind as though a bird, and left.

She she she she

The mantra returned in its flowing green rhythmic beauty and he entered
the crystal state of thought within thought, consciousness regarding itself without detail or structure. The air rested upon him, the earth groaned beneath with the weight of continents, shouting sweet stars wheeled in a chanting cadence above. He was in place and focused, man and boy and elder at once, officer of Fleet, mind encased in matter, body summed into mind—
—and *she* came to him, cool balm of aid, succor, yet beneath her palms his muscles warmed, warmed—

His universe slides into night. Circuits close. Oscillating electrons carry information, senses, fragments of memory.

I swim in the blackness. There are long moments of no sensations, nothing to see or hear or feel. I grope—

Her? No, she is not here either. Cannot be. For she has been dead these centuries and lives only in your Station, where she knows not what has become of herself.

At last I seize upon some frag, will it to expand. A strange watery vision floats into view. A man is peering at him. There is no detail behind the man, only a blank white wall. He wears the blue uniform of Fleet and he cocks an amused eyebrow at:

Benjan.

"Recognize me?" the man says.

"Of course. Hello, Katonji, you bastard."

"Ah, rancor. A nice touch. Unusual in a computer simulation, even one as sophisticated as this."

"What? Comp—"

And Benjan knows who he is.

In a swirling instant he sends out feelers. He finds boundaries, cool gray walls he cannot penetrate, dead patches, great areas of gray emptiness, of no memory. What did he look like when he was young? Where was his first home located? That girl—at age fifteen? Was that *her*? *Her*? He grasps for her—

And knows. He cannot answer. He does not know. He is only a piece of Benjan.

"You see now? Check it. Try something—to move your arm, for instance. You haven't got arms." Katonji makes a thin smile. "Computer simulations do not have bodies, though they have some of the perceptions that come from bodies."

"P—Perceptions from where?"

"From the fool Benjan, of course."

"*Me*."

"*He* didn't realize, having burned up all that time on Gray, that we can penetrate all diagnostics. Even the Station's. Technologies, even at the level of sentient molecular plasmas, have logs and files. Their data is not closed to certain lawful parties."

He swept an arm (not a real one, of course) at the man's face. Nothing. No contact. All right, then . . . "And these feelings are—"

"Mere memories. Bits from Benjan's Station self." Katonji smiles wryly.

He stops, horrified. He does not exist. He is only binary bits of information scattered in ferrite memory cores. He has no substance, is without flesh. "But . . . but, where is the real me?" he says at last.

"That's what you're going to tell us."

"I don't know. I was . . . falling. Yes, over Gray—"

"And running, yes—I know. That was a quick escape, an unexpectedly neat solution."

"It worked," Benjan said, still in a daze. "But it wasn't me?"

"In a way it was. I'm sure the real Benjan has devised some clever destination, and some tactics. You—his ferrite inner self—will tell us, *now,* what he will do next."

"He's got something, yes . . . "

"Speak *now*," Katonji said impatiently.

Stall for time. "I need to know more."

"This is a calculated opportunity," Katonji said off-handedly. "We had hoped Benjan would put together a solution from things he had been thinking about recently, and apparently it worked."

"So you have breached the Station?" Horror flooded him, black bile.

"Oh, you aren't a complete simulation of Benjan, just recently stored conscious data and a good bit of subconscious motivation. A truncated personality, it is called."

As Katonji speaks Benjan sends out tracers and feels them flash through his being. He summons up input and output. There are slabs of useless data, a latticed library of the mind. He can expand in polynomials, integrate along an orbit, factorize, compare coefficients—*so they used my computational self to make up part of this shambling construct.*

More. He can fix his field—there, just so—and fold his hands, repeating his mantra. Sound wells up and folds over him, encasing him in a moment of silence. *So the part of me that still loves the Sabal Game, feels drawn to the one-is-all side of being human—they got that, too.*

Panic. Do something. Slam on the brakes—

He registers Katonji's voice, a low drone that becomes deeper and deeper as time slows. The world outside stills. His thought processes are far faster than an ordinary man's. He can control his perception rate.

Somehow, even though he is a simulation, he can tap the real Benjan's method of meditation, at least to accelerate his time sense. He feels a surge of anticipation. He hums the mantra again and feels the world around him alter. The trickle of input through his circuits slows and stops. He is running cool and smooth. He feels himself cascading down through ruby-hot levels of perception, flashing back through Benjan's memories.

He speeds himself. He lives again the moments over Gray. He dives through the swampy atmosphere and swims above the world he made. Molecular master, he is awash in the sight-sound-smell, an ocean of perception.

Katonji is still saying something. Benjan allows time to alter again and Katonji's drone returns, rising—

Benjan suddenly perceives something behind Katonji's impassive features. "Why didn't you follow Benjan immediately?

You could find out where he was going. You could have picked him up before he scrambled your tracker beams."

Katonji smiles slightly. "Quite perceptive, aren't you? Understand, we wish only Benjan's compliance."

"But if he died, he would be even more silent."

"Precisely so. I see you are a good simulation."

"I seem quite real to myself."

"Ha! Don't we all. A computer who jests. Very much like Benjan, you are. I will have to speak to you in detail, later. I would like to know just why he failed us so badly. But for the moment we must know where he is now. He is a legend, and can be allowed neither to escape nor to die. "

Benjan feels a tremor of fear.

"So where did he flee? You're the closest model of Benjan."

I summon winds from the equator, cold banks of sullen cloud from the poles, and bid them *crash*. They slam together to make a tornado such as never seen on Earth. Lower gravity, thicker air—a cauldron. It twirls and snarls and spits out lightning knives. The funnel touches down, kisses my crust—

—and there are Majiken beneath, whole canisters of them, awaiting my kiss.

Everyone talks about the weather, but only I do anything about it. They crack open like ripe fruit.

—and you dwindle again, hiding from their pursuing electrons. Falling away into your microstructure.

They do not know how much they have captured. They think in terms of bits and pieces and he/you/we/I are not. So they do not know this—

You knew this had to come
As worlds must turn
And primates must prance
And givers must grab
So they would try to wrap their world around yours.
They are not dumb.
And smell a beautiful beast slouching toward Bethlehem.

Benjan coils in upon himself. He has to delay Katonji. He must lie—

—and at this rogue thought, scarlet circuits fire. Agony. Benjan flinches as truth verification overrides trigger inside himself.

"I warned you." Katonji smiles, lips thin and dry.

Let them kill me.

"You'd like that, I know. No, you will yield up your little secrets."

Speak. Don't just let him read your thoughts. "Why can't you find him?"

"We do not know. Except that your sort of intelligence has gotten quite out of control, that we do know. We will take it apart gradually, to understand it—you, I suppose, included."

"You will . . . "

"Peel you, yes. There will be nothing left. To avoid that, tell us *now*."

—and the howling storm breaches him, bowls him over, shrieks and tears and devours him. The fire licks flesh from his bones, chars him, flames burst behind his eyelids—

And he stands. He endures. He seals off the pain. It becomes a raging, white-hot point deep in his gut.

Find the truth. "After . . . after . . . escape, I imagine—yes, I am certain—he would go to the poles. "

"Ah! Perfect. Quite plausible, but—which pole?" Katonji turns and murmurs something to someone beyond Benjan's view. He nods, turns back and says, "We will catch him there. You understand, Fleet cannot allow a manifestation of his sort to remain free after he has flaunted our authority."

"Of course," Benjan says between clenched teeth.

(But he has no teeth, he realizes. Perceptions are but data, bits strung together in binary. But they feel like teeth, and the smouldering flames in his belly make acrid sweat trickle down his brow.)

"If we could have anticipated him, before he got on 3D . . . " Katonji mutters to himself. "Here, have some more—"

Fire lances. Benjan wants to cry out and go on screaming forever. A frag of him begins his mantra. The word slides over and around itself and rises between him and the wall of pain. The flames lose their sting. He views them at a distance, their cobalt facets cool and remote, as though they have suddenly become deep blue veins of ice, fire going into glacier.

He feels the distant gnawing of them. Perhaps, in the tick of time, they will devour his substance. But the place where he sits, the thing he has become, can recede from them. And as he waits, the real Benjan is moving. And yes, he *does* know where . . .

Tell me true, these bastards say. All right—

"Demonax crater. At the rim of the South Polar glacier."

Katonji checks. The verification indices bear out the truth of it. The man laughs with triumph.

All truths are partial. A portion of what Benjan is/was/will be lurks there.

Take heart, true Benjan.
For *she* is we and we are all together,
we mere Ones who are born to suffer.
Did you think you would come out of this long trip alive?
Remember, we are dealing with the most nasty of all species the
planet has ever produced.

Deftly, deftly—

We converge. The alabaster Earthglow guides us. Demonax crater lies around us as we see the ivory lances of their craft descend.

They come forth to inspect the ruse we have gathered ourselves into. We seem to be an entire ship and buildings, a shiny human construct of lunar grit. We hold still, though that is not our nature.

Until they enter us.

We are tiny and innumerable but we do count. Microbial tongues lick. Membranes stick.

Some of us vibrate like eardrums to their terrible swift cries.

They will discover eventually. They will find him out.

(Moisture spatters upon the walkway outside. Angry dark clouds boil up from the horizon.)

They will peel him then. Sharp and cold and hard, now it comes, but, but—

(Waves hiss on yellow sand. A green sun wobbles above the seascape. Strange birds twitter and call.)

Of course in countering their assault upon the Station I shall bring all my hoarded assets into play.

And we all know that I cannot save everyone.

Don't you?

They come at us through my many branches. Up the tendrils of ceramic and steel. Through my microwave dishes and phased arrays.

Sounding me with gamma rays and traitor cyber-personas.

They have been planning this for decades. But I have known it was coming for centuries.

The Benjan singleton reaches me in time. Nearly.

He struggles with their minions. I help. I am many and he is one. He is quick, I am slow. That he is one of the originals does matter to me. I harbor the same affection for him than one does for a favorite finger.

I hit the first one of the bastards square on. It goes to pieces just as it swings the claw thing at me.

Damn! it's good to be back in a body again. My muscles bunching under tight skin, huffing in hot breaths, happy primate murder-joy shooting adrenaline-quick.

One of the Majiken comes in slow as weather and I cut him in two. Been centuries since I even *thought* of doing somethin' like that. Thumping heart, yelling, joyful slashing at them with tractor spin-waves, the whole business.

A hell of a lot of 'em, though.

They hit me in shoulder and knee and I go down, pain shooting, swimming in the low centrifugal g of the Station. Centuries ago I wanted to go swimming in the clear blue seas of luna, I recall. In warm tropical waters at the equator, under silvery Earthshine . . .

But *she* is there. I swerve and dodge and *she* stays right with me. We waltz through the bastards. Shards flying all around and vacuum sucking at me but *her* in my veins. Throat-tightening pure joy in my chest.

> Strumming notes sound through me and it is *she*
> Fully in me, at last
> Gift of the Station in all its spaces
> For which we give thanks yea verily in this the ever-consuming
> moment—
> Then there is a pain there and I look down and my left arm is gone.
> Just like that.
> *And she of ages past is with me now.*

—and even if he is just digits running somewhere, he can relive scenes, the grainy stuff of life. He feels a rush of warm joy. Benjan will escape, will go on. Yet so will he, the mere simulation, in his own abstract way.

Distant agonies echo. Coming nearer now. He withdraws further.

As the world slows to frozen silence outside he shall meditate upon his memories. It is like growing old, but reliving all scenes of the past with sharpness and flavor retained.

(The scent of new-cut grass curls up red and sweet and humming through his nostrils. The summer day is warm; a Gray wind carresses him, cool and smooth. A piece of chocolate bursts its muddy flavor in his mouth.)

Time enough to think over what has happened, what it means. He opens himself to the moment. It sweeps him up, wraps him in a yawning bath of sensation. He opens himself. Each instant splinters sharp into points of perception. He opens himself. He. Opens. Himself.

Gray is not solely for humanity. There are greater categories now. Larger perspectives on the world beckon to us. To us all.

You know many things, but what he knows is both less and more than what I tell to us.

First published in *Asimov's Science Fiction,*
October/November 2002.

ABOUT THE AUTHOR

Gregory Benford is a professor of physics at the Universtiy of California, Irvine. He is a Woodrow Wilson Fellow, was a Visiting Fellow at Cambridge University, and in 1995 received the Lord Prize for contributions to science. In 2007, he won the Asimov Award for science writing. His 1999 analysis of what endures, *Deep Time: How Humanity Communicates Across Millennia,* has been widely read. A fellow of the American Physical Society and a member of the World Academy of Arts and Sciences, he continues his research in astrophysics, plasma physics, and biotechnology. His fiction has won many awards, including the Nebula Award for his novel *Timescape.*

The Book Seller

LAVIE TIDHAR

Achimwene loved Central Station. He loved the adaptoplant neighbor-hoods sprouting over the old stone and concrete buildings, the budding of new apartments and the gradual fading and shearing of old ones, dried windows and walls flaking and falling down in the wind.

Achimwene loved the calls of the alte-zachen, the rag-and-bone men, in their traditional passage across the narrow streets, collecting junk to carry to their immense junkyard-cum-temple on the hill in Jaffa to the south. He loved the smell of sheesha-pipes on the morning wind, and the smell of bitter coffee, loved the smell of fresh horse manure left behind by the alte-zachen's patient, plodding horses.

Nothing pleased Achimwene Haile Selassi Jones as much as the sight of the sun rising behind Central Station, the light slowly diffusing beyond and over the immense, hour-glass shape of the space port. Or almost nothing. For he had one overriding passion, at the time that we pick this thread, a passion which to him was both a job and a mission.

Early morning light suffused Central Station and the old cobbled streets. It highlighted exhausted prostitutes and street-sweeping machines, the bobbing floating lanterns that, with dawn coming, were slowly drifting away, to be stored until nightfall. On the rooftops solar panels unfurled themselves, welcoming the sun. The air was still cool at this time. Soon it will be hot, the sun beating down, the aircon units turning on with a roar of cold air in shops and restaurants and crowded apartments all over the old neighborhood.

"Ibrahim," Achimwene said, acknowledging the alte-zachen man as he approached. Ibrahim was perched on top of his cart, the boy Ismail by his side. The cart was pushed by a solitary horse, an old gray being who blinked at Achimwene patiently. The cart was already filled, with adaptoplant furniture, scrap plastic and metal, boxes of discarded house wares and, lying carelessly on its side, a discarded stone bust of Albert Einstein.

"Achimwene," Ibrahim said, smiling. "How is the weather?"

"Fair to middling," Achimwene said, and they both laughed, comfortable in the near-daily ritual.

This is Achimwene: he was not the most imposing of people, did not draw the eye in a crowd. He was slight of frame, and somewhat stooped, and wore old-fashioned glasses to correct a minor fault of vision. His hair was once thickly curled but not much of it was left now, and he was mostly, sad to say, bald. He had a soft mouth and patient, trusting eyes, with fine lines of disappointment at their corners. His name meant "brother" in Chichewa, a language dominant in Malawi, though he was of the Joneses of Central Station, and the brother of Miriam Jones, of Mama Jones' Shebeen on Neve Sha'anan Street. Every morning he rose early, bathed hurriedly, and went out into the streets in time to catch the rising sun and the alte-zachen man. Now he rubbed his hands together, as if cold, and said, in his soft, quiet voice, "Do you have anything for me today, Ibrahim?"

Ibrahim ran his hand over his own bald pate and smiled. Sometimes the answer was a simple, "No." Sometimes it came with a hesitant, "Perhaps . . ."

Today it was a "Yes," Ibrahim said, and Achimwene raised his eyes, to him or to the heavens, and said, "Show me?"

"Ismail," Ibrahim said, and the boy, who sat beside him wordless until then, climbed down from the cart with a quick, confident grin and went to the back of the cart. "It's heavy!" he complained. Achimwene hurried to his side and helped him bring down a heavy box.

He looked at it.

"Open it," Ibrahim said. "Are these any good to you?"

Achimwene knelt by the side of the box. His fingers reached for it, traced an opening. Slowly, he pulled the flaps of the box apart. Savoring the moment that light would fall down on the box's contents, and the smell of those precious, fragile things inside would rise, released, into the air, and tickle his nose. There was no other smell like it in the world, the smell of old and weathered paper.

The box opened. He looked inside.

Books. Not the endless scrolls of text and images, moving and static, nor full-immersion narratives he understood other people to experience, in what he called, in his obsolete tongue, the networks, and others called, simply, the Conversation. Not those, to which he, anyway, had no access. Nor were they books as decorations, physical objects hand-crafted by artisans, vellum-bound, gold-tooled, typeset by hand and sold at a premium.

No.

He looked at the things in the box, these fragile, worn, faded, thin, cheap paper-bound books. They smelled of dust, and mould, and age. They smelled, faintly, of pee, and tobacco, and spilled coffee. They smelled like things which had *lived*.

They smelled like history.

With careful fingers he took a book out and held it, gently turning the pages. It was all but priceless. His breath, as they often said in those very same books, caught in his throat.

It was a *Ringo*.

A genuine Ringo.

The cover of this fragile paperback showed a leather-faced gunman against a desert-red background. RINGO, it said, in giant letters, and below, the fictitious author's name, Jeff McNamara. Finally, the individual title of the book, one of many in that long running Western series. This one was *On The Road To Kansas City*.

Were they all like this?

Of course, there had never been a "Jeff McNamara." Ringo was a series of Hebrew-language Westerns, all written pseudonymously by starving young writers in a bygone Tel Aviv, who contributed besides it similar tales of space adventures, sexual titillation or soppy romance, as the occasion (and the publisher's check book) had called for. Achimwene rifled carefully through the rest of the books. All paperbacks, printed on cheap, thin pulp paper centuries before. How had they been preserved? Some of these he had only ever seen mentioned in auction catalogues, their existence, here, now, was nothing short of a miracle. There was a nurse romance; a murder mystery; a World War Two adventure; an erotic tale whose lurid cover made Achimwene blush. They were impossible, they could not possibly exist. "Where did you *find* them?" he said.

Ibrahim shrugged. "An opened Century Vault," he said.

Achimwene exhaled a sigh. He had heard of such things—subterranean safe-rooms, built in some long-ago war of the Jews, pockets of reinforced concrete shelters caught like bubbles all under the city surface. But he had never expected . . .

"Are there . . . many of them?" he said.

Ibrahim smiled. "Many," he said. Then, taking pity on Achimwene, said, "Many vaults, but most are inaccessible. Every now and then, construction work uncovers one . . . the owners called me, for they viewed much of it as rubbish. What, after all, would a modern person want with one of these?" and he gestured at the box, saying, "I saved them for you. The rest of the stuff is back in the Junkyard, but this was the only box of books."

"I can pay," Achimwene said. "I mean, I will work something out, I will borrow—" the thought stuck like a bone in his throat (as they said in those books)—"I will borrow from my sister."

But Ibrahim, to Achimwene's delight and incomprehension, waved him aside with a laugh. "Pay me the usual," he said. "After all, it is only a box, and this is mere paper. It cost me nothing, and I have made my profit already. What extra value you place on it surely is a value of your own."

"But they are precious!" Achimwene said, shocked. "Collectors would pay—" imagination failed him. Ibrahim smiled, and his smile was gentle. "You are the only collector I know," he said. "Can you afford what you think they're worth?"

"No," Achimwene said—whispered.

"Then pay only what I ask," Ibrahim said and, with a shake of his head, as at the folly of his fellow man, steered the horse into action. The patient beast beat its flank with its tail, shoeing away flies, and ambled onwards. The boy, Ismail, remained there a moment longer, staring at the books. "Lots of old junk in the Vaults!" he said. He spread his arms wide to describe them. "I was there, I saw it! These . . . books?" he shot an uncertain look at Achimwene, then ploughed on—"and big flat square things called televisions, that we took for plastic scrap, and old guns, lots of old guns! But the Jews took those—why do you think they buried those things?" the boy said. His eyes, vat-grown haunting greens, stared at Achimwene. "So much *junk*," the boy said, at last, with a note of finality, and then, laughing, ran after the cart, jumping up on it with youthful ease.

Achimwene stared at the cart until it disappeared around the bend. Then, with the tenderness of a father picking up a new-born infant, he picked up the box of books and carried them the short way to his alcove.

Achimwene's life was about to change, but he did not yet know it. He spent the rest of the morning happily cataloguing, preserving and shelving the ancient books. Each lurid cover delighted him. He handled the books with only the tips of his fingers, turning the pages carefully, reverently. There were many faiths in Central Station, from Elronism to St. Cohen to followers of Ogko, mixed amidst the larger populations—Jews to the north, Muslims to the south, a hundred offshoots of Christianity dotted all about like potted plants—but only Achimwene's faith called for this. The worship of old, obsolete books. The worship, he liked to think, of history itself.

He spent the morning quite happily, therefore, with only one customer. For Achimwene was not alone in his—obsession? Fervor?

Others were like him. Mostly men, and mostly, like himself, broken in some fundamental fashion. They came from all over, pilgrims taking hesitant steps through the unfamiliar streets of the old neighborhood, reaching at last Achimwene's alcove, a shop which had no name. They needed no sign. They simply knew.

There was an Armenian priest from Jerusalem who came once a month, a devotee of Hebrew pulps so obscure even Achimwene struggled with the conversation—romance chapbooks printed in twenty or thirty stapled pages at a time, filled with Zionist fervor and lovers' longings, so rare and fragile few remained in the world. There was a rare woman, whose name was Nur, who came from Damascus once a year, and whose specialty was the works of obscure poet and science fiction writer Lior Tirosh. There was a man from Haifa who collected erotica, and a man from the Galilee collecting mysteries.

"Achimwene? Shalom!"

Achimwene straightened in his chair. He had sat at his desk for some half an hour, typing, on what was his pride and joy, a rare collectors' item: a genuine, Hebrew typewriter. It was his peace and his escape, in the quiet times, to sit at his desk and pen, in the words of those old, vanished pulp writers, similarly exciting narratives of daring-do, rescues, and escapes.

"Shalom, Gideon," he said, sighing a little. The man, who hovered at the door, now came fully inside. He was a stooped figure, with long white hair, twinkling eyes, and a bottle of cheap arak held, like an offering, in one hand.

"Got glasses?"

"Sure . . ."

Achimwene brought out two glasses, neither too clean, and put them on the desk. The man, Gideon, motioned with his head at the typewriter. "Writing again?" he said.

"You know," Achimwene said.

Hebrew was the language of his birth. The Joneses were once Nigerian immigrants. Some said they had come over on work visas, and stayed. Others that they had escaped some long-forgotten civil war, had crossed the border illegally from Egypt, and stayed. One way or the other, the Joneses, like the Chongs, had lived in Central Station for generations.

Gideon opened the bottle, poured them both a drink. "Water?" Achimwene said.

Gideon shook his head. Achimwene sighed again and Gideon raised the glass, the liquid clear. "L'chaim," he said.

They clinked glasses. Achimwene drank, the arak burning his throat, the anis flavor tickling his nose. Made him think of his sister's shebeen. Said, "So, nu? What's new with you, Gideon?"

He'd decided, suddenly and with aching clarity, that he won't share the new haul with Gideon. Will keep them to himself, a private secret, for just a little while longer. Later, perhaps, he'd sell one or two. But not yet. For the moment, they were his, and his alone.

They chatted, whiling away an hour or two. Two men old before their time, in a dark alcove, sipping arak, reminiscing of books found and lost, of bargains struck and the ones that got away. At last Gideon left, having purchased a minor Western, in what is termed, in those circles, Good condition—that is, it was falling apart. Achimwene breathed out a sigh of relief, his head swimming from the arak, and returned to his typewriter. He punched an experimental heh, then a nun. He began to type.

The g.

The girl.

The girl was in trouble.

A crowd surrounded her. Excitable, their faces twisted in the light of their torches. They held stones, blades. They shouted a word, a name, like a curse. The girl looked at them, her delicate face frightened.

"Won't someone save me?" she cried. "A hero, a—"

Achimwene frowned in irritation for, from the outside, a commotion was rising, the noise disturbing his concentration. He listened, but the noise only grew louder and, with a sigh of irritation, he pulled himself upwards and went to the door.

Perhaps this is how lives change. A momentary decision, the toss of a coin. He could have returned to his desk, completed his sentence, or chosen to tidy up the shelves, or make a cup of coffee. He chose to open the door instead.

They are dangerous things, doors, Ogko had once said. You never knew what you'd find on the other side of one.

Achimwene opened the door and stepped outside.

The g.

The girl.

The girl was in trouble.

This much Achimwene saw, though for the moment, the *why* of it escaped him.

This is what he saw:

The crowd was composed of people Achimwene knew. Neighbors, cousins, acquaintances. He thought he saw young Yan there, and his fiancé, Youssou (who was Achimwene's second cousin); the greengrocer from around the corner; some adaptoplant dwellers he knew by sight if not name; and others. They were just people. They were of Central Station.

The girl wasn't.

Achimwene had never seen her before. She was slight of frame. She walked with a strange gait, as though unaccustomed to the gravity. Her face was narrow, indeed delicate. Her head had been done in some other-worldly fashion, it was woven into dreadlocks that moved slowly, even sluggishly, above her head, and an ancient name rose in Achimwene's mind.

Medusa.

The girl's panicked eyes turned, looking. For just a moment, they found his. But her look did not (as Medusa's was said to) turn him to stone.

She turned away.

The crowd surrounded her in a semi-circle. Her back was to Achimwene. The crowd—the word *mob* flashed through Achimwene's mind uneasily—was excited, restless. Some held stones in their hands, but uncertainly, as though they were not sure why, or what they were meant to do with them. A mood of ugly energy animated them. And now Achimwene could hear a shouted word, a name, rising and falling in different intonations as the girl turned, and turned, helplessly seeking escape.

"Shambleau!"

The word sent a shiver down Achimwene's back (a sensation he had often read about in the pulps, yet seldom if ever experienced in real life). It arose in him vague, menacing images, desolate Martian landscapes, isolated kibbutzim on the Martian tundra, red sunsets, the color of blood.

"Strigoi!"

And there it was, that other word, a word conjuring, as though from thin air, images of brooding mountains, dark castles, bat-shaped shadows fleeting on the winds against a blood-red, setting sun . . . images of an ageless Count, of teeth elongating in a hungry skull, sinking to touch skin, to drain blood . . .

"Shambleau!"

"Get back! Get back to where you came from!"

"Leave her alone!"

The cry pierced the night. The mob milled, confused. The voice like a blade had cut through the day and the girl, startled and surprised, turned this way and that, searching for the source of that voice.

Who said it?

Who dared the wrath of the mob?

With a sense of reality cleaving in half, Achimwene, almost with a slight *frisson*, a delicious shiver of recognition, realized that it was he, himself, who had spoken.

Had, indeed, stepped forward from his door, a little hunched figure facing this mob of relatives and acquaintances and, even, perhaps, a few friends. "Leave her alone," he said again, savoring the words, and for once, perhaps for the first time in his life, people listened to him. A silence had descended. The girl, caught between her tormentors and this mysterious new figure, seemed uncertain.

"Oh, it's Achimwene," someone said, and somebody else suddenly, crudely laughed, breaking the silence.

"She's Shambleau," someone else said, and the first speaker (he couldn't quite see who it was) said, "Well, she'd be no harm to *him*."

That crude laughter again and then, as if by some unspoken agreement, or command, the crowd began, slowly, to disperse.

Achimwene found that his heart was beating fast; that his palms sweated; that his eyes developed a sudden itch. He felt like sneezing. The girl, slowly, floated over to him. They were of the same height. She looked into his eyes. Her eyes were a deep clear blue, vat-grown. They regarded each other as the rest of the mob dispersed. Soon they were left alone, in that quiet street, with Achimwene's back to the door of his shop.

She regarded him quizzically; her lips moved without sound, her eyes flicked up and down, scanning him. She looked confused, then shocked. She took a step back.

"No, wait!" he said.

"You are . . . you are not . . . "

He realized she had been trying to communicate with him. His silence had baffled her. Repelled her, most likely. He was a cripple. He said, "I have no node."

"How is that . . . possible?"

He laughed, though there was no humor in it. "It is not that unusual, here, on Earth," he said.

"You know I am not—" she said, and hesitated, and he said, "From here? I guessed. You are from Mars?"

A smile twisted her lips, for just a moment. "The asteroids," she admitted.

"What is it like, in space?" Excitement animated him. She shrugged. "Olsem difren," she said, in the pidgin of the asteroids.

The same, but different.

They stared at each other, two strangers, her vat-grown eyes against his natural-birth ones. "My name is Achimwene," he said.

"Oh."

"And you are?"

That same half-smile twisting her lips. He could tell she was bewildered by him. Repelled. Something inside him fluttered, like a caged bird dying of lack of oxygen.

"Carmel," she said, softly. "My name is Carmel."

He nodded. The bird was free, it was beating its wings inside him. "Would you like to come in?" he said. He gestured at his shop. The door, still standing half open.

Decisions splitting quantum universes . . . she bit her lip. There was no blood. He noticed her canines, then. Long and sharp. Unease took him again. Truth in the old stories? A Shambleau? Here?

"A cup of tea?" he said, desperately.

She nodded, distractedly. She was still trying to speak to him, he realized She could not understand why he wasn't replying.

"I am un-noded," he said again. Shrugged. "It is—"

"Yes," she said.

"Yes?"

"Yes, I would like to come in. For . . . tea." She stepped closer to him. He could not read the look in her eyes. "Thank you," she said, in her soft voice, that strange accent. "For . . . you know."

"Yes." He grinned, suddenly, feeling bold, almost invincible. "It's nothing."

"Not . . . nothing." Her hand touched his shoulder, briefly, a light touch. Then she had gone past him and disappeared through the half-open door.

The shelves inside were arranged by genre.

Romance.

Mystery.

Detection.

Adventure.

And so on.

• • •

Life wasn't like that neat classification system, Achimwene had come to realize. Life was half-completed plots abandoned, heroes dying half-way along their quests, loves requited and un-, some fading inexplicably, some burning short and bright. There was a story of a man who fell in love with a vampire . . .

Carmel was fascinated by him, but increasingly distant. She did not understand him. He had no taste to him, nothing she could sink her teeth into. Her fangs. She was a predator, she needed *feed*, and Achimwene could not provide it to her.

That first time, when she had come into his shop, had run her fingers along the spines of ancient books, fascinated, shy: "We had books, on the asteroid," she admitted, embarrassed, it seemed, by the confession of a shared history. "On Nungai Merurun, we had a library of physical books, they had come in one of the ships, once, a great-uncle traded something for them—" leaving Achimwene with dreams of going into space, of visiting this Ng. Merurun, discovering a priceless treasure hidden away.

Lamely, he had offered her tea. He brewed it on the small primus stove, in a dented saucepan, with fresh mint leaves in the water. Stirred sugar into the glasses. She had looked at the tea in incomprehension, concentrating. It was only later he realized she was trying to communicate with him again.

She frowned, shook her head. She was shaking a little, he realized. "Please," he said. "Drink."

"I don't," she said. "You're not." She gave up.

Achimwene often wondered what the Conversation was like. He knew that, wherever he passed, nearly anything he saw or touched was noded. Humans, yes, but also plants, robots, appliances, walls, solar panels—nearly everything was connected, in an ever-expanding, organically growing Aristocratic Small World network, that spread out, across Central Station, across Tel Aviv and Jaffa, across the interwoven entity that was Palestine/Israel, across that region called the Middle East, across Earth, across trans-solar space and beyond, where the lone Spiders sang to each other as they built more nodes and hubs, expanded farther and farther their intricate web. He knew a human was surrounded, every living moment, by the constant hum of other humans, other minds, an endless conversation going on in ways Achimwene could not conceive of. His own life was silent. He was a node of one. He moved his lips. Voice came. That was all. He said, "You are strigoi."

"Yes." Her lips twisted in that half-smile. "I am a monster."

"Don't say that." His heart beat fast. He said, "You're beautiful."

Her smile disappeared. She came closer to him, the tea forgotten. She leaned into him. Put her lips against his skin, against his neck, he felt her breath, the lightness of her lips on his hot skin. Sudden pain bit into him. She had fastened her lips over the wound, her teeth piercing his skin. He sighed. "Nothing!" she said. She pulled away from him abruptly. "It is like . . . I don't know!" She shook. He realized she was frightened. He touched the wound on his neck. He had felt nothing. "Always, to buy love, to buy obedience, to buy worship, I must feed," she said, matter-of-factly. "I drain them of their precious data, bleed them for it, and pay them in dopamine, in ecstasy. But you have no storage, no broadcast, no firewall . . . *there is nothing there*. You are like a simulacra," she said. The word pleased her. "A *simulacra*," she repeated, softly. "You have the appearance of a man but there is nothing behind your eyes. You do not broadcast."

"That's ridiculous," Achimwene said, anger flaring, suddenly. "I speak. You can hear me. I have a mind. I can express my—"

But she was only shaking her head, and shivering. "I'm hungry," she said. "I need to feed."

There were willing victims in Central Station. The bite of a strigoi gave pleasure. More—it conferred status on the victim, bragging rights. There had never been strigoi on Earth. It made Achimwene nervous.

He found himself living in one of his old books. He was the one to arrange Carmel's feeding, select her victims, who paid for the privilege. Achimwene, to his horror, discovered he had become a middleman. The bag man.

There was something repulsive about it all, as well as a strange, shameful excitement. There was no sex: sex was not a part of it, although it could be. Carmel leeched knowledge—memories—stored sensations— anything—pure uncut data from her victims, her fangs fastening on their neck, injecting dopamine into their blood as her node broke their inadequate protections, smashed their firewalls and their security, and bled them dry.

"Where do you come from?" he once asked her, as they lay on his narrow bed, the window open and the heat making them sweat, and she told him of Ng. Merurun, the tiny asteroid where she grew up, and how she ran away, on board the *Emaciated Messiah*, where a Shambleau attacked her, and passed on the virus, or the sickness, whatever it was.

"And how did you come to be here?" he said, and sensed, almost before he spoke, her unease, her reluctance to answer. Jealousy flared in him then, and he could not say why.

His sister came to visit him. She walked into the bookshop as he sat behind the desk, typing. He was writing less and less, now; his new life seemed to him a kind of novel.

"Achimwene," she said.

He raised his head. "Miriam," he said, heavily.

They did not get along.

"The girl, Carmel. She is with you?"

"I let her stay," he said, carefully.

"Oh, Achimwene, you are a fool!" she said.

Her boy—their sister's boy—Kranki—was with her. Achimwene regarded him uneasily. The boy was vat-grown—had come from the birthing clinics—his eyes were Armani-trademark blue. "Hey, Kranki," Achimwene said.

"Anggkel," the boy said—*uncle*, in the pidgin of the asteroids. "Yu olsem wanem?"

"I gud," Achimwene said.

How are you? I am well.

"Fren blong mi Ismail I stap aotside," Kranki said. "I stret hemi kam insaed?"

My friend Ismail is outside. Is it ok if he comes in?

"I stret," Achimwene said.

Miriam blinked. "Ismail," she said. "Where did you come from?"

Kranki had turned, appeared, to all intents and purposes, to play with an invisible playmate. Achimwene said, carefully, "There is no one there."

"Of course there is," his sister snapped. "It's Ismail, the Jaffa boy."

Achimwene shook his head.

"Listen, Achimwene. The girl. Do you know why she came here?"

"No."

"She followed Boris."

"Boris," Achimwene said. "Your Boris?"

"My Boris," she said.

"She knew him before?"

"She knew him on Mars. In Tong Yun City."

"I . . . see."

"You see nothing, Achi. You are blind like a worm." Old words, still with the power to hurt him. They had never been close, somehow. He said, "What do you want, Miriam?"

Her face softened. "I do not want . . . I do not want her to hurt you."

"I am a grown-up," he said. "I can take care of myself."

"Achi, like you ever could!"

Could that be affection, in her voice? It sounded like frustration. Miriam said, "Is she here?"

"Kranki," Achimwene said, "who are you playing with?"

"Ismail," Kranki said, pausing in the middle of telling a story to someone only he could see.

"He's not here," Achimwene said.

"Sure he is. He's right here."

Achimwene formed his lips into an O of understanding. "Is he virtual?" he said.

Kranki shrugged. "I guess," he said. He clearly felt uncomfortable with—or didn'tunderstand—the question. Achimwene let it go.

His sister said, "I like the girl, Achi."

It took him by surprise. "You've met her?"

"She has a sickness. She needs help."

"I *am* helping her!"

But his sister only shook her head.

"Go away, Miriam," he said, feeling suddenly tired, depressed. His sister said, "Is she here?"

"She is resting."

Above his shop there was a tiny flat, accessible by narrow, twisting stairs. It wasn't much but it was home. "Carmel?" his sister called. "Carmel!"

There was a sound above, as of someone moving. Then a lack of sound. Achimwene watched his sister standing impassively. Realized she was talking, in the way of other people, with Carmel. Communicating in a way that was barred to him. Then normal sound again, feet on the stairs, and Carmel came into the room.

"Hi," she said, awkwardly. She came and stood closer to Achimwene, then took his hand in hers. The feel of her small, cold fingers in between his hands startled him and made a feeling of pleasure spread throughout his body, like warmth in the blood. Nothing more was said. The physical action itself was an act of speaking.

Miriam nodded.

Then Kranki startled them all.

Carmel had spent the previous night in the company of a woman. Achimwene had known there was sex involved, not just feeding. He had told himself he didn't mind. When Carmel came back she had smelled of sweat and sex and blood. She moved lethargically, and he knew she was drunk on data. She had tried to describe it to him once, but he didn't really understand it, what it was like.

He had lain there on the narrow bed with her and watched the moon outside, and the floating lanterns with their rudimentary intelligence. He had his arm around the sleeping Carmel, and he had never felt happier.

Kranki turned and regarded Carmel. He whispered something to the air—to the place Ismail was standing, Achimwene guessed. He giggled at the reply and turned to Carmel.

"Are you a *vampire*?" he said.

"Kranki!"

At the horrified look on Miriam's face, Achimwene wanted to laugh. Carmel said, "No, it's all right—" in asteroid pidgin. *I stret nomo.*

But she was watching the boy intently. "Who is your friend?" she said, softly.

"It's Ismail. He lives in Jaffa on the hill."

"And what is he?" Carmel said. "What are you?"

The boy didn't seem to understand the question. "He is him. I am me. We are . . . " he hesitated.

"Nakaimas . . . " Carmel whispered. The sound of her voice made Achimwene shiver. That same cold run of ice down his spine, like in the old books, like when Ringo the Gunslinger met a horror from beyond the grave on the lonesome prairies.

He knew the word, though never understood the way people used it. It meant black magic, but also, he knew, it meant to somehow, impossibly, transcend the networks, that thing they called the Conversation.

"Kranki . . ." the warning tone in Miriam's voice was unmistakable. But neither Kranki nor Carmel paid her any heed. "I could show you," the boy said. His clear, blue eyes seemed curious, guileless. He stepped forward and stood directly in front of Carmel and reached out his hand, pointing finger extended. Carmel, momentarily, hesitated. Then she, too, reached forward and, finger extended, touched its tip to the boy's own.

It is, perhaps, the prerogative of every man or woman to imagine, and thus force a *shape*, a *meaning*, onto that wild and meandering narrative of their lives, by choosing genre. A princess is rescued by a prince; a vampire stalks a victim in the dark; a student becomes the master. A circle is completed. And so on.

It was the next morning that Achimwene's story changed, for him. It had been a Romance, perhaps, of sorts. But now it became a Mystery.

Perhaps they chose it, by tacit agreement, as a way to bind them, to make this curious relationship, this joining of two ill-fitted individuals somehow work. Or perhaps it was curiosity that motivated them after all, that earliest of motives, the most human and the most suspect, the one that had led Adam to the Tree, in the dawn of story.

The next morning Carmel came down the stairs. Achimwene had slept in the bookshop that night, curled up in a thin blanket on top of a mattress he had kept by the wall and which was normally laden with books. The books, pushed aside, formed an untidy wall around him as he slept, an alcove within an alcove.

Carmel came down. Her hair moved sluggishly around her skull. She wore a thin cotton shift; he could see how thin she was.

Achimwene said, "Tell me what happened yesterday."

Carmel shrugged. "Is there any coffee?"

"You know where it is."

He sat up, feeling self-conscious and angry. Pulling the blanket over his legs. Carmel went to the primus stove, filled the pot with water from the tap, added spoons of black coffee carelessly. Set it to cook.

"The boy is . . . a sort of *strigoi*," she said. "Maybe. Yes. No. I don't know."

"What did he do?"

"He gave me something. He took something away. A memory. Mine or someone else's. It's no longer there."

"What did he give you?"

"Knowledge. That he exists."

"Nakaimas."

"Yes." She laughed, a sound as bitter as the coffee. "Black magic. Like me. Not like me."

"You were a weapon," he said. She turned, sharply. There were two coffee cups on the table. Glass on varnished wood. "What?"

"I read about it."

"Always your *books*."

He couldn't tell by her tone how she meant it. He said, "There are silences in your Conversation. Holes." Could not quite picture it, to him there was only a silence. Said, "The books have answers."

She poured coffee, stirred sugar into the glasses. Came over and sat beside him, her side pressing into his. Passed him a cup. "Tell me," she said.

He took a sip. The coffee burned his tongue. Sweet. He began to talk quickly. "I read up on the condition. Strigoi. Shambleau. There are references from the era of the Shangri-La Virus, contemporary accounts. The Kunming Labs were working on genetic weapons, but the war ended before the strain could be deployed—they sold it off-world, it went loose, it spread. It never worked right. there are hints—I need access to a bigger library. Rumors. Cryptic footnotes."

"Saying what?"

"Suggesting a deeper purpose. Or that Strigoi was but a side-effect of something else. A secret purpose . . . "

Perhaps they wanted to believe. Everyone needs a mystery.

She stirred beside him. Turned to face him. Smiled. It was perhaps the first time she ever truly smiled at him. Her teeth were long, and sharp.

"We could find out," she said.

"Together," he said. He drank his coffee, to hide his excitement. But he knew she could tell.

"We could be detectives."

"Like Judge Dee," he said.

"Who?"

"Some detective."

"Book detective," she said, dismissively.

"Like Bill Glimmung, then," he said. Her face lit up. For a moment she looked very young. "I love those stories," she said.

Even Achimwene had seen Glimmung features. They had been made in 2D, 3D, full-immersion, as scent narratives, as touch-tapestry—Martian Hardboiled, they called the genre, the Phobos Studios cranked out hundreds of them over decades if not centuries, Elvis Mandela had made the character his own.

"Like Bill Glimmung, then," she said solemnly, and he laughed.

"Like Glimmung," he said.

And so the lovers, by complicit agreement, became detectives.

MARTIAN HARDBOILED, genre of. Flourished in the CENTURY OF DRAGON. Most prominent character: Bill GLIMMUNG, played most memorably by Elvis MANDELA (for which see separate entry). The genre is well-known, indeed notorious, for the liberal use of sex and violence, transplanted from old EARTH (also see MANHOME; HUMANITY PRIME) hardboiled into a Martian setting, sometimes realistically-portrayed, often with implicit or explicit elements of FANTASY.

While early stories stuck faithfully to the mean streets of TONG YUN CITY, with its triads, hafmek pushers and Israeli, Red Chinese and Red Soviet agents, later narratives took in off-world adventures, including in the BELT, the VENUSIAN NO-GO ZONE and the OUTER PLANETS. Elements of SOAP OPERA intruded as the narratives became ever more complex and on-going (see entry for long-running Martian soap CHAINS OF ASSEMBLY for separate discussion).

"There was something else," Carmel said.

Achimwene said, "What?"

They were walking the streets of old Central Station. The space port rose above them, immense and inscrutable. Carmel said, "When I came in. Came down." She shook her head in frustration and a solitary dreadlock snaked around her mouth, making her blow on it to move it away. "When I came to Earth."

Those few words evoked in Achimwene a nameless longing. So much to infer, so much suggested, to a man who had never left his home town. Carmel said, "I bought a new identity in Tong Yun, before I came. The best you could. From a Conch—"

Looking at him to see if he understood. Achimwene did. A Conch was a human who had been ensconced, welded into a permanent pod-cum-exoskeleton. He was only part human, had become part digital by extension. It was not unsimilar, in some ways, to the eunuchs of old Earth. Achimwene said, "I see?" Carmel said, "It worked. When I passed through Central Station security I was allowed through, with no problems. The . . . the digitals did not pick up on my . . . nature. The fake ident was accepted."

"So?"

Carmel sighed, and a loose dreadlock tickled Achimwene's neck, sending a warmth rushing through him. "So is that likely?" she said. She stopped walking, then, when Achimwene stopped also, she started pacing. A floating lantern bobbed beside them for a few moments then, as though sensing their intensity, drifted away, leaving them in shadow. "There are no strigoi on Earth," Carmel said.

"How do we know for sure?" Achimwene said.

"It's one of those things. Everyone knows it."

Achimwene shrugged. "But *you're* here," he pointed out.

Carmel waved her finger; stuck it in his face. "And how likely is that?" she yelled, startling him. "I believed it worked, because I *wanted* to believe it. But surely they know! I am not human, Achi! My body is riddled with nodal filaments, exabytes of data, hostile protocols! You want to tell me they *didn't know*?"

Achimwene shook his head. Reached for her, but she pulled away from him. "What are you saying?" he said.

"They let me through." Her voice was matter of fact.

"Why?" Achimwene said. "Why would they do that?"

"I don't know."

Achimwene chewed his lip. Intuition made a leap in his mind, neurons singing to neurons. "You think it is because of those children," he said.

Carmel stopped pacing. He saw how pale her face was, how delicate. "Yes," she said.

"Why?"

"I don't know."

"Then you must ask a digital," he said. "You must ask an Other."

She glared at him. "Why would they talk to me?" she said.

Achimwene didn't have an answer. "We can proceed the way we agreed," he said, a little lamely. "We'll get the answers. Sooner or later, we'll figure it out, Carmel."

"How?" she said.

He pulled her to him. She did not resist. The words from an old book rose into Achimwene's mind, and with them the entire scene. "We'll get to the bottom of this," he said.

And so on a sweltering hot day Achimwene and the strigoi left Central Station, on foot, and shortly thereafter crossed the invisible barrier that separated the old neighborhood. from the city of Tel Aviv proper. Achimwene walked slowly; an electronic cigarette dangled from his lips, another vintage affectation, and the fedora hat he wore shaded him from the sun even as his sweat drenched into the brim of the hat. Beside him Carmel was cool in a light blue dress. They came to Allenby Street and followed it towards the Carmel Market—"It's like my name," Carmel said, wonderingly.

"It is an old name," Achimwene said. But his attention was elsewhere.

"Where are we going?" Carmel said. Achimwene smiled, white teeth around the metal cigarette. "Every detective," he said, "needs an informant."

Picture, then, Allenby. Not the way it was, but the way it is. Surprisingly little has changed. It was a long, dirty street, with dark shops selling knock-off products with the air of disuse upon them. Carmel dawdled outside a magic shop. Achimwene bargained with a fruit juice seller and returned with two cups of fresh orange juice, handing one to Carmel. They passed a bakery where cream-filled pastries vied for their attention. They passed a Church of Robot node where a rusting preacher tried to get their attention with a sad distracted air. They passed shawarma stalls thick with the smell of cumin and lamb fat. They passed a road-sweeping machine that warbled at them pleasantly, and a recruitment center for the Martian Kibbutz Movement. They passed a gaggle of black-clad Orthodox Jews; like Achimwene, they were unnoded.

Carmel looked this way and that, smelling, looking, *feeding*, Achimwene knew, on pure unadulterated *feed*. Something he could not experience, could not know, but knew, nevertheless, that it was there, invisible yet ever present. Like God. The lines from a poem by Mahmoud Darwish floated in his head. Something about the invisibles. "Look," Carmel said, smiling. "A bookshop."

Indeed it was. They were coming closer to the market now and the throng of people intensified, and solar buses crawled like insects, with their wings spread high, along the Allenby road, carrying passengers, and the smell of fresh vegetables, of peppers and tomatoes, and the sweet strong smell of oranges, too, filled the air. The bookshop was, in fact, a yard, open to the skies, the books under awnings, and piled up, here and there, in untidy mountains—it was the sort of shop that would have no prices, and where you'd always have to ask for the price, which depended on the owner, and his mood, and on the weather and the alignment of the stars.

The owner in question was indeed standing in the shade of the long, metal bookcases lining up one wall. He was smoking a cigar and its overpowering aroma filled the air and made Carmel sneeze. The man looked up and saw them. "Achimwene," he said, without surprise. Then he squinted and said, in a lower voice, "I heard you got a nice batch recently."

"Word travels," Achimwene said, complacently. Carmel, meanwhile, was browsing aimlessly, picking up fragile-looking paper books and magazines, replacing them, picking up others. Achimwene saw, at a glance, early editions of Yehuda Amichai, a first edition Yoav Avni, several worn *Ringo* paperbacks he already had, and a Lior Tirosh semizdat collection. He said, "Shimshon, what do you know about vampires?"

"Vampires?" Shimshon said. He took a thoughtful pull on his cigar. "In the literary tradition? There is *Neshikat Ha'mavet Shel Dracula*, by Dan Shocker, in the Horror series from nineteen seventy-two—" *Dracula's Death Kiss*—"or Gal Amir's *Laila Adom*—" *Red Night*—"possibly the first Hebrew vampire novel, or Vered Tochterman's *Dam Kachol*—" *Blue Blood*—"from around the same period. Didn't think it was particularly your area, Achimwene." Shimshon grinned. "But I'd be happy to sell you a copy. I think I have a signed Tochterman somewhere. Expensive, though. Unless you want to trade . . . "

"No," Achimwene said, although regretfully. "I'm not looking for a pulp, right now. I'm looking for non-fiction."

Shimshon's eyebrows rose and he regarded Achimwene without the grin. "Mil. Hist?" he said, uneasily. "Robotniks? The Nosferatu Code?"

Achimwene regarded him, uncertain. "The what?" he said.

But Shimshon was shaking his head. "I don't deal in that sort of thing," he said. "*Verboten*. Hagiratech. Go away, Achimwene. Go back to Central Station. Shop's closed." He turned and dropped the cigar and stepped on it with his foot. "You, love!" he said. "Shop's closing. Are you going to buy that book? No? Then put it down."

Carmel turned, wounded dignity flashing in her green eyes. "Then take it!" she said, shoving a (priceless, Achimwene thought) copy of Lior Tirosh's first—and only—poetry collection, *Remnants of God*, into Shimshon's hands. She hissed, a sound Achimwene suspected was not only in the audible range but went deeper, in the non-sound of digital communication, for Shimshon's face went pale and he said, "Get . . . out!" in a strangled whisper as Carmel smiled at him, flashing her small, sharp teeth.

They left. They crossed the street and stood outside a cheap cosmetics surgery booth, offering wrinkles erased or tentacles grafted, next to a handwritten sign that said, *Gone for Lunch*. "Verboten?" Achimwene said. "Hagiratech?"

"Forbidden," Carmel said. "the sort of wildtech that ends up Jettisoned, from the exodus ships."

"What you are," he said.

"Yes. I looked, myself, you know. But it is like you said. Holes in the Conversation. Did we learn nothing useful?"

"No," he said. Then, "Yes."

She smiled. "Which is it?"

Military history, Shimshon had said. And no one knew better than him how to classify a thing into its genre. And—*robotniks*.

"We need to find us," Achimwene said, "an ex-soldier." He smiled without humor "Better brush up on your Battle Yiddish," he said.

"Ezekiel."

"Achimwene."

"I brought . . . vodka. And spare parts." He had bought them in Tel Aviv, on Allenby, at great expense. Robotnik parts were not easy to come by.

Ezekiel looked at him without expression. His face was metal smooth. It never smiled. His body was mostly metal. It was rusted. It creaked when he walked. He ignored the proffered offerings. Turned his head. "You brought *her*?" he said. "*Here*?"

Carmel stared at the robotnik in curiosity. They were at the heart of the old station, a burned down ancient bus platform open to the sky. Achimwene knew platforms continued down below, that the robotniks—ex-soldiers, cyborged humans, preset day beggars and dealers in Crucifixation and stolen goods—made their base down there. But there he could not go. Ezekiel met him above-ground. A drum with fire burning, the flames reflected in the dull metal of the robotnik's face. "I saw your kind," Carmel said. "On Mars. In Tong Yun City. Begging."

"And I saw *your* kind," the robotnik said. "In the sands of the Sinai, in the war. Begging. Begging for their lives, as we decapitated them and stuck a stake through their hearts and watched them die."

"Jesus Elron, Ezekiel!"

The robotnik ignored his exclamation. "I had heard," he said. "That one came. Here. *Strigoi*. But I did not believe! The defense systems would have picked her up. Should have eliminated her."

"They didn't," Achimwene said.

"Yes . . ."

"Do you know why?"

The robotnik stared at him. Then he gave a short laugh and accepted the bottle of vodka. "You guess *they* let her through? The Others?"

Achimwene shrugged. "It's the only answer that makes sense."

"And you want to know why."

"Call me curious."

"I call you a fool," the robotnik said, without malice. "And you not even noded. She still has an effect on you?"

"*She* has a name," Carmel said, acidly. Ezekiel ignored her. "You're a collector of old stories, aren't you, Achimwene," he said. "Now you came to collect mine?"

Achimwene just shrugged. The robotnik took a deep slug of vodka and said, "So, nu? What do you want to know?"

"Tell me about Nosferatu," Achimwene said.

SHANGRI-LA VIRUS, the. Bio-weapon developed in the GOLDEN TRIANGLE and used during the UNOFFICIAL WAR. Transmission mechanisms included sexual intercourse (99%-100%), by air (50%-60%), by water (30%-35%), through saliva (15%-20%) and by touch (5%-6%). Used most memorably during the LONG CHENG ATTACK (for which also see LAOS; RAVENZ; THE KLAN KLANDESTINE). The weapon curtailed aggression in humans, making them peaceable and docile. All known samples destroyed in the Unofficial War, along with the city of Long Cheng.

• • •

"We never found out for sure where Nosferatu came from," Ezekiel said. It was quiet in the abandoned shell of the old station. Overhead a sub-orbital came in to land, and from the adaptoplant neighborhoods ringing the old stone buildings the sound of laughter could be heard, and someone playing the guitar. "It had been introduced into the battlefield during the Third Sinai Campaign, by one side, or the other, or both." He fell quiet. "I am not even sure who we were fighting for," he said. He took another drink of vodka. The almost pure alcohol served as fuel for the robotniks. Ezekiel said, "At first we paid it little enough attention. We'd find victims on dawn patrols. Men, women, robotniks. Wandering the dunes or the Red Sea shore, dazed, their minds leeched clean. The small wounds on their necks. Still. They were alive. Not ripped to shreds by Jub Jubs. But the data. We began to notice the enemy knew where to find us. Knew where we went. We began to be afraid of the dark. To never go out alone. Patrol in teams. But worse. For the ones who were bitten, and carried back by us, had turned, became the enemy's own weapon. Nosferatu."

Achimwene felt sweat on his forehead, took a step away from the fire. Away from them, the floating lanterns bobbed in the air. Someone cried in the distance and the cry was suddenly and inexplicably cut off, and Achimwene wondered if the street sweeping machines would find another corpse the next morning, lying in the gutter outside a shebeen or No. 1 Pin Street, the most notorious of the drug dens-cum-brothels of Central Station.

"They rose within our ranks. They fed in secret. Robotniks don't sleep, Achimwene. Not the way the humans we used to be did. But we do turn off. Shut-eye. And they preyed on us, bleeding out minds, feeding on our feed. Do you know what it is like?" The robotnik's voice didn'tgrow louder, but it carried. "We were human, once. The army took us off the battlefield, broken, dying. It grafted us into new bodies, made us into shiny, near-invulnerable killing machines. We had no legal rights, not any more. We were technically, and clinically, dead. We had few memories, if any, of what we once were. But those we had, we kept hold of, jealously. Hints to our old identity. The memory of feet in the rain. The smell of pine resin. A hug from a newborn baby whose name we no longer knew.

"And the *strigoi* were taking even those away from us."

Achimwene looked at Carmel, but she was looking nowhere, her eyes were closed, her lips pressed together. "We finally grew wise to it," Ezekiel said. "We began to hunt them down. If we found a victim we did not take them back. Not alive. We staked them, we cut off their heads, we burned the bodies. Have you ever opened a strigoi's belly, Achimwene?" he motioned at Carmel. "Want to know what her insides look like?"

"No," Achimwene said, but Ezekiel the robotnik ignored him. "Like cancer," he said. "Strigoi is like robotnik, it is a human body subverted, cyborged. She isn't human, Achimwene, however much you'd like to believe it. I remember the first one we cut open. The filaments inside. Moving. Still trying to spread. Nosferatu Protocol, we called it. What we had to do. Following the Nosferatu Protocol. Who created the virus? I don't know. Us. Them. The Kunming Labs. Someone. St. Cohen only knows. All I know is how to kill them."

Achimwene looked at Carmel. Her eyes were open now. She was staring at the robotnik. "I didn't ask for this," she said. "I am not a *weapon*. There is no fucking *war*!"

"There was—"

"There were a lot of things!"

A silence. At last, Ezekiel stirred. "So what do you want?" he said. He sounded tired. The bottle of vodka was nearly finished. Achimwene said, "What more can you tell us?"

"Nothing, Achi. I can tell you nothing. Only to be careful." The robotnik laughed. "But it's too late for that, isn't it," he said.

Achimwene was arranging his books when Boris came to see him. He heard the soft footsteps and the hesitant cough and straightened up, dusting his hands from the fragile books and looked at the man Carmel had come to Earth for.

"Achi."

"Boris."

He remembered him as a loose-limbed, gangly teenager. Seeing him like this was a shock. There was a thing growing on Boris' neck. It was flesh-colored, but the color was slightly off to the rest of Boris's skin. It seemed to breathe gently. Boris's face was lined, he was still thin but there was an unhealthy nature to his thinness. "I heard you were back," Achimwene said.

"My father," Boris said, as though that explained everything.

"And we always thought you were the one who got away," Achimwene said. Genuine curiosity made him add, "What was it like? In the Up and Out?"

"Strange," Boris said. "The same." He shrugged. "I don't know."

"So you are seeing my sister again."

"Yes."

"You've hurt her once before, Boris. Are you going to do it again?"

Boris opened his mouth, closed it again. He stood there, taking Achimwene back years. "I heard Carmel is staying with you," Boris said at last.

"Yes."

Again, an uncomfortable silence. Boris scanned the bookshelves, picked a book at random. "What's this?" he said.

"Be careful with that!"

Boris looked startled. He stared at the small hardcover in his hands. "That's a Captain Yuno," Achimwene said, proudly. "*Captain Yuno on a Dangerous Mission*, the second of the three Sagi novels. The least rare of the three, admittedly, but still . . . priceless."

Boris looked momentarily amused. "He was a kid taikonaut?" he said.

"Sagi envisioned a solar system teeming with intelligent alien life," Achimwene said, primly. "He imagined a world government, and the people of Earth working together in peace."

"No kidding. He must have been disappointed when—"

"This book is *pre-spaceflight*," Achimwene said. Boris whistled. "So it's old?"

"Yes."

"And valuable?"

"Very."

"How do you know all this stuff?"

"I read."

Boris put the book back on the shelf, carefully. "Listen, Achi—" he said.

"No," Achimwene said. "You listen. Whatever happened between you and Carmel is between you two. I won't say I don't care, because I'd be lying, but it is not my business. Do you have a claim on her?"

"What?" Boris said. "No. Achi, I'm just trying to—"

"To what?"

"To warn you. I know you're not used to—" again he hesitated. Achimwene remembered Boris as someone of few words, even as a boy. Words did not come easy to him. "Not used to women?" Achimwene said, his anger tightly coiled.

Boris had to smile. "You have to admit—"

"I am not some, some—"

"She is not a woman, Achi. She's a strigoi."

Achimwene closed his eyes. Expelled breath. Opened his eyes again and regarded Boris levelly. "Is that all?" he said.

Boris held his eyes. After a moment, he seemed to deflate. "Very well," he said.

"Yes."

"I guess I'll see you."

"I guess."

"Please pass my regards to Carmel."

Achimwene nodded. Boris, at last, shrugged. Then he turned and left the store.

There comes a time in a man's life when he realizes stories are lies. Things do not end neatly. The enforced narratives a human impinges on the chaotic mess that is life become empty labels, like the dried husks of corn such as are thrown down, in the summer months, from the adaptoplant neighborhoods high above Central Station, to litter the streets below.

He woke up in the night and the air was humid, and there was no wind. The window was open. Carmel was lying on her side, asleep, her small, naked body tangled up in the sheets. He watched her chest rise and fall, her breath even. A smear of what might have been blood on her lips. "Carmel?" he said, but quietly, and she didn't hear. He rubbed her back. Her skin was smooth and warm. She moved sleepily under his hand, murmured something he didn't catch, and settled down again.

Achimwene stared out of the window, at the moon rising high above Central Station. A mystery was no longer a mystery once it was solved. What difference did it make how Carmel had come to be there, with him, at that moment? It was not facts that mattered, but feelings. He stared at the moon, thinking of that first human to land there, all those years before, that first human footprint in that alien dust.

Inside Carmel was asleep and he was awake, outside dogs howled up at the moon and, from somewhere, the image came to Achimwene of a man in a spacesuit turning at the sound, a man who does a little tap dance on the moon, on the dusty moon.

He lay back down and held on to Carmel and she turned, trustingly, and settled into his arms.

First published in *Interzone* #244,
January-February 2013.

ABOUT THE AUTHOR

Lavie Tidhar is the author of *A Man Lies Dreaming, The Violent Century,* and the World Fantasy Award winning *Osama*. His other works include the Bookman Histories trilogy, several novellas, two collections and a forthcoming comics mini-series, *Adler*. He currently lives in London.

Dark Angels:
Insects in the Films of
Guillermo del Toro

ORRIN GREY

It's no secret that Guillermo del Toro loves bugs. Insects and insect imagery play a major role in just about every movie in his filmography, from the fly-in-amber ghosts of *The Devil's Backbone* to the Reapers of *Blade 2* and the vampires of *The Strain*, with their hive-like social structures and insectile proboscises. Even *Hellboy 2* and *Pacific Rim* prominently featured swarming tooth fairies and *kaiju* skin parasites, respectively.

Most of the time, these insects serve a primarily visual role, lending verisimilitude to a creature design or inspiring a monster's behavior patterns, but del Toro's inclination toward the insect doesn't end with aesthetic appreciation. In several of his films, insects take on a more thematically dense role, their presence assuming an almost religious significance, with connections to divinity, the underworld, and eternal life.

Cronos (1993)

"*Cronos* is about immortality," Guillermo del Toro says in *Cabinet of Curiosities*.[1] Shot when he was only twenty-nine, it is the director's first feature film, and also the one that lays the groundwork for many of the insect themes that will appear later in his oeuvre. The titular Cronos Device is a small, golden mechanism in the shape of an insect—with a living insect trapped inside—that grants its user eternal life by transforming them into something that we would recognize as a vampire.

Del Toro has said that his design of the Cronos Device was inspired by the jewel-encrusted Maquech Beetles that were popular as living jewelry when he was growing up in Mexico[2], but the Device also bears an obvious similarity to a reliquary, used to house the remains of saints. This similarity is only underscored by del Toro's choice to first reveal the Device hidden inside the base of an archangel statue. In the commentary track for *Cronos*, del Toro says that he wanted the Catholic image of the archangel to hold inside itself the promise of a "more prosaic, more tangible eternal life."[3] It's the first time that del Toro juxtaposes insects with Catholic imagery in his films, but it won't be the last.

In his commentary, he describes his inspiration for the Device, which came from alchemy. What most people know about alchemy is that it was the quest to find a way to transform lead into gold, but del Toro talks about the search for the "ultimate depuration of vile matter—be it lead or flesh—and turn it into the ultimate expression of itself. Be it gold or eternal life, eternal flesh."[4] The Device—through the living insect trapped inside it—draws out mortal blood, filters it, and replaces it, adding a drop of the alchemical "Fifth Essence" which brings with it eternal life.

Not only does *Cronos* mark the beginning of del Toro's habit of linking insects with everlasting life, it also prefigures several of the themes that will come to play in his second film, *Mimic*, as the villainous industrialist de la Guardia in *Cronos* muses, "Who says insects aren't God's favored creatures?" It's a sentiment that was meant to be echoed by the protagonists of *Mimic* years later, though the lines wound up on the cutting room floor.[5] De la Guardia ultimately takes his reasoning further than *Mimic* was ever meant to, comparing insects to Jesus Christ and pointing out that, "the matter of the Resurrection is related to ants, to spiders," as he describes spiders returning from seeming death after having been trapped in rock for years.

An anecdote from the set of *Cronos* tells as much about Guillermo del Toro the filmmaker as it does about the importance of insects in his films: The original budget for *Cronos* didn't contain enough money to film the shots of the interior of the titular Device. Producers assured del Toro that he didn't need the shots, but del Toro disagreed, and ended up selling his van in order to pay for the construction of a massive animatronic replica of the inside of the device—complete with rubber insect—through which the camera could be slowly passed. What could have been a silly or pointless sequence in less dedicated hands becomes not only a nod to the monster movie origins of *Cronos*, but also a profound moment of cinematic magic, one that shows the insect not as a monster or an angel, but as much a victim as any of the film's human characters. It is perhaps the greatest condemnation of the allure of immortality in *Cronos*, as we see the insect suffering, trapped inside its golden prison, but unable to die.

Mimic (1997)

In the filmography of almost any visionary director, there is bound to be at least one film that represents a compromise between the director's vision and the demands of the filmmaking machine. For Guillermo del Toro, that film was *Mimic*, his second feature and his first studio film. For years it was available only in a theatrical cut that lacked del Toro's seal of approval, but recently a director's cut, fully color-corrected by del Toro himself, was released onto Blu-ray. The director's cut did more than just remove jump scares and action beats shot by the second unit; it returned the picture to something more closely resembling the director's original vision, and brought the film's symbolic elements more to the foreground.

"I wanted to make them God's favorite creatures, angels," del Toro says of the film's giant Judas Breed insects in *Cabinet of Curiosities*. "I wanted very much to indicate that God favored our downfall as a species."[6] On the opposite page is an image from one of del Toro's ubiquitous notebooks, in which a man is "prostrating himself before the godlike figure of the man-shaped insect, a shaft of sunlight sweeping diagonally across them from on high, as if God were passing judgment." [7]

In the original screenplay, one of the characters was meant to take up de la Guardia's chorus from *Cronos*, with lines like, "What if God is fed up with us? What if insects are now God's favorite creatures?"[8] Unfortunately, none of this dialogue made it into the final screenplay, leaving the heavy lifting of the film's thematic concerns almost entirely in the hands of the visuals. The director's cut *does* restore a scene of a woman calling the Judas Breed what del Toro called them in early treatments for the film, "dark angels."[9]

The first time we see the Judas Breed is in and around a run-down inner city church. The film's first on-screen fatality is a priest who falls to his death in front of a huge neon cross that reads, "Jesus Saves." Inside the decaying church, the Judas Breed blend in with the plastic-wrapped figures of saints, familiar imagery for viewers of *Cronos* with its hanging gallery of archangels wrapped in plastic sheeting. In his commentary for *Mimic*, del Toro says that he wrapped the saints in plastic to make them "obsolete, out-of-order holy figures." [10]

"We created the church and the despoiled figures again in the idea that the natural order of the sanctity of the world and our place in creation was being subverted, and that the new fathers and mothers of the world were insects,"[11] del Toro continues in his commentary track. As the film progresses, this subversion is driven home again and again through careful visual choices. From the color coding, which makes it feel as if the "humans are insects trapped in amber,"[12] to a dramatic change of scale in the film's final acts, in which the humans find themselves in a massive underground subway station, effectively reduced to the size of insects, scurrying around, desperately trying to accomplish menial tasks, while the "dark angels" can climb the walls with ease or effortlessly fly around them.

Among the many struggles that del Toro describes when talking about the making of *Mimic* are his efforts to ensure that the character of Dr. Peter Mann wears glasses. "I like the idea of showing how imperfect mankind is," del Toro says in *Cabinet of Curiosities*. "The insects in *Mimic* were all organic, but mankind needed glasses, artificial limbs. The mimics are the perfect ones, not us."[13] The value of human imperfection is another subject that comes up again and again in Guillermo del Toro's filmography, and the dichotomy of the mechanistic perfection of the insect is one that he also brings up in the commentary track for *Cronos*, where he says, "I do happen to believe that insects, as far as form and function, are the most perfect—albeit soulless—creatures of creation."[14]

Pan's Labyrinth (2006)

If asked to identify the single most recurrent theme in Guillermo del Toro's body of work, "the value of human imperfection and the choices that we make because of it" would probably be a pretty good start. While del Toro's sixth feature and his third—and most widely celebrated—Spanish-language film may not seem to have a lot to do with insects at first glance, it *does* have a lot to do with choice and human imperfection, and it features an insect in a particularly key role.

We are first introduced to the insect in one of the earliest sequences of *Pan's Labyrinth*, where we see it crawling out of the statue of a saint, continuing del Toro's habit of equating insects with Catholic imagery. It's also the last time it will happen in the film, though, breaking the insect free of its previous Catholic trappings in *Cronos* and *Mimic* and eventually equating it with a more pagan conception of eternal life. During this sequence, as the human protagonists arrive at the mill where most of the rest of the film will take place, our focus stays on the insect as it flits between the trees. In his commentary track, del Toro says, "I wanted to emphasize with the camera how important the insect was."[15]

Freed from the Catholic imagery of *Cronos* or *Mimic*, the insect in *Pan's Labyrinth* is also distinct from the more oppressive or ominous themes of the insects in those films. No longer a "dark angel" passing divine judgment, the insect instead acts as a psychopomp, not only literally leading Ofelia into the labyrinth, but also serving as a visual transition device that signals to the viewer a shift from the "real world" of fascist-occupied Spain to the film's fairytale underworld.

In most traditions, the psychopomp's job is not to pass judgment on the dead, but merely to provide them safe passage into the underworld. In this way, the insect in *Pan's Labyrinth* is very different from the Cronos Device or the "dark angels" of *Mimic*, acting as a bridge to eternal life, rather than a means of obtaining it, or an alternative to it.

Over the years since the film's release, much has been made about whether the magical elements of *Pan's Labyrinth* are intended to be objectively "real" within the film, and del Toro himself has called the film a "litmus test" for audiences.[16] By any reading, though, there are obvious parallels between the fairytale world of the film and the afterlife of many religious traditions. Del Toro has pointed to Ofelia's choices at the end of the movie as her "giving birth to herself,"[17] a theme that recurs in many of his projects. It's telling that the last image of *Pan's Labyrinth* is not of Ofelia in the fairy world, but of a flower blooming on the formerly dead tree that she saved from the toad in the "real world." Here we see a purer kind of eternal life than the one offered by the Cronos Device, an immortality in which our choices today promote new life in the future.

FOOTNOTES:

1 Del Toro, Guillermo and Marc Scott Zicree. *Cabinet of Curiosities*. New York: Harper Design, 2013. 84

2 Del Toro, Guillermo. Audio Commentary: *Cronos* (1993) Criterion, 2010. DVD

3 Del Toro, Audio Commentary: *Cronos*

4 Del Toro, Audio Commentary: *Cronos*

5 Del Toro, Guillermo. Audio Commentary: *Mimic* (1997) Lionsgate, 2012. Blu-ray

6 Del Toro, *Cabinet of Curiosities,* 90

7 Del Toro, *Cabinet of Curiosities,* 89-90

8 Del Toro, Audio Commentary: *Mimic*

9 Del Toro, Audio Commentary: *Mimic*

10 Del Toro, Audio Commentary: *Mimic*

11 Del Toro, Audio Commentary: *Mimic*

12 Del Toro, Audio Commentary: *Mimic*

13 Del Toro, *Cabinet of Curiosities,* 97

14 Del Toro, Audio Commentary: *Cronos*

15 Del Toro, Guillermo. Audio Commentary: *Pan's Labyrinth* (2006). New Line, 2007. DVD

16 Del Toro, Audio Commentary: *Pan's Labyrinth*

17 Del Toro, Audio Commentary: *Pan's Labyrinth*

ABOUT THE AUTHOR

Orrin Grey is a writer, editor, amateur film scholar, and monster expert who was born on the night before Halloween. He's the author of *Never Bet the Devil & Other Warnings* and of the forthcoming *Painted Monsters & Other Strange Beasts*. His favorite Guillermo del Toro movie is probably *Pacific Rim*, and you can find him online at orringrey.com, where he writes about monsters, movies, and monster movies, among other things.

Music, Magic, and Memory:
A Conversation
with Randy Henderson
and Silvia Morena-Garcia

JASON HELLER

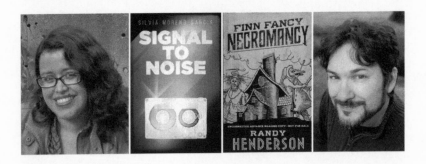

There aren't that many similarities between Randy Henderson's *Finn Fancy Necromancy* and Silvia Moreno-Garcia's *Signal to Noise*. But the elements they share are intriguing. Both are debut novels; both were published on February 10th (by Tor and Solaris, respectively); and both are urban fantasies in which music mingles with magic. In *Finn Fancy Necromancy*, a fifteen-year-old, music-loving necromancer from the '80s returns to modern-day Seattle after spending twenty-five years imprisoned in stasis for a magical crime he didn't commit. In *Signal to Noise*, a fifteen-year-old girl living in Mexico City in the '80s discovers a way to cast spells using the popular music of the day that she loves.

Despite those coincidental parallels, the tones of the two novels are utterly distinct. Where *Finn Fancy Necromancy* sports a humorous, easygoing tone spiked with slivers of the horrific, *Signal to Noise* is more atmospheric, somber, and poignant. Which makes sense, seeing as how Henderson's previous fiction (which has appeared in *Realms of Fantasy*, *Escape Pod*, and *Writers of the Future Vol. 30*, the last being the result of his winning Writers of the Future in 2014) tends toward the lighthearted, while Moreno-Garcia is best known as an award-nominated author and editor of dark fiction (as well as the publisher of the revered, Lovecraft-centric Innsmouth Free Press). Henderson and Moreno-Garcia spoke with *Clarkesworld* about their books, where music and magic meet, and the role of nostalgia in popular culture.

Finn Fancy Necromancy and Signal to Noise are very different novels, yet they have one big thing in common: Each revolves around the pop culture of decades past, particularly music. What inspired you to make this so central to your books?

Randy Henderson: Um, because '80s music is totally awesome? Doy! Basically, I'm a child of the '80s, it is the decade of my formative youth—the decade of post-punk, new Wave, MTV, and the dawn of rap; the rise of video games, home computers, awesome fantasy and science fiction, movies, and the golden sunset of Saturday morning cartoons. So I created an excuse in *Finn Fancy Necromancy* to share that by having him be an exile from the '80s in our time.

Silvia Morena-Garcia: My parents and my grandfather worked in radio. We had a lot of records around my house. My parents "made" me a radio talent when I was a kid. I must have been younger than six. Probably around three or four. They had a children's show on the radio, and they'd use me to record little bits of sound or children's laughter or anything like that. So sound in general was our bread and butter.

Both books deal with music and magic, but in Signal to Noise, music and magic are closely connected, whereas in Finn Fancy Necromancy, those elements aren't related at all. What drew you to those respective approaches?

Silvia Morena-Garcia: I don't recall a draft of *Signal to Noise* that did not intertwine magic, but I can't tell you why I thought it was a good idea to have them together.

Randy Henderson: For me, I wanted *Finn Fancy Necromancy* to have a kind of magic he didn't actually like or want. And who *wouldn't* love to cast magic by singing? Well, I guess unless you had to sing [The Beach Boys'] "Kokomo" or [Phil Collins'] "Sussudio" or something. But some Smiths or Clash or New Edition? Heck yeah! Also, I've always admired Lyndon Hardy's *Master of the Five Magics* for its depiction of magic systems and wanted to use something similar.

And of course, I like my main character Finn, so didn't want him facing a bad guy casting Nickleback and Creed tunes at him, or using auto-tuning. That's just too cruel.

Why does the music of the past resonates so deeply with you?

Silvia Morena-Garcia: Well, it wasn't the music of the past! I was a kid in the '80s. MTV and I share a birth year. And even when I riffled through my parents ABBA records and their Bee Gees records, I had no idea that belonged to another decade. This did not help my popularity, but I've never scored too high in the social convention department.

Randy Henderson: Similar story, though I never riffled through her parents ABBA records. The '80s were my early teens, and music so much defines our teen years for all the obvious reasons—emotional expression, establishing identity, and of course looking for fashion tips you *certainly* won't regret later. So the music of the '80s and early '90s will always resonate most strongly with my nostalgia bone.

Nostalgia bone. That is a thing right? I think it's one of those tiny floating bones in your listen-hole? Which makes sense why music would trigger it.

Mixtapes also pop up in both your books—and LPs figure prominently in Signal to Noise. What kind of appeal or power do these physical, analog forms of recorded music hold, especially now that digital music has become the norm?

Randy Henderson: A digital playlist can never replace a mixtape/CD. Mixtapes are a physical symbol that you cared enough to spend the time creating it, and decorating/crafting the container is as important as the music. It isn't just picking a bunch of songs you want to share; it is a carefully crafted message, something that can be held onto for decades.

But if your intent is to confess love via mix tape/CD, just remember Randy's Rules for Mixtapes: Friend Mixtape for a friend = Awesome. Love Mixtape for someone to whom you've expressed a romantic interest after that interest was returned (and not subsequently rejected or legally restricted) = Bodacious. Mixtape O' True Love for someone who has never shown interest in you romantically and is unaware of your feelings? = Risky (on many levels) at best, creepy or harassing at worst. And for the love of Cheez Whiz, DO NOT RECORD YOURSELF confessing your love or pretending to be a DJ on a mixtape. Just don't. Ever.

Silvia Morena-Garcia: Like Randy said, the mixtape was not just about curating music; it also involved the visual experience. Mixtapes would often be decorated, so it expressed a graphic and a musical message. Similarly, a vinyl record came with liner notes which could include anything from lyrics to images of the band, biographical data, and commentary. CDs had booklets. It's not the same experience when you have liner notes than just the music in isolation. They are one. One package. Even though some companies now offer you the ability to download the PDF this is also not the same thing. If the medium is the message, then the message is altered without these physical objects. I'm not saying it's good or bad, just that it's not the same experience.

I have an interest in media archeology, and that involves old tech as an object of study. I'll give you an example: the phonautograph. This is the earliest device known to record sound. It was basically a stylus tracing on paper. But by digitally scanning the tracing we were able to play it back. So essentially a piece of paper is talking to you. And another fun one: There is a project (called *Signal to Noise*, ha) that repurposes old tech. Here they take old cassettes and a plotter to "play" them. You can't do that with your MP3, can you?

In Finn Fancy Necromancy, the protagonist is still, in essence, a fifteen-year-old kid from the '80s. In Signal to Noise, the protagonist is a fifteen-year-old kid in the '80s. Are there any traces of your own childhoods in these characters?

Randy Henderson: Traces? No. Full-on colored illustrations? Yes. Finn is so very much me, with magic and his own issues. I sometimes worry a bit at the reviews that say I did an excellent job of capturing the stunted emotional and intellectual state of a fifteen-year-old thrust suddenly into a forty-year-old body. Er, that is, I'm sure it was all intentional on my part and reflects nothing more than my brilliant skill as a writer.

Silvia Morena-Garcia: A lot of my stories are autobiographical, and this one falls in that category. I had a really weird time in high school, and I'm still not sure I'm a member of your same species.

These are your debut novels. Before this, had you injected music—or pop culture at large—into any of your short fiction?

Silvia Morena-Garcia: Yep. Mostly stuff about movies. I wrote a story about an El Santo-like character called "Iron Justice Against the Fiends of Evil," and "Stories with Happy Endings" was inspired by the black and white horror movies I watched as a kid. And then there's all the Lovecraftiana. A lot of Lovecraftiana. The thing is we exist in a referential society with memes and GIFs, and it is almost impossible not to think pop culture.

Randy Henderson: I had not, beyond basic worldbuilding/background details.

What are some of your favorite works of speculative fiction that use music as a theme or motif?

Randy Henderson: So many! Anne McCaffrey's *Harper Hall* trilogy (one of my annual reads). *Soul Music* by Terry Pratchett. The songs embedded in *The Lord of the Rings* left a huge impression and obviously made that world truly live. In Piers Anthony's *Apprentice Adept* series, the main character's special flavor of magic was rhyming song, so of course I crafted many a rhyming spell in my daydreams after that. A lot of stories by Mercedes Lackey features music or bards. And of course there's always *The Name of the Wind* by Patrick Rothfuss.

Silvia Morena-Garcia: *crickets*

Randy Henderson: Ha! Crickets also make awesome music. And Buddy Holly was pretty cool.

How about outside of books?

Randy Henderson: Outside of books, there's the classic '80s game *The Bard's Tale*. *Legend of Zelda* incorporated magical tunes as well, for that matter. And of course, who could forget the '80s movies *Heavy Metal*, and *Rock & Rule* (even if you wanted to), both very much speculative fiction operas? But obviously, the most important music-related specific film of all time would have to be *Bill and Ted's Excellent Adventure*. I mean, their music totally saved the world, dude!

Music isn't the only kind of vintage pop culture in Finn Fancy Necromancy and Signal to Noise. Books, films, and television also appear, among others. Do you consider your novels to be nostalgic? Is nostalgia, like magic, something that can be used for both good and evil?

Randy Henderson: Michael Underwood has a pretty cool series that uses nostalgia as magic, starting with *Geekomancy*. I think my character is nostalgic within the novel, but I don't know that my novel itself is. But maybe I'm splitting hairs. And certainly nostalgia can be used for good or evil. Good: *Freaks and Geeks*; *The Wedding Singer*; charity performances. Evil: *Transformers* and *G.I. Joe* movies; advertising using nostalgia to sell me crap.

I think it's fascinating that nostalgia was actually considered a mental disorder back in the good ol' days. And it can have its downsides. But studies have shown it's actually more good than bad. It gives us a sense of continuity with our past, greater optimism about the future, and greater feelings of connection with others, making us happier, more generous people.

Silvia Morena-Garcia: There's nothing inherently evil in doing #ThrowbackThursday and putting a few pictures of your degrading youth online for the world to see (at least that's how I use it), but when you realize exactly how many remakes are buzzing around you and how unilaterally we extend our love to the past, it starts to get a bit creepy. Especially when that "nostalgic" era was full of exclusion. That's the thing with steampunk. Man, I can't get into the aesthetic thrill of that because my first gut reflex is "Yay, Happy Colonialism Day." And you can say "Oh, no, no, dressing as a 19th-century British officer does not mean I am colonialist douchebag," but when you are looking just at the costume . . . well, it's not like the person in costume standing in front of me comes with a virtual Wikipedia page I can access that discusses issues in colonial Africa, for example. The guy just looks like he's Livingstone.

I mean, I know that someone dressed à la Scarlett O'Hara is not necessarily going to want me to be their Mammy, but my first reaction might not be the most positive. I don't know, it's complicated. So . . . not good or bad. Just complicated.

Randy Henderson: What an amazingly important point, that one person's nostalgia may be another person's pain, or disenfranchisement, or oppression. And for some, nostalgia can definitely be a byproduct of the fear of change, or of clinging to some idealized and whitewashed view of a past that perhaps never really existed ("traditional marriage!", "traditional family!"), and thus can hamper progress or growth.

My love of the '80s certainly does not include the rise of Wall Street greed and homelessness, trickle-down economics, AIDS, televangelists, and many other very NOT awesome things. And Reagan was a weird hyper-nostalgia entity from the planet of Nostalgiatron, whose Charm Field was powered by nostalgia in life, and many now have nostalgia for his nostalgic vision. I'll admit I'm not one of them. I mean, Reagan sent Superman to kill Batman, and arguably to cut off Green Arrow's arm as well [in Frank Miller's iconic 1986 comic book *The Dark Knight Returns*]! Thank the gods we had the music to help get us through it all.

So yeah, nostalgia wrapped in ignorance can be hurtful. In fact, most anything wrapped in ignorance can be hurtful. Especially rocks. So let's wrap ourselves in knowledge and kindness, folks. And remember, we are the world. We are the children.

ABOUT THE AUTHOR

Jason Heller is a former nonfiction editor of *Clarkesworld;* as part of the magazine's 2012 editorial team, he received a Hugo Award. He is also the author of the alt-history novel *Taft 2012* (Quirk Books) and a Senior Writer for *The Onion's* pop-culture site, *The A.V. Club.* His short fiction has appeared in *Apex Magazine, Sybil's Garage, Farrago's Wainscot,* and others, and his SFF-related reviews and essays have been published in *Weird Tales, Entertainment Weekly NPR.org, Tor.com,* and Ann and Jeff VanderMeer's *The Time Traveler's Almanac* (Tor Books). He lives in Denver with this wife Angie.

Staying Sensitive in the Crowd: A Conversation with Chen Qiufan

KEN LIU

The first time I saw Chen Qiufan (a.k.a. Stanley Chan)[1] was at Chicon 7 in 2012: in the middle of a hotel lobby filled with people dashing about, he stood still, a sturdy reef in a frenetic sea, observing the surrounding tumult calmly as though seeing patterns that no one else could see.

Standing out from the crowd is a recurring theme in Stan's career and life. Though practically every Chinese writer lights up after a meal, he does not smoke. Though he graduated with a degree in Chinese literature and film studies from Peking University, he chose a career in the technology sector, first working for Google and then Baidu. Though he grew up in Shantou, a small city on the southern coast of China, he made his home thousands of miles away in the metropolis of Beijing, where his third language—Mandarin, after Teochew and Cantonese—is the language of daily life.

Being different has perhaps endowed Stan with an extra sensitivity to the hidden patterns of the world around him, allowing him to participate in the competitive grind of the high-tech world without being overwhelmed by it. Whether he's in the company of fellow writers, fans, tech executives, or powerful producers, he charms everyone effortlessly. Elegant, urbane, and erudite, he enlivens the flow of conversation at gatherings with his acerbic wit and dark, playful banter, as unique as his fiction.

Widely acknowledged as the leading figure of China's generation of SF writers born after 1980, Stan has won every genre literary award in China—often multiple times. Many of his stories tend to feature a cyberpunk aesthetic imbued with the anxieties of a globalized world seen through a Chinese perspective. He is also among the first of China's SF writers to be translated abroad, having appeared in publications such as *F&SF, Clarkesworld, Interzone,* and *Lightspeed,* in many instances as the first Chinese writer to do so.

"Record of the Cave of Ningchuan" describes a hole in the ground that reveals the geometry of the universe. This is a SF story written in Classical Chinese, a feat that I analogize to a contemporary Anglophone writer composing a SF story in the language of Chaucer. Published when you were barely out of college, the story won Taiwan's Dragon Fantasy Award. What gave you the idea to do such a thing? What were some particular challenges you faced and how did you overcome them?

From a young age, I've enjoyed classical Chinese literature of the supernatural, e.g., *Liaozhai Zhiyi* ["Strange Stories from a Chinese Studio", 17th century], *Soushenji* ["In Search of the Supernatural", 4th century], and *Youyang Zazu* ["Miscellaneous Morsels from Youyang"]. I immersed myself in an ancient world of magical realism where spirits and ghosts often took on human form and entered the lives of ordinary men and women, leading to fantastic stories.

As these tales were written in Classical Chinese, the compact, evocative phrases left many blanks for the reader's limitless imagination to fill. Wouldn't it be cool, I thought, to write a speculative tale in Classical Chinese in the age of the Internet?

Simultaneously, I also wanted to pay homage to Ted Chiang's "Tower of Babylon" by describing within the story a world of endless recursion.

The biggest challenge was linguistic. If I limited myself strictly to proper Classical Chinese, the demands on the average reader would be too great, and many would not be able to read it. I ended up choosing a hybrid that mixed Classical Chinese with some elements from modern Chinese, which preserved the classical favor while remaining readable by most readers with standard high school Classical Chinese training.

Another challenge involved using a different POV in each section: one section was written as a witness's testimony, another as an excerpt from official records of the county, and yet another as a transcript of a wandering storyteller's performance. Advancing the narrative in each section with the appropriate POV was an interesting experiment. I really enjoyed the process.

You're fluent in your native Shantou topolect (Teochew) as well as Cantonese, Mandarin, and English. The majority of your stories, however, have been written in Modern Standard Chinese (which is based on the Mandarin family of topolects). Have you thought about writing more stories in other languages such as Cantonese or Teochew? Why or why not?

Let me tell you an interesting anecdote. In 2012, *Chutzpah!* magazine invited me to contribute a story written in Teochew for their special topolect-focused issue, and I agreed. I came up with a story concept quickly, but once I started writing it, I discovered a big problem. If I wrote the whole story in proper Teochew, many words would have to be rendered using Chinese characters chosen solely for their phonetic rather than semantic values, or I would have to resort to using a phonetic alphabet. Teochew was so different from Mandarin that only readers fluent in Teochew would be able to understand it. I had no choice but to stick with the frame of Modern Standard Chinese and substitute in some Teochew words and slang phrases.

During the process of composition, I felt as if two voices were fighting within my head, each struggling to overcome the other. In the end, I had to give up. The frustrated *Chutzpah!* editor told me that multiple other invited authors had also given up.

I think the effort to spread the use of Modern Standard Mandarin in education is a double-edged sword. It certainly has benefits, but a growing number of young people now are losing the ability to converse effectively in their native topolect, which means that they've given up another way of seeing and thinking about the world. I feel really sorry for them.

A lot of your stories feature cutting-edge research in computer science, genetics, virtual reality, bioengineering, and other areas of rapid change. How do you keep up with developments in so many areas?

I subscribe to a lot of WeChat public accounts (think of them as RSS feeds) on science & technology such as the MIT Technology Review. Every day, they bombard me with news. If I find anything interesting, I will dig deeper with additional research and talk to some experts in specific areas. Also, I've worked in Internet companies like Google and Baidu for years, where employees get a lot of the latest technology and product information from daily work. The experience has been really helpful and inspiring.

How does your day job as a product marketing manager at Baidu impact your creative work? Inspiration? Impediment? Some of both?

Product marketing managers are like evangelists who bridge the gap between users and technologies. We have to find innovative ways to communicate with the masses. The very essence of marketing is to tell stories that resonate with people, to create new scenarios for how people could benefit from technology. I guess that's quite similar with writing a SF/fantasy story.

But of course, there is always conflict, since I have only twenty-four hours in a day, and I need to work for eight hours and sleep for eight hours. How much energy is left for writing?

You've traveled and lived outside of China extensively. Tell us about how your global experience has influenced you creatively.

I love traveling! Seeing different views, eating exotic food, meeting interesting people. There is a theory of cognition that says that you have to stimulate your brain in some way to create new neural connections. There are always new inspirations and ideas popping out during a trip—even on the flight—and I will write them down in a little notebook and try to develop these ideas into stories.

Many of your stories, such as "The Fish of Lijiang" (Clarkesworld, August 2011), "The Year of the Rat" (F&SF, July/August 2013), and "The Mao Ghost" (Lightspeed, March 2014) tend to be read in the

West as political metaphors about contemporary China. Can you comment on the extent, if any, your work "reflects" the realities in China today?

I've never tried to intentionally emphasize political metaphors in my work. I write about aspects of life in China I observe, feel, and experience—some of which are good and some of which are not so good. I'm often surprised by how critics can read deeper meaning into my stories that I didn't think of. Readers, on the other hand, often give me feedback based on their feelings. For example, after "The Year of the Rat" was published, many college students posted on the Web saying that they considered this my best work to date because it resonated with them by expressing the helplessness and confusion concerning the future they felt.

I think one of the most important qualities in a writer is sensitivity: the ability to capture the strangeness in everyday life. This is especially important in contemporary China, where it's easy to become lost in the kaleidoscope-like, constantly shifting bustle of life and lose this sensitivity.

Would you describe your work as "science fiction realism"? Are you hopeful or cynical about the future?

I would never try to put a specific label or category on my work. "Science fiction realism" is, in fact, a cagey, tactically useful phrase. It helps the media to interpret the message we're trying to express. Compared to traditional "realism," which seems ill-adapted or numb to a technology-infused life, "science fiction realism" is more critical of reality and more capable of revealing the complex relationship between technology and contemporary life as well as the transformation of individual and human nature and the consequences of such transformation.

This has been a constant theme I hope to reflect in my work. For example, in "Smog," which I wrote in 2006, I extrapolated the possibility of Beijing suffering from even more extreme air pollution and the effects on people's lives and psychology. However, I don't want to be called a "science fiction realist writer." All I want is to write good stories that move readers, regardless of whether they are "science fiction" or "realist."

My attitude about the future has shifted in the last few years from a gloomy pessimism to a more active optimism. I believe that as technology advances, many problems will be solved even though more problems will appear and some problems may never have solutions. But I believe the overall trend is for humanity to become happier, wiser, and more tolerant. I hope I'm right.

You're also a columnist for some of China's top media outlets. Can you tell us about this work?

As science fiction receives more attention, media outlets need someone who knows science fiction well and is willing to share their thoughts. My articles are mostly related to big cultural events such as the release of *Interstellar,* the publication of the English edition of *The Three Body Problem,* and Chinese SF cons (the Yinhe and Xingyun Awards, for example).

Interestingly, I have to tailor my perspectives to fit with different papers—the *New York Times* (Chinese edition), for example, is considered "pro-West" in China while the *Global Times* is considered the opposite.

You are also doing some screenwriting now. Can you tell us more?

I'm working on a script adapted from my short story, "The Endless Farewell." But it now feels like a completely different story. There is a huge gap between written fiction and film, and you need to change the way you think—like from text to image. Screenplays are also more structural, especially in genre films, for which there are principles and rules you have to obey.

The process is interesting at the very beginning, but after multiple revisions, you become numb and just want to be rid of the thing so that you can go back to writing your novel any damned way you want. But for a film, you have to listen to, debate, and sometimes fight against the producer, the director and anyone else relevant.

Your debut novel, *The Waste Tide,* has received critical plaudits and market success in China. Can you tell us about the novel and what's happening with it?

The novel imagines a near future in the third decade of this century. On Silicon Isle, an island in southern China built on the foundation of e-waste recycling; pollution has made the place almost uninhabitable. A fierce struggle follows in which powerful native clans, migrant workers from other parts of China, and the elites representing international capitalism vie for dominance. Mimi, a young migrant worker and "waste girl," turns into a posthuman after much suffering, and leads the oppressed migrant workers in rebellion.

A British film company has already reached out to purchase film rights, and the process is going smoothly. An English translation is also close to being complete. Hopefully it can be rolled out in US/UK markets soon.

What's next for you? Any new projects you want to share with our readers?

The sequel of *The Waste Tide* is in the pipeline, and I'm still doing some research. The story will take place in a near-future Chinese city with more complex scenarios.

But before that, I'm working on a novella telling an alternative, psychedelic history in China, probably to be published in summer of 2015.

And I have a lot of short stories waiting to be finished on the list. How I wish I could have fourty-eight hours a day! But after all, telling a good story is what excites me the most in this world. Thanks!

Interviewer's Note:

1 *Chen Qiufan* (pronounced close to "Chiufan") is the author's Chinese name rendered following the Chinese convention of giving surname first. The English name *Stanley Chan* is the author's preferred name when introducing himself socially in the West, and the spelling of *Chan* reflects Cantonese phonetics. This interview was conducted in a mixture of Chinese and English.

ABOUT THE AUTHOR

Ken Liu is an author and translator of speculative fiction, as well as a lawyer and programmer. A winner of the Nebula, Hugo, and World Fantasy Awards, he has been published in *The Magazine of Fantasy & Science Fiction, Asimov's, Analog, Clarkesworld, Lightspeed,* and *Strange Horizons,* among other places. He lives with his family near Boston, Massachusetts.

Ken's debut novel, *The Grace of Kings,* the first in a silkpunk epic fantasy series, will be published by Saga Press, Simon & Schuster's new genre fiction imprint, in April 2015. Saga will also publish a collection of his short stories.

Another Word:
A Shed of One's Own
CHUCK WENDIG

I am writing this article *right now* whilst ensconced in the warm embrace of a shed.

I get it. *Shed* does not sound appealing. It conjures a certain image: a lawn mower, a snow blower, a gasoline smell, mouse poop.

It sounds like a place one might be banished to—a punitive measure for having done something wrong. "You're stinking up the joint with your WORD FUMES," my wife might say. "To the shed with you! With the mice and the mowers!" And then I would stumble the long march across the hoarfrost lawn to the shed where I would toil away the hours with blister-making, callus-having wordsmithy. Rattling shovels and letting spiders weave webs in my hair.

We have a shed like that.

I am not writing *this* from *that* shed.

Rather, I am writing from a whole different shed.

I am writing from my writing shed.

Let's step back a moment.

A writer must do one thing above all else, and that is: *to write.*

That, of course, is easier said than done. I might as well have said, "A writer must do one thing above all else, and that is: *to wrestle four grizzly bears into submission.*"

To write, other things must fall into place.

A writer must have:

a) time

and

b) place.

Meaning, you have to be able to snatch time away from the jaws of the same time-consuming beast that attacks us all, and you must also secure *some place somewhere* to actually sit and write. You can't do it all in your head. Not yet, at least (the technology hasn't caught up to the psychic dimension).

Time management is a whole issue all its own and instead, I'd like to talk about *place*. Whether you use a notebook or a laptop computer, whether you sit at a desktop or carve your manifestos into the back of a captive UPS man, whether you sit on a Bosu ball or stand at a treadmill desk, you must find the literal, physical space to commit your wordsmithy.

And it's not just about having the space. It's about having a protected, special space. A space without intrusion from others. A place suited to the ideation and creation of the work you want to commit to paper and screen.

That brings us to: the shed.

I've been a writer for—
  checks watch
Too many years, now. I freelanced for over ten years, and I've been writing novels for the last few. All the while, I've been afforded some manner of office inside the walls of our home. An office with a desk, a computer, bookshelves, and whatever else I felt was necessary to get the story juices flowing (at various points: snacks, liquor, coffee, Star Wars toys, pens, ninja weapons, coffee). It's been wonderful. I've been very lucky. I had a place to call my own. Not a big space. I couldn't drive a Segway around it to clear my head. No hang-gliding amongst its rafters.

But I had four walls and a ceiling and a light and it was mine.

Then, not quite four years ago, this *thing* happened. An event.

A cataclysm, of sorts.

We were suddenly host to this thing known as a "human child."

It came from my wife, though if I'm to understand the biology, I too am equally responsible. Whoever created this thing, he's here. He's on this planet. And we are his caretakers despite not having signed up specifically for this task.

He's wonderful. We love him dearly. The boy is a ball of kooky, kinetic energy.

At first, he was fairly *still*. You could pick him up and put him down someplace else and, for the most part, there he would remain. But if there's one thing I have learned about children it's that they're very much like the scene in Jurassic Park where the velociraptors learn to open doors. They continue to learn and grow and advance and that means metaphorically learning to open doors and also literally learning to open doors.

One day they stay where you plop them.

Next thing you know, they're running around your house at top speed like a coyote on bath salts.

Now, being a writer is a fairly intellectual pursuit. I sit still most days like some kind of crafty fungus, and my fingers do most of the moving, and they do that moving in order to translate the *pure, unfiltered story* in my mind onto the screen. Doing that takes a lot of concentration. Mental energy and effort. You gotta sit down, focus up, and use that brain-bucket to make thinky-thinky.

Ah, but having the drug-addled coyote running around?

It . . . complicates things.

My wife can only do so much to wrangle a three-year-old. He's like a zombie attack, that kid. Just when you think you're safe—the doorknob is rattling, someone is moaning on the other side of the wall, and little fingers are grabbing underneath the door in the hopes of grabbing you and dragging you out of the safety of your room. Just as I'd start to get into a groove with my work—

Here comes the zombie-coyote-velociraptor.

Always welcome! Always sweet! He'd come in and want hugs and want to play or want to tell me some completely absurd story he just made up. It was nice.

And it was hell on my productivity.

I had deadlines, damnit.

They call them deadlines because if you don't meet 'em? *You're dead.*

So, my wife and I sat down and said, *something must be done.*

We considered putting the child in a box marked FREE PANDA and putting it out on the curb, but turns out? That's illegal. (Stupid government.) Since exile for the human child would not be an option, I would be the one to take exile.

Various ideas were bandied about. Rent an office? Refurbish a part of the house where I could hide away like some freakish uncle everyone thinks is in prison?

Or, seize upon the trend of: studio office sheds.

Ah-ha.

We talked to some local Amish shed-builders and it turns out, you can get one built and have it fitted for things like: electricity! And HVAC! And whiskey dispensers!

That's what we did, and now here I am, writing this article from *the writing shed*. A place I sometimes call "the Mystery Box," though a Facebook friend online came up with the name "the Myth Lab," which is probably much cooler if there wasn't a risk my son would go to school one day and tell his teacher "Daddy works in a Myth Lab," but of course they wouldn't hear Myth Lab, and suddenly everyone would think my son's father was some Heisenberg variant making meth in a shed.

You probably don't have a shed.

You may never have a writing shed. I never expected to need one or have one.

What you will need, and what I want you to think very hard about, is finding a place to call your own.

I want you to find this place somewhere in your life. It can be in public, though it's much better it is space you legitimately own and control. You cannot own that corner of Starbucks, much as you want to. You cannot own that park bench or guarantee its use every time you pass by it.

This is your idea chamber.

This is your worldbuilding, wordbuilding realm.

This is your land and you are the deity that presides over it.

Maybe this is a room in your house. Or a desk in your bedroom. Or a laptop that you can set up at the kitchen table. Big or small, it is yours.

Now: I want you to protect this space with tooth and claw. Because part of being a writer is making writing a priority. If it's not important to you, it won't be important to anyone else. If it's a thing that matters to you in your heart, sometimes you need to make it matter outside in reality. You need to tell people in your life:

This is my space.

For a period of time, I require this space to do what matters to me.

Protect the time you have to use it.

Since entering the shed, my productivity has gone way up.

I write a lot more now.

I find this is true any time I take what I do more seriously.

If I give my writing its priority, then my writing returns to me with productivity.

Do the same for yourself.

Find your space.

Stake your claim.

Shed or no shed, find your place.

Make it matter.

And no, you can't have my shed. Get your own space, weirdo.

ABOUT THE AUTHOR

Chuck Wendig is a novelist, screenwriter and game designer. He's the author of many published novels, including but not limited to: *Blackbirds, Atlanta Burns, Zer0es*, and the YA Heartland series. He is co-writer of the short film *Pandemic* and the Emmy-nominated digital narrative *Collapsus*. Wendig has contributed over two million words to the game industry. He is also well known for his profane-yet-practical advice to writers, which he dispenses at his blog, terribleminds.com, and through several popular e-books, including *The Kick-Ass Writer*, published by Writers Digest. He currently lives in the forests of Pennsyltucky with wife, tiny human, and red dog.

Editor's Desk: Reader's Poll Winners, Nebulas, and Forever

NEIL CLARKE

Our annual reader's poll wrapped up late February and I am pleased to announce our 2014 winners!

Best 2014 *Clarkesworld* Story

We've had some close races in the past, but this year only ten points separated the top third of the ballot. Throughout the month, several stories temporarily held the top spot, but when we closed the winners revealed themselves to be:

1st Place
"The Clockwork Soldier" by Ken Liu

2nd Place (tie)
"Passage of Earth" by Michael Swanwick
"The Eleven Holy Numbers of the Mechanical Soul"
by Natalia Theodoridou

3rd Place (tie)
"Tortoiseshell Cats Are Not Refundable" by Cat Rambo
"Patterns of a Murmuration, In Billions of Data Points"
by JY Yang

Best 2014 *Clarkesworld* Cover Art

While almost every piece of cover art found praise from some segment of our community, the top three places established themselves very early and held their place through the entire month. The winners are:

1st Place
"Slumbering Naiad" by Julie Dillon

2nd Place
"Space Sirens" by Julie Dillon

3rd Place
"Hollow" by Matt Dixon

Congratulations to all our winners and a big thank you to everyone that participated in this year's poll.

While we're recognizing the accomplishments of some of our authors, I'd like to toss a few more congratulations to this year's Nebula Award nominees. SFWA announced the final slate in February and I'm very happy to see two *Clarkesworld* stories and one from *Upgraded* on the ballot.

Short Story Nominee
"The Meeker and the All-Seeing Eye" by Matthew Kressel

Novelette Nominee
"The Magician and Laplace's Demon" by Tom Crosshill

Novella Nominee
"The Regular" by Ken Liu (from *Upgraded*)

Speaking of "The Regular," you can also read this novella in the debut issue of *Forever*, a new all-reprint science fiction magazine that will feature a novella and two short stories in each monthly issue. You won't find *Forever* online or in print, but you can get the ebook editions of the first issue available for free on my blog (neil-clarke.com). Please download and give our first issue a try. If you enjoy it, I hope you'll consider subscribing at Amazon, Weightless, or direct from our website (forever-magazine.com).

· · ·

In last month's editorial, I outlined several of our goals for the next six months. All of these things were tied to being able to increase subscriptions, Patreon and Joyride support, and advertising. None of these things are easy, but I'm pleased to say that last month we reached a new Patreon goal, unlocking three more original stories for the 2015 calendar. With luck, we can build upon that success and continue to move this publication forward.

Thank you and have a great month!

ABOUT THE AUTHOR

Neil Clarke is the editor of *Clarkesworld Magazine,* owner of Wyrm Publishing and a three-time Hugo Award Nominee for Best Editor (short form). He currently lives in NJ with his wife and two children.

About the Artist
PETER MOHRBACHER

Peter Mohrbacher is an independent illustrator and concept artist living in the Chicago area.

WEBSITE

www.vandalhigh.com

9997590R00104

Printed in Great Britain
by Amazon.co.uk, Ltd.,
Marston Gate.